In Another Time

by

Bill Brown

Illustrated by Stephen Phipps

In Another Time

by

Bill Brown

Illustrated by Stephen Phipps

Publisher
Best Books Online
Mediaworld PR Ltd

ISBN: 1-904502-71-7

Printed and bound by Antony Rowe Ltd, Eastbourne

ACKNOWLEDGEMENTS

Jean and Mike Glendinning
For their tireless work on the original manuscript.

David Humphries
For his patient computer check and compilation into book form.
***Sadly since we worked together some months ago,
David died on the 29th December 2004***

Stephen Phipps
For his illustrations and his sense of humour at all times.

Bill Brown was born in February 1925 and educated at Kingswood Grammar School and Loughborough College, where he qualified as a teacher, specialising in handicraft.

On leaving college he was called up into the Army Intelligence Corps and served in India and the Andaman Islands. His main task was the investigation of Japanese war crimes and was recommended for a commission for his work on the Tarmugli Incident.

Following demobilisation on a Class 'B' release, he taught in several local schools until 1985, retiring as Head of Technical Studies at Wellsway Comprehensive School, Keynsham.

He and his wife, Margaret, have been life long worshippers at Hanham Baptist Church where they married in 1948. They have two daughters, three grand-daughters and a great grand-daughter.

Bill has written one other book: *Sparks From Our Blakeys,* a collection of pre-war boyhood memories.

Contents

Forward 1

The Old Baptist Chapel 3

Chapter One - The City 7

Chapter Two - The Printer 29

Chapter Three - The Butchers.. ... 36

Chapter Four - The Forest 48

Chapter Five - The Trek 71

Chapter Six - The Good Samaritan ... 80

Chapter Seven - The Widow's Tale ... 92

Chapter Eight - The Chapel 101

Chapter Nine - Contact 117

Chapter Ten - Haberdashery. ... 127

Chapter Eleven - The Weddings. ... 136

Chapter Twelve - Sons 146

Chapter Thirteen - Dark Days 154

Chapter Fourteen - News From Afar ... 161

Chapter Fifteen - The Assizes 174

Chapter Sixteen - A Story To Tell ... 177

Chapter Seventeen - Where Now?.. ... 184

Chapter Eighteen - The Gathering Of The Clan. 188

Chapter Nineteen - Life Is Full Of Surprises ... 197

Chapter Twenty - Five Years Later ... 208

Chapter Twenty-one - The Confession ... 227

Extract from the diary of Charles & Martha Curtis.. 231

Epilogue - 237

Illustrations

Map of Hanham 5

The Notice In The Window 28

Two Magificent Creatures Drinking From A Pool ... 50

On The Spit Was A Fish... 53

His Favourite Caravan 79

A Simple Dwelling 90

The Chapel 103

The Blue Bowl 125

The Hall 139

Those Travelling Against Their Will 207

The Darting Of The Flying Fish 214

Australian Shelter 220

Foreword

The location for this story is the village of Hanham. Situated on the outskirts of Bristol, astride the old roman road to Bath; the Via Julia, and close to the River Avon. The earliest possessor of Hanham was Ernulf de Hesding who came to England with William the Conqueror.

The area for many centuries was part of the ancient forest of Kingswood, a Royal Chase, which covered a large expanse to the east of Bristol; continuing along the southern side of the River Avon into Somerset and some seven miles north east to the village of Pucklechurch.

A. Braine in his "History of Kingswood Forest," published in 1891, describes it as "a piece of country of the most varied and interesting character - pleasingly undulating and most prettily interspersed with hills and vales; and which when formerly covered with luxuriant woods, must have presented one of those charming pictures so characteristic of ancient English scenery."

However, the inhabitants of the forest, especially a group from Kingswood known as the Cockroad Gang, were fierce and lawless. They virtually ruled the area by fear until a combined force of city watchmen and city guards overcame them in a surprise night-raid. Some of the gang were transported, others were hanged at Bristol and Gloucester, very few were liberated.

A religious revival inspired by the Dissenters and Field Preachers started about 1658 and was continued by the Baptists who erected a Chapel in 1714. The revival blossomed under the influence of George Whitefield together with John and Charles

Wesley.

This imaginary story takes place during the latter half of the 18th Century.

This book is dedicated to the memory of those folk who had the faith and vision to build the Old Chapel and establish a witness, which has continued for nearly three hundred years.

The Old Baptist Chapel

The Old Baptist church was built in a clearing, which in 1658 was an open-air meeting place where Dissenters met to worship as they wished, and not as the state decreed. This meant that they were persecuted by the authorities and betrayed by their fellow citizens; at least one preacher was pursued and drowned in the River Avon and one imprisoned in Gloucester gaol where he met his death.

The building was completed in 1714 using local stone and timber. The long windows finished in a graceful arch and an inner, parallel line of blue glass, emphasised and enhanced their shape. A sizeable porch gave entry to the main building; this was equipped with a solid foot scraper set into the outside wall. The pulpit was central and set behind a baptistry in the floor of the building. The churchyard, opened in 1721, contains victims of a cholera epidemic and was finally closed in 1965.

During the life of the chapel it was enlarged with a brick wall being constructed at the east end and inside a large platform was built behind the pulpit. At the west end of the chapel, a second floor, almost like a balcony, was erected and could be screened off. Various lean-to buildings came into use as a vestry, kitchen and storeroom. One lean-to building was used as a base for the men's Bible class on a Sunday and, during the week, it became a small shooting range for the Home Guard.

When the New Chapel was erected in 1907 the building was used mainly for a large Sunday School, mid-week activities and social events, such as Harvest Supper.

In March 1958 the New Chapel suffered a disastrous fire and the Old Chapel once again became the main sanctuary until the re-opening of the building in September 1959.

Because of the poor condition of the roof timbers the Old Chapel was demolished in 1971 and replaced with a modern building.

Map of Hanham
1843

Chapter One

The City

Bright moonlight played upon the waters of the estuary, creating rippling stars and forming them into a ribbon of silver which followed the full tide as it pushed the river back up the deep gorge and beyond the centre of the city. The tethered craft rose and fell on the gentle swell, their tall masts casting bent shadowy fingers along the riverbank and on the quiet wharf. Rats and water voles scurried away in search of higher burrows, or explored the many man-made shelters on the riverside as the murky waters rose. Along the quay, large warehouses with their roofs silhouetted against the night sky stood as silent guardians over the city's growing wealth, only the watchmen broke the stillness as they pursued their regular duties. At curfew all the fires in the city had been extinguished to ensure that there was no re-occurrence of the ever-present menace, which had marred its recent history.

Sharp shadows fell across the narrow streets where the timbered houses inclined their heads and almost embraced each other. The shadows were kind to the city, they placed a dark blanket over the hovels of the narrow twisting streets where an open sewer ran down a central gutter carrying away to the river the human waste and garbage of the day. During the night hours these compact dwellings provided a safe haven for the unfortunate beings of society as they plied their doubtful trades amid the shadows. The tavern close by the quayside displayed a warmth of candlelight, the air inside alive with heavy, blue tobacco smoke, twisting its rising path to a nicotine stained ceiling, or curling around a solid wooden beam as it became an integral part of the atmosphere. Raucous revellers were being dispensed cheap ale by a buxom barmaid; it lubricated the tongues luring their owners to express the opinions of muddled minds, liberated by alcohol. So they argued the issues of the day or devised provocative comments concerning their immediate neighbours. These caustic asides provided bait for physical conflict, inducing the drunken individuals to become participants in a bare-fisted brawl with supporters of each faction voicing their encouragement, or adding to the confusion by creating their own eruptions of violence. The female company in the tavern viewed this display of manliness from their ringside seats, or from the comparative safety of the sawdust-strewn floor where some of their number had already collapsed into a gin fed stupor.

A ragged ribbon of men emerged from the darkness of the quay, staggering under the heavy kegs upon their shoulders and enjoying the protection of several batmen armed with stout staves, they moved from shadow to shadow making their way with great caution to the rear of the tavern. Having secured a safe passage from the quay to a waiting, willing taverner, the men faded into the night, thankful once again they had not been apprehended.

Several hours earlier, two male figures both of solid if rather lean stature, were deep in conversation as they walked purposefully from the quay where they had secured their flat bottomed trow. They picked their way through the rubbish of the streets, disturbing the alien livestock endeavouring to find a resting place for the long night hours.

Tom Stafford and his father were wending their way home; he had a prayer upon his lips, and also in his heart, that his dear wife Hannah would have been safely delivered of their second child.

He had hoped the news would have reached him during the day, but the hours had passed and no one had sought him out to bring the expected intelligence.

They finally arrived at the door of their rented, ground floor tenement situated a short distance outside the remnants of the old wall that once surrounded the city. The proud castle that at one time had dominated the skyline was now a ruin, taken apart stone by stone, by the citizens of the city. Tom arrived after this event had taken place, having spent his early years living in the forest that spread to the east, north and south outside the city's limits. It was a vast forest, a King's chase, and home for Tom for more than a score of years.

His family lived within the confines of the forest, in a small cottage constructed from outcrops of stone and roofed with local timbers It had been completed and inhabited in a day, with smoke issuing from the straight chimney by nightfall, thus giving the family squatters rights and they could now improve their dwelling at their leisure. His father, a miner, had introduced Tom to the pit at an early age; he had laboured with other young boys moving the drams of coal along dark, narrow workings. They pushed with their heads, or pulled using a shoulder harness, the heavy loads. It was exhausting, dangerous and frightening as they laboured in conditions that had already sent many of their kind to an early grave.

Together with his father they would trudge home in the evening, blackened by coal dust and bleeding from injuries sustained underground, completely drained of energy and with no desire to resume their labours on the morrow. There was one saving grace appertaining to the pits in the area; they were free from gas and this meant that their badge of trade, a metal candle holder, designed with a spike at one end, could be safely driven into the coal face in order to shed a little light to their advantage; but they found small consolation in this.

Thankfully, the roof fall in the pit occurred during the night and later investigations were to confirm a large fault in the seam. Despite serious efforts to re-open the section it soon became evident the situation was fraught with danger and would never be a profitable concern. Much against the owner's wishes, the area was shut down adding father and son to the growing number of unemployed within the forest.

Over the next few years life for the family was hard. As Tom grew, his mother made sacrifices, denying herself so that her son and his father might have the stamina to take on seasonal jobs, but no permanent situations could be found. There were times when the quarries offered employment, earnings from the spelter works, and pin making all helped to keep the family together, and it was during a spell of the latter that Tom met and married Hannah. Despite their poverty, they had a sense of belonging in the family, hoping against hope that at some point fortune would smile on them. Two years later the union of Tom and Hannah produced their first child, a daughter who they named Emma, she proved to be a bright girl and became inseparable from her mother. The joy brought to the household by the little granddaughter helped to raise the spirits of all concerned, but the strain of maintaining an acceptable standard of living began to take its toll on the grandmother. Gradually she became weaker and as the days passed, her strength was insufficient to ward off an attack of fever, which brought about her sudden death. The distraught family laid her to rest beneath a large beech tree within the forest, marking the grave with a simple wooden cross. Now all were concerned for the future and what it might hold.

Tom and his father desired more fulfilling labours than those found in the bowels of the earth or within the confines of the forest, so their attentions strayed to the concerns of the city.

Fortune favoured them both. Fairly sturdy of frame, gifted with innate intelligence and of honest appearance, they made their way into the city on several occasions searching for employment. They were finally successful in securing positions with a merchant in the dock area, whose business was rapidly expanding as the trade of the city extended far beyond its shores.

The vast dock, crowded with tall ships, reached into the centre of the city, it required a number of small craft to transfer cargo from ship to shore, shore to ship and ship to ship. The flat-bottomed trows used for this purpose would settle upstream on the mud when the tide ebbed, until they were resurrected on the incoming flow into a new life and a new working day.

The subject of their conversation as they walked from the quay was the naming of the next generation. They finally agreed on the name Samuel, this being their first choice; provided the new arrival was a son. United in this conclusion they entered the door of the building to be greeted by the news that the birth had not yet taken place. Tom embraced his wife who assured him there was nothing to be concerned about as she did not think the birth was imminent. There was a quick hug with Emma, who then ran to her grandfather to inform him of the happenings of the day and together they prepared the table for the evening meal. Wishing to be of service little Emma placed the dishes on the table then watched with hungry enthusiasm as her grandfather served out portions of the rabbit stew that had been simmering on the hob for several hours.

Hannah had always marvelled at her daughter's insatiable appetite and today was no exception. With the bowl tipped to her lips, the chattering tongue was made speechless by the taste of the warm liquid, whilst her eyes registered grateful approval as they smiled at her mother. With a small residue of stew remaining in the bowl, Emma proceeded to break off a chunk of crusty bread and with it she wiped her bowl clean. Having decided that further labours on the vessel in her hand would be non productive, she placed the bowl upon the table and looked intently at the faces of her seniors with childish expectancy. There was no reproach on the faces she gazed at, nor was there any offer of further sustenance, just a quiet indication that the hour was getting late and they would all soon be settling down for the night.

It was to be a long night, the little girl and the old man both slept soundly, but for her parents there was no real rest. Tom concerned himself with the welfare of his wife as she was certain her labour had commenced. As time passed and between them they had only managed brief periods of sleep, Hannah implored Tom to seek out her good friend and neighbour. She was a mother herself and lived a few minutes away in the same building, she assured Tom she had every confidence in her for any eventuality. Reluctantly Tom left his wife to comply with her orders, and the good woman agreed to come to Hannah and remain with her until she was confident that it would be safe to leave her.

The curfew had passed; Tom turned his attention to the kindling of the fire and preparation of warm water, then seated himself near the hearth awaiting the birth. He was soon joined by his daughter and his father who demanded to hear an up-to-date account of the happenings throughout the night.

With a good deal of emotion in his voice, Tom explained the events that had taken place during the previous hours and how Hannah required the help and comfort of her neighbour, who was willing to come and in fact was with her now. He was pleased this was so, but he felt ill at ease sitting by the fire unable to be of any real service. Time seemed to stand still and more than once they were grateful for the incessant babble of their young companion.

Without warning, after what appeared to be hours of tense waiting, there came an unmistakeable infant cry, it transfixed the three generations producing immobile gazes followed by exclamations of joyful relief. The minutes passed as they waited for a call into the room in order to see this little wonder who had just joined their world, when to their complete and utter amazement a second infant cry became audible. Tom, unable to contain himself any longer, rushed into the room to be greeted by the news that he was now the proud father of, not one, but two sons.

Emma for the first time that day became speechless, but her joy radiated and filled the room when she realised she now had two brothers, whilst her grandfather ruefully informed his son that the conversation which occupied their thoughts on the way home, did not supply them with a complete answer. In point of fact, in agreeing on one name they had only half a solution to the situation. Together they stood by the bedside looking down on the two newly born babes, pink faces topped with unruly black hair emerging from the blankets bound around them. Hannah regarded Tom with an understanding that advertised their great bond, their deep love for each other and their mutual respect. The world was theirs in that wonderful moment of new birth.

His father broke the silence as he playfully reminded Tom the boy's name they had discussed was still applicable, but only to one of his newborn babes. Hannah demanded to have some knowledge of this pre-emptive conversation and Tom readily agreed to fully inform his wife of the deliberations between his father and himself whilst they were walking home from their labours.

Hannah listened with interest and when Tom offered to tell her the outcome of their discussion she whole-heartedly concurred.

"That being agreed," said Tom, he picked up his first-born son from the bed and holding him high in the air, at arms length, he announced; "We name you Samuel, may God bless and keep you."

He then gently kissed his son on the forehead and placed him in the arms of his father. Turning to his wife and daughter he invited them to take on the responsibility of naming their second son who was now nestling in the arms of Hannah. Emma ran to her mother's side and looking at her baby brother being tenderly nursed began to pour out a series of possibilities, all the while looking at her mother's face for signs of approval. Their combined efforts finally gave rise to the name Joseph, the men nodded in approval and the issue was settled. Tom lifted him high as he had done to his brother, and so Sam and Joe Stafford came into the world.

Tom and his father ate a quick meal, took a final look at the new offspring, and then ventured out into the autumn sunshine. They picked their way through the narrow streets, shielding their faces against the stench from the gutter, the contents of which were still being augmented by fresh loads of garbage descending from the overhanging windows to land on random targets. The dogcarts on their morning missions also vied for a safe passage, their owners breaking into an explosion of oaths if the shower of filth dropped in their vicinity. Reaching the quayside, they meandered to the point where the trow was moored, glad they could breath the somewhat fresher air of the estuary rather than the putrid city atmosphere. The docks were alive with ships and shipping, several large merchantmen demonstrating the increase in trade from the near and far continents, these provided a full day's labour that gladdened their hearts.

It was during the next few days Hannah reluctantly came to the conclusion her body could not bear the strain of suckling both of her sons. Her neighbour suggested that a young mother in the next tenement, having recently lost her new offspring, would be a worthy candidate for wet nursing. The young mother was willing to comply and terms were agreed for her to suckle Joseph whilst Samuel was suckled at his mother's breast.

~*~

The years quickly passed, walks along the riverbank into the forest area cemented a strong bond between Hannah and her daughter, the old man with Joseph and Tom with Sam.

They traversed the path along the river stopping to watch the wild life, the river traffic, and to pass the time of day with acquaintances they encountered on their various wanderings. It was in these couplings they could be found on market day in the city, exploring the various stalls erected to display a colourful variety of goods. Local produce, much of it grown or reared on the fringes of the city, included meat from many kinds of livestock and a variety of fruit and vegetables according to the season; all were available for those who could afford to buy. On other stalls, shining trinkets reflected the sun's rays and rich fabrics caught the eye, but if purchased, emptied the coffers. An array of household items could be seen in the established shops, they offered a better way of life to careful purchasers. Tom would move towards the bakers at the cross roads where the inviting aroma of freshly baked bread permeated the atmosphere, attracting customers from all quarters of the city. Hannah would buy her purchases for the daily meals, discussing them with Emma and passing them to her for safekeeping. Meanwhile, the old man with Joseph, pondered over the bric-a-brac of sundry stalls, where, after prolonged bargaining, they would procure small books or leaflets which provided information on the world about them, or which appeared to be little gems of literature. Despite his austere childhood the old man possessed a love of learning, which he had imparted to his son and was now attempting to plant the seeds of knowledge in his dealings with his grandsons; especially Joseph. Tom, with Sam at his side, explored the areas in the city where the craftsmen held sway. They would search out the wheelwrights, the sawyers, the carpenters, the potters and the smiths, or wander into the shipbuilding yards intent on watching the skill of the men employed in the various trades. Sam, despite his young years, would stand enthralled displaying a mature appreciation and asking questions which at times were beyond the limits of his father's knowledge.

When the mid-summer days were at their warmest, the fun of the fair could be found on the Downs. A long winding hill from the city centre brought the traveller to a large expanse of open greenery set high upon the edge of the gorge. Here the market had been transported from the city, to be set up beneath and between the majestic trees gracing the main area. It was here the crowds flocked to enjoy tumblers and acrobats, or to cringe as bare-fisted fighters fought endless rounds inflicting bloody wounds upon each other, but there was no submission, until one dropped to the floor through utter exhaustion, or a knockout blow that would have felled an ox. Even then it was not unknown for the seconds of the prone individual to apply copious amounts of cold water and much verbal encouragement in order to get him back on his feet and fighting again, in the faint hope they would still realise some profit on their wager. Later in the day, following a tour of the stalls offering a variety of merchandise and tempting morsels, there would be a taste of pork from the pig roasting.

The atmosphere was infectious as Tom and his family found to their great delight as they rested awhile on the green sward beneath a large plane tree, following, the long climb from the city and an exhausting but enjoyable day at the fair. Here they could espy the young flower girls, dodging in and out of the crowds endeavouring to sell their posies for a pittance. As they watched, the crowd would part as if controlled by an unseen force as a swarthy group of individuals swaggered from stall to stall. Thickset, fierce of eye and of intimidating appearance they made an unhurried approach to the victim of their selection. A fearful stallholder with a look of complete despair, would deftly withdraw a small moneybag from its secret hiding place, passing it with a nervous reaction to the leading thug. The cash deposit became an insurance for the year so that wherever the vendor decided to set his stall within the area; he was safe from being molested or his monies stolen. The gang doffed their hats as they departed towards their next victim, indicating the bargain had been sealed and they would be ready to do business again next year.

On the far side of the Downs, where the ground fell away into scrubland with dwarfed, windswept trees bending towards the city, a slight, weedy individual was hurriedly collecting his belongings. Hoping to make an unseen exit from the scene. Dewdrop was using all his guile in an effort to give his persecutors the slip, unfortunately his activities were noted and he knew he had been seen.

Hannah, with Emma by her side drifted to the main walkway across the Downs, here the gentry paraded with their ladies who were adorned in the fashions of the day. Mother and daughter were awestruck by the display; the arrogant, the proud, the dignified, the demure, were all there to capture the admiration of the onlookers and perhaps just one individual in particular. The sight of a small, dark-skinned boy dressed in western style snobbishness and attentive to every whim of his mistress's pleasure, made our two onlookers turn away in disgust to the stalls where their combined attentions could result in procuring a bargain. The old man, with Joseph probed the grasses, the trees, the bushes for treasures of nature, consulting with their newly acquired literature to glean further knowledge of the wonders of life around them. Tom, accompanied by Sam, was drawn to the far edge of the Downs, where one could look down from several hundred feet on to the dwarfed river traffic leaving the harbour on the evening tide. They stood and stared, man and boy, as the tall ships were coerced to a point of freedom then rounding the bend of the gorge into the full estuary and beyond. Tom wondered what lay before the travellers, what horizons they would see, what wonders they would behold and he would share these thoughts with his son as they made their way back to rejoin the rest of the family. Life for all of them, although not rich in material things, was good in many ways and the two men, by sheer hard labour, were progressing at a good rate in paying for the boat that was the mainstay of their livelihood. They were completely unaware of the change in their fortunes which was about to take place.

~*~

The twins had enjoyed their tenth birthday and the year had reached its festive close when the New Year brought a great change in the weather. A cold, heavy mist hung over the city and filled the deep gorge as if it was solid, the February sun failed to disperse the gloom and the cold, dank conditions prevailed.

"This cold penetrates my very bones," complained the old man and it came to Tom's notice that as they were working, his father would be fighting for breath, a legacy of his mining days now exacerbated by the prolonged unhealthy conditions. There were rumours of a fever outbreak in parts of the city, which folk blamed on the visiting crews of some of the ships. A few of these had been confined to the harbour for several weeks and would not be able to sail until the conditions improved with the lifting of the mist. Although there was no real proof of the fever scare, his father was not making progress, and Tom began to wonder if the rumours had some substance in them. His fears were heightened when young Joseph began to mirror the old man's symptoms, a worrying situation made worse when the lad would climb on his grandfather's lap in an endeavour to provide some comfort.

March came in like a lion. The wind blew strongly from the northeast, dispersing the misty fog and replacing it with cold, crisp days as the temperature began to fall. The old man and the boy grew weaker and despite every effort made by Hannah and Tom, they could not prevent the fever taking hold of both of them, it became impossible for the old man to go to work. In the freezing conditions Tom endeavoured to carry on their business single handed, finding the task overwhelming as he fought the ice, the river currents and the heavy loads; all too much for one man. Gradually he had to set his sights on smaller burdens in calmer waters, his earnings dropping to a level which brought them close to the poverty line and like many others in the city they supplemented their income by scavenging from the loose outcrops of coal on the fringes of the forest, or collecting waste timbers in and around the dock area, in order to provide a measure of warmth.

The wind suddenly dropped, an uneasy calm settled on the city and a strange light prevailed. The overcast sky became a leaden grey then, towards evening, the first flakes of snow began to fall, deadening the sounds of the city and creating an eerie silence. The quietness took possession of the city as the snow settled in an even, white covering and the streets became deserted. Joseph and his grandfather, both huddled in blankets, sat watching the changing scene. In the fading light they noticed all sharp edges had become rounded and small landmarks exaggerated.

"If this keeps on throughout the night it will be fairly deep by morning," the old man muttered, as he drew away from the window and snuggled down under the blankets with his young grandson who had not displayed his normal enthusiasm for the snow.

Morning dawned, the last flutter of white flakes adding the final flourish to the thick, white blanket which had created a new world, a different world, a world without blemish. Tom looked out on the silent scene and, more by habit than design, he began to rekindle the fire. By some miracle of fate the water pump in an adjoining street was still in use, so braving the elements he made his way to fill two buckets with water for the day's use. Returning to the tenement and ridding his footwear of the clinging snow, he enquired of Hannah how the invalids were fairing, she told him that as they were both still slumbering and the morning was very chill, she did not wish to disturb them. Tom looked in at the sleeping pair but he could observe no movement and he suddenly had a great sense of foreboding. Outside was a silent world, here inside their dwelling was an uncanny stillness and despite all efforts to arouse the sleepers, he was finally forced to interpret the absence of response in the only way he could. The old man and the boy, wrapped in each other's arms, had died peacefully during the night.

The realisation that his father and his son were no longer going to be part of their household reduced Tom to an utterly dejected being, he was unable to control his grief as he looked down upon the still figures in the bed. He could not come to terms with the fact his father would no longer pass onto him the wisdom of his years and that both members of his family would not rise, or see, or speak, or hear, or laugh again. Hannah, Emma and Sam endeavoured to console the new head of the family and shared in his grief, although death was a frequent visitor to the city, the family were heartbroken over the double tragedy. It had always been the old man's wish that he be buried with his wife within the forest, but the prevailing conditions, plus the uncertainty of finding the exact location, made Tom realise that he would not be able to comply with the final wish of his father. He therefore made arrangements for the oldest and the youngest in the family to be laid to rest in one of the churchyards within the city.

The family mourned the old man; his understanding, his knowledge, his patience, all these attributes they had taken for granted when he was with them, his death had caused a vacuum that could not be filled. Gone too was the constant questioning and the bright smile of little Joseph who, during his short lifetime, was forever seeking answers to the perplexities of his lively world. As well as losing his father, Tom had also lost his workmate and the partnership they had created was now torn asunder. The future would be bleak and unbearable without him. Mother and daughter both shed copious tears and as the family endeavoured to comfort each other they eased their own grief.

Some months later Emma brought a ray of hope to the family when she secured a situation with a seamstress, as well as being taught the trade she would also have a day at school each week until she was proficient at reading and writing. Although her contribution to the weekly finances would be comparatively small, the very fact she had been successful in obtaining the post meant a good deal, and hopefully augured well for the future.

Tom was making every effort to come to terms with his situation and he would sit trying to analyse his position, then discuss the various options with Hannah, both of them knowing full well they could not continue without more weekly income. He finally, very reluctantly, decided to sell his boat and seek work within the city. Hannah gave him her blessing, assuring him she would support him in whatever was required to secure their future together. The news that the trow was for sale was soon circulated around the dock and within a few days was common knowledge. One evening, as he was finishing his day's labours, he was approached by a tall stranger who was well versed in all the circumstances surrounding his situation, and who offered his help in finding a buyer for the trow. He explained to Tom he knew of a possible purchaser and made the suggestion of meeting with Tom and this third party a few days hence. Accordingly, they agreed to meet at the same spot and at the same time, three days from now when the prospective buyer would also be in attendance.

Three days later following the completion of his day's operations, Tom remained at the quayside close to the landing stage where the trow was moored. The evening was fairly calm, a light, offshore wind prevailed and the light had not faded, but for some reason, which he could not fathom, Tom felt ill at ease. The tavern was unusually quiet whilst the quayside was almost deserted, a state of affairs which did not help to bolster his confidence as he waited for the gentlemen he had promised to meet. He suddenly became aware of a presence; a tall, well-built stranger wearing a long dark blue cloak approached him and made his business clear. Yes, Tom had a boat for sale, he had fixed a price in his mind but this could be discussed once the stranger had inspected the craft. Together they moved along the quayside until they came upon a short flight of steps leading to the landing stage where the trow was gently pulling at its moorings. As they descended the steps, Tom began to point out to the stranger the merits of his craft and the qualities he thought made it ideal for the work, which he and his father had undertaken. The two men descended the steps to get a closer view and whilst Tom was extolling the characteristics of his beloved trow, he felt a thundering blow on the back of his head, he then collapsed into a lifeless heap at the feet of the stranger.

Out of the shadows of the bank, a jolly boat glided silently towards the landing stage, the two-man crew raised their oars and threw a rope to the tall stranger who pulled the boat towards the jetty, securing it to the little bollard. Tom was quickly bound and gagged then unceremoniously dumped into the stern of the boat as the seamen, now joined by the stranger, began to pull away from the bank heading for the middle of the river and the estuary beyond.

The cool breeze brought Tom back to part consciousness and as he painfully opened his eyes, he sensed the movement of the boat and saw beneath the long coat of the stranger the unmistakeable blue of a sailor's uniform. A deep sorrow overwhelmed him, he was lost, his family might never see him again and would possibly not survive this new trauma that had been thrust upon them. He feared for the future of his loved ones and himself with a dread that tore at his very soul. He had been press-ganged and there was nothing he could do to rectify the situation. He felt a greater swell beneath the boat and realised they were leaving the shelter of the gorge and moving towards a man-of-war anchored in the estuary. He was roughly handled upon to the deck where he lay, an untidy, half conscious bundle, as the man-of-war became a hive of activity. He painfully turned his head to look back up the gorge where he noticed, with full irony, he had passed the point, which he and Sam had viewed from the Downs and wondered what lay beyond. He now knew that he would soon have the answer to this question. Orders were shouted, men began running hither and thither, climbing the rigging unfurling the sails, raising the anchor, no-one noticed he was there. He could not look up, he lay utterly dejected and partly oblivious to all that was happening as the sails caught the breeze and the ship began to journey south.

Back at the tavern, which was now showing greater signs of life, a shifty, weedy individual, with a mean face that housed a large, hooked nose was pocketing a bag of money. He sat alone, drinking his own health and fully confident he would be able to pay his tormentors wherever he chose to set up his stall during the next two fairs.

~*~

23

Hannah sat with her children awaiting the arrival of Tom and hoping he would be the bearer of good news concerning the sale of the boat. They speculated about the price he had managed to raise and how they might use this financial gain to further their lot, whether they would remain in the city or return to the forest. There appeared to be several options open to them, but then they would remember Emma had her situation in the city and Tom would have to find some alternative employment now that the boat was sold. During their deliberations the time had ebbed away and Hannah was beginning to get anxious, her concern deepened when she realised evening had glided into night. The hours passed, there was still no sign of Tom, his evening meal remained untouched and would require re-heating when he arrived. Their discomfort grew as an uneasy silence settled on the family and words seemed to have little impact upon their mood, they sat with heads lowered and hearts full of misgivings as the night passed. Dawn began to break over three tired, unbelieving individuals who could find no explanation for their predicament, nor see any way forward without the guiding hand of the head of the household.

Morning came and as soon as she thought it safe to venture along the quay, Hannah resolved to walk to the spot where the boat was usually moored in order to glean any information concerning the happenings of the previous night. As Emma departed to her workplace, Hannah turned to her son and informed him of her intentions and he pleaded with her to let him accompany her. For several minutes Sam found his mother immovable and he almost gave up the argument, but finally she succumbed to his wishes and together they set out on their mission.

The quay was busy and as she threaded her way through the human traffic of the dock she encountered several of Tom's acquaintances, but their eyes averted her gaze and they gave no sign of recognition to mother or son. Sam noticed the trow before his mother, his keen young eyes searching for clues that might help them to solve the mystery of the previous, fatal night. He jumped down on the landing stage, but there were no indications as to what might have taken place, perhaps at this very spot. The boat was moored as they had seen it on other occasions but there was no sign of Tom or any of his belongings.

Dejectedly, they turned away from the trow and began to walk towards a group of folk who were gathered near the tavern, they were talking in undertones and Hannah dared to move closer to catch any snippets of conversation. She heard whispers of a man-of-war being anchored in the estuary but it must have sailed on the evening tide as the early workers on the quay noticed when they arrived that morning, she had already departed. There was a strong possibility a press gang had been at work in the city before she had weighed anchor, because extra hands were in great demand to crew two large vessels being commissioned on the south coast. It was rumoured the vessels would be away on a voyage of discovery for several years, this would take them to the other side of the world, and no man in his right mind wished to be dragged into such a situation. Hannah had heard sufficient of the conversation to confirm her worst fears and without a word to anyone she took hold of her son's hand and began to walk away from the quay and towards the city, her heart at breaking point and her mind in a whirl.

As she walked, with Sam at her side, she began to fear the worst for herself and her children. With Tom as her strength she could endure anything and the last few years had stretched them to the limits, but by some means or other they had prevailed and come through their troubles. Now, with her strength taken away from her, she was drifting on the sea of life without a pilot.

The next few days were lost to all the family; their grief was such they desired to see no one, or to venture outside of their tenement. On the third day, as the family were seated around the fire which Sam had managed to kindle, they were endeavouring to find some explanation for the sequence of events that had taken place, when a sharp rap on the door brought them all to a sense of expectation. As Hannah opened the door she recognised the voice of one of Tom's acquaintances, as he sought permission to enter. The immediate euphoria this friendly contact created was quickly turned to pessimism when the lighterman revealed he had no news of Tom's whereabouts, but he did know he had been abducted on the night the man-of-war was anchored in the estuary.

"The talk in the city concerning two large vessels being commissioned seems to be correct," said the man. "Tom was not the only river man to be press ganged that evening, we are aware of at least one other, but it is Tom we are concerned about and it is his family we have pledged to help."

Hannah's heart sank, this kindly, rough, dockworker had confirmed her worst fears but she was at a loss to know how this man, or any of his colleagues, could be of service to herself and her children. With an awkward gesture he reached into the folds of his outer garment producing a moneybag, which he placed on the table in front of Hannah. Absent-mindedly she lifted the bag from its resting place noticing it was a good deal heavier than she had anticipated. The man continued with some hesitation.

"When we discovered how Tom had been set up whilst trying to sell his boat, several of his friends decided they could be of service on two counts. Firstly, they would attempt to finalise the sale of the boat, several lightermen were interested in effecting a purchase, and secondly, they determined to seek out the individual who was responsible for selling Tom down the river. On the first count, a generous offer had been made for the boat, therefore on Hannah's behalf they had accepted and sealed the bargain; on the second count, several of the dock workers at the tavern, had an inkling as to the identity of the traitor who had made it possible for Tom to be abducted. When the man was taken to task on the issue, he was found to be in possession of a large sum of money and when further questioned, by one of the larger members of the company, he agreed he had arranged for Tom's capture. This weedy, little customer has therefore made a sizeable contribution to the amount in the bag, as he was generous enough to hand over his ill gotten gains, his name is Dewdrop so if you should have the misfortune to meet him, you can treat him with utter contempt, or thank him for the gift."

Hannah stood and stared at the man in utter amazement, she had not reckoned on this turn of events and to be shown favourable consideration by such a rough body of men, robbed her of her reasoning. Finally, she managed to summon sufficient courage to thank the man for all he and his friends had accomplished on her behalf, and for the sake of the two children, who obviously would also benefit from their generosity of thought and deed. She prevailed on him to deliver her grateful thanks and good wishes to his workmates back at the quay. As he departed he wished the family well, adding, "You cannot mistake Dewdrop, he is like a little river rat, with a large hooked nose from which hangs his nickname, but I feel that he may be missing from the area for some time."

The Notice In The Window

Chapter Two

The Printer

Outside the forest and towards the east, along a very rough road reputed to be one of the worst highways in England, called the Bath Waye, the Spa city housed the printing success of a family concern, trading under the name of 'Manpitt'. Occupying a prime sight near the imposing abbey, the business had exceeded all expectations, enabling the owner to purchase a fine dwelling on the outskirts of the city. Set in several acres of land, the house was home for Mr and Mrs Matthew Manpitt and their son Richard. Matthew had inherited a situation that gave him a freedom of choice, to continue with his father's business, or to set up and develop his own interest in printing. He chose the latter course of action and now employed several men at his printing works in the city. His wife, unfortunately, was becoming increasingly infirm and although they employed several servants, he required a trustworthy housekeeper who could oversee the daily running of the household and also act in the capacity of a companion to his wife. To this end he prepared and printed several leaflets advertising the situation, and these had been displayed in the area, with a few being delivered to the busy port to the west.

One of these notices exhibited in a shop window near the market, had caught Hannah's attention whilst she was on one of her shopping trips, she informed her daughter of some of the content of the notice but admitted she did not fully understand the implications of all that was printed therein. Mother and daughter therefore, returned to the shop where the notice was displayed and were fortunate enough to encounter the shopkeeper, who appraised them of the fact that Mr Manpitt would be in the city in two days time; he would be in contact with him and would inform him of their interest. Two days later Hannah and Emma positioned themselves near the shop being visited by the printer and awaited his arrival. Unaware of his appearance, stature or bearing, mother and daughter received several false hopes. However, as customers arrived and then departed from the premises, the businesslike approach of the shopkeeper gave them a gleam of hope. His desire to make an impression on his customers meant he would accompany them to the door of his abode, wish them well and then with a gesture of the hand usher them through the door, which he had already opened for their departure, uttering their name as he bid them good day. Their patience was finally rewarded when the name they had been waiting to hear was announced by the shopkeeper, as a man of medium build, with slightly greying hair and rather refined features, emerged from the shop. With their pulses racing and wondering how to seize the opportunity, Emma suddenly took the initiative and almost curtseying to the stranger, blurted out: "Sir my mother would like to speak with you."

Completely startled by this intrusion into his privacy and being accosted in the street, especially by a woman, Mr Manpitt stopped and came face to face with Hannah. Quickly she asked for his forgiveness for the intrusion and then unfolded her desire to glean more details concerning the situation advertised in the shop window; as she would like to be considered for the post. In reply the gentleman gave Hannah a small printed card.

"This," he said, "is my name, and the address of my premises near the market here in this city, and if you present yourselves at this office, on the morrow at noon, I will be available to talk further with you."

Hannah and her daughter took their leave of the gentleman, thanking him for his consideration and kindness and confirmed they would be at the appointed place at midday. Accordingly, on the following day, as the city clock was striking twelve, mother and daughter approached the address on the card. They made a very cautious entrance to a small office, situated in a side street just off the market square and were requested to wait in a rather bare, outer room, by a young lad who appeared to be in charge of the situation. After a few minutes of nervous anxiety the young lad announced that Mr Manpitt was ready to see them, accordingly he ushered them up a couple of bare wooden steps and directed them through a solid oak door into an office, where the gentleman they had conversed with the previous day, was seated. Hannah, her heart pounding, but everyone of her senses alert, climbed the two steps leading in to the office whilst holding firmly on to the hand of her daughter.

Mr Manpitt bade them be seated as he pointed out wooden chairs close to a rather fine mahogany desk, behind which he reclined at ease. After listening to a description of her circumstances and why she was seeking this particular post, he explained at length the duties, the pay and conditions of the situation for Hannah, then added that with Emma's training as a seamstress, despite the fact she had not yet completed her apprenticeship, he was certain he could make use of her services. Hannah decided this was the opportune moment to acquaint her possible employer with the complete picture of her present circumstances, and set about explaining her concern for Sam. Mr Manpitt regarded her with a rather serious look, hesitated for a few moments, then expressed his desire to comply with her wishes with regard to keeping the family together, but he had no position for Sam and he could not envisage one in the near future. Seated in the alien surroundings of the office, with a possible solution to their future being mapped out before them, Hannah was suddenly full of misgivings, as she fully contemplated the inevitable splitting up of the family.

Not recognising that the lady seated in front of him was deeply concerned over matters of a personal nature, Mr Manpitt made the situation more complex by supplying the knowledge he had already interviewed a second lady in Bath, that she had been offered the post and was at the moment, considering her answer. This lady had made a firm promise to acquaint him with her final decision in three days time, he therefore proposed they meet again, at the same time and in the same place four days from now. As they parted company at the door of his office Mr Manpitt noticed in Hannah's countenance, despite her mental wrestling with all the knowledge she had just gleaned, a quality of character that had not been apparent in the lady he had made his first choice. They both agreed the interlude would give them a time for contemplation on a variety of solutions, in particular the future well being of Sam.

On returning home the main topic of conversation was the question of Sam's future, should Hannah have a favourable outcome to her next meeting with the printer? All the avenues presenting possibilities were explored, the one big stumbling block to each solution was the resources required for placing Sam into a reasonably secure situation. One of their final discussions encompassed placing Sam under the ever-watchful eye of the local butcher and his wife, a Mr and Mrs Streer. For a young lad in Sam's circumstances, there were very few possibilities within the city, but this particular situation offered some hope, especially now Hannah could afford to make a contribution towards Sam's keep. She concluded she would make her way to the shop and ascertain the full details from the two people concerned.

~.*.~

The butcher stood upright and proud, confident in his ability to deal with all that was thrown at him on a physical plane; his massive arms and shoulders had been developed over the years by wrestling with the various livestock delivered to his premises for slaughter. The slaughterhouse stood at the rear of the shop and housed the fierce looking pole-axes with which he could fell, at one stroke, the beasts brought to him for butchering. Having established that Hannah was not a customer, but that she had come to make inquiries concerning the vacancy he had for a butcher's boy, he called for his wife to join him, whereupon a small, 'Sparrow' like creature entered and stood by the side of the butcher, being completely dwarfed by his presence.

Money was the key; for an amount Hannah could now afford, the couple agreed to house the lad whilst he was being trained as a delivery boy, then if required, he could enter into a full apprenticeship to train as a qualified butcher. His earnings during this time would not be great, but he would finally be in a good trade.

"Meat is always required by the populace," piped up Mrs Streer in a funny high-pitched voice.

"Yes," added her husband, "and good meat at that." His booming tones were pitched well over an octave lower and issued forth from a cavern set between two mighty red cheeks. "If he stays here with us, Mrs Streer will provide nothing but the best," he continued, "but you must decide, and quickly please Mam, because I have other boys who are interested." He finished his discourse with a flourish of the meat cleaver, which he had been brandishing in the air throughout the conversation and as his wife retreated away from her husband, he brought the blade down with such forceful precision that the pork chop, was severed with one blow, and almost flew off the block.

Hannah left the premises wondering if her son would be safe

in such an environment, then she reasoned that there were many questions to be resolved before Sam would be sleeping above the shop. Most of these imponderables were outside of her control, so much depended on the second visit to the printer, but the butcher offered a possible solution to Sam's need.

Equipped with a partial solution to Sam's future, the next meeting with the printer was awaited with great eagerness but also much trepidation. Finally, the moment came when Hannah and her daughter were seated, as before, in the inner office and it became very apparent the printer was agitated and focused on some issue that was beyond their comprehension. Mr Manpitt suddenly came to life, he smiled and then gently informed his guests that he was in a predicament concerning the lady he had mentioned at their previous meeting.

"As yet she has not honoured the commitment she made concerning her final answer. I will await the arrival of the next London coach, which is due shortly, but if there is no message delivered I cannot extend the period of grace, we must proceed with our discussion."

Mr Manpitt was watching the effect his words had upon Hannah and was attempting to analyse the full spectrum of her feelings, in particular the look of dejection, which was appearing as the moments passed. The atmosphere suddenly changed, as a knock on the door was followed by the entry of the young lad from the outer office, clutching a note. He passed the message to the printer who, on receiving it, unfolded the document with a very deliberate action and began to read. Hannah watched his face, scrutinizing all the changes of expression, as the printer perused every word of the letter laid out on his desk before him, but she gained no comfort from her observations and her spirits sank.

Placing the letter in front of him Mr Manpitt looked up and fixing his gaze on Hannah said, "This letter, which has arrived much later than it should have done, has given me the information we require, we can now proceed. The lady concerned has declined the post I offered her, as she has now accepted a far more lucrative position in London. I must, therefore be acquainted with your feelings in the matter."

Hannah failed to hide her emotions as she realised there was a strong possibility that her prospects, together with Emma's, were assured for the foreseeable future and hopefully Sam would be able to join them later. Her joy at accepting the post for a trial period of six months was beyond all bounds as she acquainted the printer with the news of Sam's placement at the Streer's butchery.

The printer continued, "Now that we are of one mind in this matter, I will make arrangements for you and your daughter to accompany me on the morning stagecoach, some time next week and I wish your son well in his new venture, I will contact you again when everything is finalised."

He rose to his feet, directed them to the outer office where they were politely ushered from the building by the lad who had delivered the note.

Chapter Three

The Butchers

Mr Streer was grateful for a speedy answer to his suggestion and agreed to Hannah's request to allow Sam to remain with his mother and sister for the next two days. Having spent a joyous time together, Sam collected his few belongings, bade farewell then strode purposefully away from the tenement towards his new surroundings. Hannah had deemed it politic to establish Sam with the Streers before they departed for their future home, as she was full of misgivings concerning the family being separated. Sam assured her he would be happy with the butcher and in any event, he would see her from time to time when she called to pay his lodgings. Even if they did not meet, they would be able to exchange messages concerning their well-being and she would, in all probability, be given a progress report from the butcher.

"Your room is the one at the front over the shop," the shrill voice of Mrs Streer echoed in his head as he climbed the narrow, wooden staircase and entered the room, which would now be his domain. Void of any home comforts, Sam investigated the simple abode and decided that it could be worse; he therefore resolved he would make every endeavour to succeed. A few days, later standing at the roadside he watched the carriage bearing his mother and sister away from the city, and then he turned with misty eyes and a large lump in his throat in the direction of the butchers.

~*~

"When you are in the shop, you are under my control," the stentorian command reverberated down the little corridor leading to the slaughterhouse, "this area is out of bounds, for the present, as far as you are concerned and if you are required in the hothouse then Mrs Streer will give you full instructions."

Sam heeded the directions, making every effort to comply with the wishes of his master, or the twittering chatter of his wife. Under the ever-watchful eyes of both of them he made a good start and, to his surprise, he derived a degree of pleasure from his work, making quite certain that he did not encroach on any of the territory leading to the slaughterhouse. He enjoyed the freedom of delivering individual orders in the city, as well as to some of the larger establishments; in the shop he swept up the bloodied sawdust, replacing it with sweet smelling, white, pine dust from the local sawyers. When the command came to join Mrs Streer in the hothouse, he was shown the delicate art of pulling the feathers out of the warm bodies of the hens as they hung by their feet.

"If you do as I do, while the birds are still warm, it is much easier, with a little care you do not bruise the flesh and the fact they are hanging by their feet means all the blood is collecting in the head," she twittered. Later when she demanded that he now draw the birds, as well as pluck them, his courage failed and it was then he found the 'sparrow' could become a 'hawk'. Having steeled himself to carry out her wishes, a further test came when he was presented with several rabbits with instructions to skin and gut them, without spoiling the fur.

Sam enjoyed seeking out the drovers at the city boundary, so he could accompany them on the return trip directing them to the establishment where he was being trained. Once the shop was in view he always found an excuse to leave the drovers to their task just in case there was a steer that could 'smell the blood,' as the butcher described the resistance of the animal embarking on its final journey. He then sought solace in the shop with the creatures that had already been subjected to Mr Streer's attentions.

The hothouse was worthy of its name, when Mrs Streer required to boil some beef, or to salt meat strips for the needs of the mariners in the docks. Sam would finish the day with raw, red hands, his head full of muddled instructions and a lingering odour in his nostrils, which also permeated his clothing. The hot water she supplied for a final cleansing, coupled with the salt did nothing to ease the discomfort of the many small cuts and chaps sustained as he endured the complete domination of the 'sparrow', with her incessant cry of, "The populace will always require meat, whether on land or at sea, and Mr Streer can fulfil the need, boy. Do you agree?"

Sam could not disagree as he watched her swinging a rather wet cloth with evil intent, he had felt the sting of this subtle chastiser on several occasions in past days and he had no desire to renew any acquaintance with it.

It was always "BOY," whether called for service by the double bass voice of the butcher, or the squeak of his wife, but one evening the typical tone of the butcher carried a greater compulsion.

"Boy," he said, as he drew Sam closer to his side. "We will require you to move your belongings from your present situation to the room at the rear of the premises, the one over the slaughterhouse."

Before Sam could utter a word of inquiry as to why the move was necessary, the voice boomed again. "My nephew George, is going to join us, he is coming from Somerset to undertake a course in butchery so that he may be of greater use on the farm owned by his father, my brother. Of course he will be making some payment to me for my services, but this will be in kind; unlike the pittance brought to me by your mother. I therefore wish to place George in your room, firstly because he is family, and secondly because he will be making a greater contribution to the coffers of the Streers."

Sam realised he could not make out a case of appeal against the sentence he had just received, so with great reluctance he carried out the wishes of his employer. That night he lay awake as his imagination ran riot with the thoughts of what could happen in the room below him and when he found an ill fitting, old trap door, in the floor of this room, he wondered if, through the spaces in the woodwork, he might bear witness to some of these atrocities.

~*~

George duly appeared, larger than Sam in stature and several years his senior, but on their first meeting they struck a friendly chord; the one great difference was the fact that George was family and Sam was not. The arrival of George had the immediate effect of putting Sam's training on hold, he did not progress to the full butchery programme as he was expecting to do, and instead he was placed with the 'sparrow' to be instructed by her. A few days after the arrival of the nephew, two roosters were brought to the shop, accompanied by a note, which simply stated '*for the attention of Mrs Streer.*' Taking hold of the small crate that housed the birds, she placed it in the hothouse and instructed Sam to come to the room at dusk. Sam duly arrived to be witness to the following:

"Now boy, you do it this way," said his mentor, and taking the live rooster, which had just settled for the evening, by its feet, she placed the bird under her left armpit, gently stroked the back of its head with a tenderness that amazed Sam, then with a firm, quick movement she lowered its head, pulling and twisting at the same time. The bird had made no sound, there was no resistance, no flurry of feathers, it just lay lifeless in the arms of the butcher's wife, its neck broken. Sam could hardly believe his eyes and his brain did not really comprehend when the order came to try his hand on the remaining bird. He managed to take hold of the bird's feet and with a struggle he finally positioned it under his armpit, the stroking he carried out with great feeling, but the pulling and twisting was not as confident as it should have been, so that when he released his hold the neck sprung back into it normal position; the bird was still alive.

The 'sparrow' was obviously enjoying the entertainment, "Have another try, boy, only this time finish the creature off because we are going to stay here until you get it right." Her admonition motivated Sam to a second attempt, but unfortunately for the bird it required a third effort before the rooster lay lifeless in Sam's grasp.

"I reckon it died of exhaustion," cackled the woman, "but in all fairness you did the job in three, I have seen trainees make as many as six attempts before they accomplished their first killing. Now I know you can do it, I will leave you in charge of this particular aspect of our work." She cackled again as she added, "See they are both plucked and drawn before you turn in, as you are aware it is so much easier when they are still warm." She turned leaving Sam on his own looking down at the dead birds requiring his attention.

~*~

Jack the carter, who boasted he could move anything anywhere as long as he was back in his own home by nightfall, possessed a very useful form of transport which had been christened, the 'meat wagon.' The reasoning behind this was the fact that it was basically a large, square box mounted on wheels and drawn by his trusted nag. The rear of the box housed a door, this enabled small animals to be loaded, or off loaded, with ease. The Streers usually employed the carter when the butcher had effected animal purchases in the area outside the city and they required transport from the farm. Sam had noticed the meat wagon was used every month or so and somewhere in the back of his mind the seed of an idea began to germinate.

The notion was further nurtured when Sam witnessed scenes that were to change his life. The carter had delivered a live pig to the butchers and this was housed in the premises to the rear of the building. That night, following a full day with the 'sparrow' slaving in the hothouse, and with no thought for the Streers, George (who was family), or the pig, Sam slept like a log. Fairly early the following day Sam was awakened by the protesting squeals of the pig coming from the room below. He heard the crunching noise of the poleaxe and the muffled bass voice of the butcher congratulating his nephew on a perfect kill. "You can always tell when it's family," said the butcher. "I could not have done a better job myself. Come, we will let the pig bleed while we have our breakfast and then later we can butcher it."

Sam was aware the family breakfast was more substantial in quantity and quality, than the meal that would be placed out for him, but then he was not family and the family, including George, ate together. As Sam dined alone he wondered about the pig and decided it might be possible to observe the scene through the trap door. His efforts were rewarded when by lying prone on the floor, and twisting his body to get a better view, he found he could see clearly through a wide gap. The pig lay dead on the floor, its lifeblood draining away into a trough whilst the family finished their breakfast and Sam awaited their return. Later that morning the butcher informed his wife he had work to be completed in the slaughterhouse and he would take George to assist him. Sam listened to the conversation with ears agog and as soon as he was able, he made an excuse to go to his room. The 'sparrow' endeavoured to impede his progress but with customers in the shop demanding attention, she was forced to let her busyness override natural curiosity as to the purpose of Sam's mission.

As he settled himself in the same position over the trap door, he could clearly see that the pig had now been raised from the floor and was hanging from two hooks on the side wall. The butcher looked at his nephew and, placing a large, shining knife in his hand, urged him to open up the pig. Sam froze in horror, as the nephew with obvious delight, raised his hand and with one swift, confident cut, opened up the soft underside of the pig so the entrails came tumbling out like a waterfall. Sam did not even notice the container which had been placed in position to collect the offal of the pig, he almost lost his breakfast and he knew if he lived to be one hundred, he could never undertake the task which George had just performed. His days in the butchery business were numbered. He had to escape. He could cope with the chickens, the rabbits and perhaps a hare, but when in his imagination he envisaged a bullock hanging from the meat hook and his master passing him the knife, there was no possibility of him ever becoming family.

How was he going to escape? Where would he go? How would he live? He did not know. These questions occupied most of his waking thoughts and he was being brought back, on a fairly regular basis, to the task in hand by the swinging, wet cloth of the 'sparrow'. He consoled himself by remembering the good times when the family lived in the tenement, life was hard for all of them, especially his parents, but he was loved and he loved in return. Here he was alone, he was perhaps being fed very well in comparison with the frugal fare his mother could afford, and this reminded him of one of this grandfather's sayings about a dinner of herbs where love is, but he could not remember the exact words.

As he lay on his bed one evening, one of those rare evenings when he had not been called to the hothouse, he could hear someone talking in the room below.

"Have you managed to make the appointment with my father to come and visit you, Uncle?"

There was a slight pause before the unmistakeable tones of the butcher made reply, "We have not finalised the date, because I am hoping that I can couple the coming of my brother with a task I have for Jack the carter. I have purchased two sheep from a farm in the forest and he will transport them for me. At the same time I am hoping he will agree to take the boy with him, it means we shall have just family on the premises so that our business will not be overheard."

Sam had absolutely no desire to eavesdrop on the family chatter, but what he had just heard was music to his ears and his mind was now settled, all he had to do was to wait and, in the meantime, endure the ravings of the 'sparrow'. He worked with a light heart over the next weeks and to the surprise of the 'sparrow', did not shirk any of the tasks she gave him.

He did ponder on something he never quite understood and that was, despite the fact his mother had made several visits to the shop, he had never been informed of her coming and had only been given very brief details concerning her visit after her departure. Somehow he was always on duties, which took him away from the premises when her visits were imminent and he perceived that this was a deliberate policy of the butcher. He now felt confident with his escape plan, fostering the idea in his mind that if he was going towards the Spa city then there was a possibility he might meet up with his mother and sister once again.

The arrival of the butcher's brother made Sam's heart pound in his body, this must be the day he had been waiting for, now all that was required was the meat wagon with Jack the carter in charge.

"Boy," the call that required an immediate response thundered down the little corridor to his room where he was alert and eagerly waiting.

"I wish you to take a trip with the carter today, he is visiting a farm in the forest and will be returning this evening with two sheep I have purchased. The weather is good and he wishes to leave directly, so look lively and come and meet him."

Sam almost fell down the small flight of steps which brought him to the same level as the Streers, passing them without a word he ran out on to the street to see his salvation, the meat wagon. Jack was already aboard on the only seat available, so he invited his passenger to climb on to a small plank of wood, which he had placed across the corner of the wagon.

Sam managed to scramble on to the plank arranged by the carter, making himself as secure as he was able. Jack ran the reins through his fingers giving them a slight jerk, at the same time uttering some incomprehensible command, which stirred the horse into life as they moved away from the butchers towards the market square. Sam's spirits sank as some of the scenes he now witnessed reminded him of the family days when they perused the market together, but his heart was uplifted as they travelled eastwards towards the forest, leaving behind the sounds and smells of the city. The tall buildings were replaced by single storey dwellings; many of them stone cottages which increased in number as they made progress towards the forest. Jack came to life as they approached a division in the highway.

"We journey on the Bath Waye here my lad," explained the carter as he took the right-hand fork in the road, "The other road is the London Waye, and they be both as bad as each other when it comes to wear and tear on the cart." This was quite a speech from the carter and although he was not aware of the condition of the London road, Sam was in full agreement concerning the state of the surface on which they were travelling.

"I agree this road is rather bumpy and there are a number of large holes in its surface, which makes my situation a little uncomfortable," he replied.

"If you need to stretch your legs lad, you can do one of two things; jump down and walk, or slide down into the cart and stand up. Tis' spread with good, new straw so you'll come to no harm."

Sam was glad he had not kept his peace, as he usually did with the butcher, so easing his sore buttocks from the plank he turned and slid down into the meat wagon giving himself a vantage point where he had an all round view of his surroundings.

They were now travelling rather hilly terrain and the March sun silhouetted the forest against the skyline. There were majestic oaks and elms, interspersed with sturdy beeches, sycamores and chestnuts with the lacelike tracery of emerging leaves on the silver birches almost transparent against the sunlight. The ash bursting its black buds with new green life heralded the arrival of another spring, another summer, and Sam, as he looked upon these wonders, hoped it also predicted another chance. Here and there the trees had been felled with the result that the furzes together with the hollies had taken up residence; there were also areas of rather poor grazing with stony outcrops breaking through the soil. Sam studied the landscape with renewed interest as they approached a small village, which the carter called, Annum.

"Here," he informed his passenger, "Our journey comes to its turning point, but before we visit the farm to collect the sheep, I intend to take some refreshment at the Blue Bowl."

Sam wandered a little way down the lane that adjoined the inn and to his surprise came upon a thriving timber yard with a large sawpit in obvious use. He made himself comfortable on the bank of the lane oblivious to the time slipping away, as he watched the activities of the sawyers and the carter refreshed himself for the homeward journey.

Having collected the sheep from the farm, situated across the Bath Waye from the Blue Bowl, Sam secured his plank on the corner of the cart and settled himself for the homeward trip. He looked down through the large mesh net the carter had placed over the top of the cart to see two, woolly, sad eyed sheep with busy tails. His thoughts were immediately transferred to his room with the trap door, the sight of the pig and George. He was now absolutely certain that he had to escape and in his imagination he wondered if he could take the sheep with him, but he dismissed this latter flight of fancy when he reminded himself that stealing a loaf of bread was a hanging offence, so the sentence for two sheep was too horrible to contemplate.

The cart rumbled on, the return journey was pleasant with the warm sun overhead and when Sam looked at the carter it was obvious that the refreshment he had taken in the Blue Bowl had a soporific effect, he was asleep, the reins slack in his grasp, his chin resting on his chest and his eyes closed. Without thinking of the consequences Sam nudged the carter who came to life with a start and asked why his slumbers had been so rudely interrupted, Sam spluttered out some excuse, which was simply nonsense and was immediately taken to task by his inebriated companion.

"The horse knows the way lad, if I nod off after a hard day's work, then so be it, leave me alone."

Realising a sleeping partner could not be a witness to his disappearance, Sam watched with confidence as the drowsy carter drifted back into the land of nod, leaving him in peace to plan his moment of freedom.

He was watching the passing scenery, waiting for the high point on the road where he decided he would have the best chance of making his escape. The horse slowed to a gentle gait and slowed even further when the hill began to take its toll, and there was no reprimand from his sleeping master. Sam decided this was the moment he had planned for, with a quick, final glance at the sheep and unobserved by the carter, he jumped. He had chosen the spot well, landing on the verge where the grass was lush and green he rolled over in a somersault, tumbling down a small embankment between the trees. Picking himself up he began to run as fast as his legs would carry him, his young body had been strengthened by the diet given to him by the 'sparrow' and the fact that he was now free increased his desire to get away as quickly as possible. He knew the river lay to the south and he could tell from the contours of the land in which direction he had to run, urging himself onwards over the rough ground between the trees and dodging the furzes and hollies. As he ran to the south, but away from the city, he became conscious of the small cottages dotted between the trees, there seemed to be no pattern to their placement and he would be suddenly surprised by the movement of rough looking adults, or dirty children as they moved about their business. Driving his body to the limit he kept the fear of being caught in mind, telling himself he must pull away from the city and get into the forest as far as he was able.

Chapter Four

The Forest

By chance he came across a small, clear stream, cupping his hands he refreshed himself with some of its cool liquid. His mouth was dry from fear, as well as exertion and as the water restored and enlivened his palate he suddenly realised how hungry he was, he had not eaten since leaving the butchers. Several possibilities came to mind but he decided that as it was getting dark he would push on for as long as he could, seek a place to sleep the night and endeavour to find food on the morrow. The evening became darker and amid the shadows of the trees he began to stumble over exposed roots. Still making his way towards the river he found it easier to follow the stream that had provided him with refreshment, until it suddenly disappeared into a crevice in the ground.

He made greater headway across patches of poor grazing; these formed uneven patterns and were the result of forest felling. Feeling fairly secure he decided to seek out a place to rest. Rather hungry and more than a little frightened, he finally settled himself beneath a large beech tree and endeavoured to adjust his weary limbs to the contours of the bare, stony soil. Before he drifted into sleep the first misgivings tumbled into his mind, his room above the slaughterhouse was far from palatial but he usually managed a reasonable slumber, especially when it was preceded by a helping of Mrs Streer's soup. Tonight he would not have the comfort of either; he just hoped the hours of darkness would not bring rain so that the morrow might give him time for exploration in dry clothing.

With this and many other thoughts swimming around in his young head he gradually fell into oblivion. He was not educated in the night noises of the forest and several times he was disturbed by what he believed to be the padding of small animals moving across the forest floor, but his desire to rest his tired body decided him against investigating any of these interruptions to his sleep.

The bright, low, morning sun came streaming through the fresh green foliage of the overhanging canopy, warming his young muscles into activity. Sam shielded his eyes against the brightness and began to stretch his limbs to relieve them of an ache and stiffness he had not experienced before. As he did so he came upon two animals drinking from a shallow pool not many yards away. He stifled his surprise, endeavouring to maintain a stillness and a silence leaving these magnificent creatures undisturbed. Watching with growing admiration he noticed the delicate build of the smaller of the two, its wonderful colour in the morning sun, the lighter almost round blotches on the main body skin, the restless tail and the noble head. Drinking slowly whilst maintaining a majestic stance, it was as if one kept watch for the other and from where he stood, Sam could see the darkness of the eyes, the neat muzzle and the slender sinewy legs. The larger animal raised its head to display a set of horns such as Sam had never seen before and he almost exploded with admiration when the two animals slipped away into the forest and were lost to view.

Slowly he walked towards the spot where the animals had been drinking to find a shallow stream running across the forest floor, hoping this would meander to lower ground and finally to the river, he decided to follow its course. A short distance away the stream tumbled over a rocky outcrop creating a natural waterfall, which seemed to possess a myriad rainbows in the morning sunlight. Cupping his hands beneath the edge of the fall he drank deeply of the sparkling water and then refreshed his facial skin.with the cool spring flow.

The number of dwellings increased as he made his way along the path beside the stream and signs of life came from a number of them. Adult men, unkempt and dirty, were accompanied by young lads who were in the same poor condition, their general gait gave the impression they had little desire to pursue their daily labours whether it be in the mine, the quarry or on the farm. He managed to dodge several groups of individuals and was working his way across to a thicker part of the forest when he noticed that the ground fell away into a deep recess.

Two Magnificent Creatures Drinking From A Pool

Here, he thought, there must have been a quarry of some kind, or folk had simply removed the stone for their own use, or perhaps it was just a natural fault. Whatever the explanation the situation provided a good hiding-place, especially as several large hollies had taken root and flourished. Behind the hollies Sam noticed a tiny whiff of smoke rising in the clear air and he decided to investigate further.

Carefully working his way towards the area where he'd seen the smoke, and rounding one of the biggest hollies, he was astonished to see a young lad sitting on a large, flat stone. He was turning a wooden spit which was resting in the forks of two sturdy twigs placed upright in the ground, one each side of a fire that was contained within a circle of stones. On the spit was a fish, gutted and speared down the length of its body, it appeared and smelt almost ready to eat. Sam felt his hunger pains even stronger than before and he moved forward to ascertain if the lad was alone or if he was a member of a larger group. As he edged closer he heard the crack of a dead branch underfoot. The sudden noise had an immediate effect upon the lad, as quick as lightning he turned and he and Sam were transfixed for several moments. Both of them were rather apprehensive until Sam noticed the fish was beginning to burn. Breaking the silence he pointed out to the stranger he was about to lose the fine fish, which he had prepared and cooked. The lad responded by removing the spit from its resting place and, looking directly at Sam, said in a very matter of fact tone, "And who are you?"

For a moment or two there was no response, the smell of the fish and his desire for something to eat was all too much. "Is the fish good to eat?" spluttered Sam.

"They are exceedingly tasty," came the reply, "Would you like to share this one with me?"

Sam did not require a second invitation he quickly joined his new acquaintance and together they began to devour the fish. The fresh-faced lad who had made the kind offer to share his breakfast with a complete stranger was watching the interloper with a shrewd expression.

"You were hungry my friend, I have a notion you have not eaten for a while and, if your appetite has not been satisfied, we can cook a second fish, and I think I have a little bread we can share.

Sam was at a loss, this complete stranger had welcomed him, he had shared one fish with him and now he was prepared to share another. The boy moved away from the fire and disappeared from sight. Before Sam could comprehend he had returned holding a shining fish which he had unwrapped from some large leaves. He skilfully pushed the wooden spit down through the fish and placed it over the fire.

"Now we can talk for a while until the fish is cooked, and I did have a little bread in store so we can share that as well."

Sam was speechless, how and where did this delicious food come from and where did the boy go?

"We will formally introduce ourselves," said the boy as he gently turned the spit. "Who are you and where have you come from?" He gave Sam a look that demanded a truthful answer. There was no need for any cover story, the simple truth of why he was in the forest could be explained fairly quickly and so the family history of life in the city, the troubles within the family, the final split from his mother and sister all came rattling off the tongue. He made light of life with the butcher and how he had planned his escape, he told of his first night in the forest and how he awoke to the sight of two beautiful, wonderful creatures. "And my name is Sam," he concluded in triumph.

He sighed with relief and waited for his newfound companion to complete the introductions.

On The Spit Was A Fish

"Our stories are quite similar in one or two respects but very different in others. My name is David, David Bell, but I am known by my nickname, Ding Dong, or if you prefer just Ding or just Dong, I do not object to any of these. I was born somewhere in the north of the forest, actual place unknown, day and month not sure and year not recorded. My mother came from Ireland with a group of Romanies and met my father in the forest area, he was a military man but he had suffered a severe leg wound in France. This made life very difficult for both of them, even more so when I arrived, however the folk in the group were very kind and when my parents died from pneumonia within days of each other, I was adopted into the larger family. Therefore, my friend I have now a number of fathers and mothers, all of whom will willingly house me in the wintertime. Here in the forest I can stay in my cave during the summer months, I call it my 'summer palace' and I live off the land plus a few extras, such as the bread we shared together. These extras are provided by a very special friend of mine and, if you are intending to stay in the area for any length of time, I will try and arrange an introduction."

Sam was dumbfounded, for a few moments he could not move, there were so many questions in his mind, but most of all he was intrigued by the idea of the summer palace.

"Where is your cave, the one you call your summer palace, is it far from here?" he asked.

"Sam, I will now call you Sam, because that is your name, you are looking at it but you do not see it. Over there behind the largest of the hollies you will find a natural wall of stone covered in ivy, part of the wall has fallen away and formed a cave-like structure. I have adapted the cave part, built a small extension to the front to make it cosier and to keep out the worst of the weather, that is why I am only a summer resident. The caravans the Romanies have are so much warmer and far more comfortable when the winter storms begin. At one time I did spend all the year with them, they took me on all their travels and I have much to thank them for. They gave me the knowledge and taught me the skills that have made me independent, but now I am older I like to divide my year into two, spending the summer here and the winter with them. This is my third year here, some of the local people know I am in residence but they tolerate me and we co-exist, how much longer it will last I do not know, but you are my first guest and you are welcome. Come, the fire is almost extinguished, we have dined well, I will show you the palace and then perhaps we can take a stroll along through the woods by the river."

Sam readily agreed and together they walked over to the large holly. Here Sam noticed the ground was very stony and fell away quite steeply and he was advised by his companion to tread rather warily.

"This gives my cave good protection because anyone who approaches finds it very difficult to do so in complete silence," he added.

They reached the entrance to the palace and Sam could see the inside was equipped with all the necessities to sustain a reasonable existence within the forest.

"I have been fortunate with my adopted parents, they have given me many items to make my life here fairly comfortable. As they travel around the countryside, especially to fairs in Somerset, they have a golden opportunity to purchase items, which can be of service to them and also to me. I will tell you more about the adventures we have had, the special times we shared and no doubt you have some stories which are of interest, we can talk during the evenings in the cave but now I will show you some of the local attractions."

Leaving the cave the two companions threaded their way through the trees along a rather narrow path. The track, which in places was quite overgrown, was also steep and Ding Dong pointed out the advantage of having the summer palace in a position where the water drained away into the river.

"We shall see the river in a moment or two, also several men working in the quarry by the riverbank and there are always coal miners moving about the forest; then at different seasons of the year the farm labourers are joined by their families who work on a daily basis as casual labour."

The river finally came into view, it was a different river and yet the same. Sam commented that in the city the river was much wider and fuller, especially when the incoming tide was running and was deep enough for tall ships to be anchored amongst the buildings of the docks.

"This part of the river is still tidal," said Ding, "I have crossed it at low tide by walking across the weir and then scrambling along the lock gates, but I do not recommend it, especially when the river is running high as there are many strong currents which you would be unable to swim against."

They stood on a raised mound watching the river traffic, several barges were to be seen most of them heading downstream towards the city.

"Those are carrying coal," observed Ding, "I have seen loads of timber, stone and other commodities being transported this way and, on rare occasions, a barge travelling upstream bearing exotic hardwoods, which are destined to be ground to a pulp and used as dyes for fabrics. I love to see the sturdy horses pulling the barges as they walk along the towpath for they remind me of the horses owned by my adopted parents. You must remind me to tell you of the special fair that we attend, it is held in Somerset and there is a great deal of horse trading done in a rather unusual way, our group of Romanies have a great time there."

Moving along the towpath away from the city they encountered a number of stone dwellings, all very similar, rather small and obviously very primitive. The arrangement was haphazard, like mushrooms, and Ding commented that the number of cottages within the forest area of Annum had greatly increased since he first became acquainted with the place. When Sam asked if there was any particular reason for this, Ding stated that the coal mining was increasing over a wide area. "But the miners are a rough, mainly uncivilised group, many of them given to drinking too much cheap ale. I usually try to keep out of their way," said Ding, "for they have caused a great deal of trouble, both individually and collectively, and I have no desire to be associated with any of the ones I have seen. We will continue to climb this road to our left, it takes us away from the river and back to the main village, on the way I will show you some of the larger houses in the area and with a little good fortune you might meet my friend."

He indicated a pathway that traversed a steep rise through the trees and as they began to climb, the signs of human habitation became more numerous.

"There are several farms in this part of the village," said Ding, "they are fairly small, mainly because a number of folk keep only one domestic animal, in fact one of the men is known as 'Farmer One Cow'. The larger fields for growing grain tend to be in the flatter part of the village, where the trees have been felled and the ground cleared. When I came to the forest some years ago, we travelled along the Bath Waye going south into Somerset, I remember there were far more trees and many deer."

Sam looked a little puzzled at the mention of deer until Ding continued, "They are the magnificent creatures you encountered on your first night in the forest and it is illegal to kill them for food, but when times are hard many get slaughtered by the locals to prevent their families from starving. For your information Sam, those wonderful horns as you called them are known as antlers and the meat from the deer, which is very good to eat; we call venison."

The pathway had emerged on to a narrow, steep road, which twisted up through the forest and on reaching the top they rounded the corner and stopped to admire a large house with tall chimneys and to the rear of the building, a small church. Ding began again; "this house is known as The Court and there are many grand banquets held here at various times of the year. I could willingly eat some of the scraps that are fed to the dogs. If you look over the rear wall beyond the garden, you will notice some stone built kennels where the dogs are housed, it would be fairly simple to edge along the wall and relieve their dishes of some of the more tasty morsels, but I venture to say the dogs would probably make a meal of me. The same is true of the garden, the growing vegetables are a great temptation and although the rabbits can breach the defences and take their fill, I cannot follow their example."

They stayed for a while admiring the house, the church and the grounds, as well as endeavouring to imagine what one of the banquets would be like with roast swan as the main course.

Turning their backs on the oldest and grandest house in the area, they directed their path towards a rough lane, which Sam was told, led to the Bath Waye, the main road through the village.

As they journeyed a second large stone built house became visible through the trees and Sam learnt from his companion that this was a much happier hunting ground. Approaching the rear of the building and threading their way along a shallow ditch, which ran almost the length of a perimeter wall, enclosing the garden, Ding suddenly stopped and motioned Sam to be quiet.

"This is where I usually find the small gifts of food which are placed here by a girl named Ruth, she works for the Squire who lives in this large house, which is known as The Hall. The bread and cake from the kitchen are most welcome, as I cannot produce anything like it at the palace and it gives a very homely touch to my meals."

Having made his case clear to Sam, he plucked a thick piece of rye grass, laid the blade flat along his left thumb then placed his right thumb against the left so the blade of grass was trapped between them. His fingers were intertwined behind his thumbs. He raised his hands to his mouth and began to blow on to the edge of the grass producing some weird high-pitched tones. Satisfied he had given the signal he sat back to wait. For some time there was no sign of life or response to the signal given. Then, almost without warning, as if by magic, a young kitchen maid appeared. She hesitated when she noticed Ding was not alone, but quietly placed a parcel, as close to them as possible and then she was gone before a word was spoken.

Sam indicated that at least they could have thanked her for her kindness, but was rather nonplussed by the reaction he received.

"On Sunday," said Ding, "her master, together with some of the servants, travel up the lane to attend worship at the chapel, situated near the Bath Waye. As they follow his horse along the route I hide in a clump of bushes and give her a big wave of thanks as she passes."

Sam was delighted to hear this explanation, but he was unaware of what day it was today, so how were they to know when it was Sunday. His companion recognised his bewilderment, but at that moment a noise from across the lane attracted Sam's attention and immediately he remembered. He stopped and looking intently at Ding, enquired; "Is that a saw I can hear?"

"Yes," came the reply, "there is a sawpit in the lane just a short distance from the rear of the inn, the one named the Blue Bowl."

It gradually dawned on Sam that he had travelled in a large circle. Some days before he had left this very inn in the meat wagon, but he could not fathom how all these various pointers informed Ding when it was Sunday.

"I was going to explain," said Ding, "the day is Sunday, when the saw pit is quiet, there are no men working in the quarry and the miners are above ground. You see, there are plenty of indications to inform you which day to come to the lane and await the Squire with his retinue, and to say thank you to Ruth."

Sam was satisfied with the explanation he received, adding that he looked forward to putting it into practice at the next opportunity. Comforted by their agreement they left the lane and began to return to the summer palace.

"We were fairly close to the chapel and another large house," said Ding, as they turned from the lane to walk across a field. "Keep your eyes open, Sam, as we return to the palace because there are some silly hens hereabouts. They escape from their inadequate pens and very often lay their eggs in the open field before they are taken into custody again. So tread gently and with a little good fortune we may dine on boiled eggs this evening."

Sam was still lost in wonder at the sight of the sawpit with all the memories it recalled. Once again he was standing with his father watching the chalk lines snapping down the log and listening to the sweet sound of the heavy ripsaw as it incised its way down through the timber. He could hear the familiar voice of the bottom sawyer, a friend of his father, who would threaten his partner up above with all manner of oaths if he received more than his fair share of the falling dust. He was lost in a world of memories, to the point where he was unaware of Ding's jubilation on his discovery of a new laid, brown egg. It became beholden upon him to prove his worth and thus make their journey as profitable as possible, so it filled him with pride when he could rejoice with Ding, he had also found one and it was still warm.

The parcel given to them by Ruth contained the bread and cake that Ding had predicted and in fact was hoping for, so on their return to the palace the immediate task was to build a fire to cook the eggs they had collected. Going into the palace Ding showed Sam the dry materials stored for such an event. "I have a policy to explain, Sam, whenever this store of dry materials runs low, it is preferable to replenish the stock so we are not caught out by the vicissitudes of our English weather. I like to use some of the wonderful words I have learned from my Romany friends, it helps to keep by brain alive, but I feel I am confusing you. Putting it simply, I suggest that whilst I kindle and cook, you search and store."

Their combined efforts soon resulted in ample provision of dry materials, which brought compliments from Ding, and a meal they devoured with relish.

Sitting over the embers of the fire and watching the evening sunset, Sam requested his new found friend to inform him of any knowledge he may possess concerning the interesting sights they had observed during their afternoon hike. Ding was more than happy to oblige, "I was once told that I have inherited the gift of the blarney from my dear mother, so if you wish me to, I can talk from now until dawn and thoroughly enjoy the exercise given to my tongue and vocal chords, you see Sam, it is very rare that I have an appreciative audience. Now, what in particular do you find of real interest?"

"I am aware," replied Sam, "that you supplied certain information as we travelled, but anything to do with the Hall, the village, the sawpit, or the Blue Bowl would be of interest to me and I will treasure your knowledge."

This final statement made Ding sit up, puff out his chest and launch himself into his narrative. "The large house, known as The Hall, is owned by a very respected and much loved family. Ruth became an orphan when her mother and father were both unfortunately killed in an accident on the farm, which is joined to The Hall. The Squire employed them both and he allowed Cook to take Ruth into her care. Since that time many years ago, Ruth has matured into a fine young girl and the bond between her and Cook is very real and durable, certainly as strong as any mother and daughter. She has also endeared herself to the rest of the household, to the Squire and to me; it is because of her I can survive these months in the summer place. Her parcels of food help to make a very frugal diet far more acceptable and although Cook is aware of the situation, she turns a blind eye to the parcels placed out by our angel of mercy. The Squire is very good to all his employees and, from time to time, he gives them a chance to celebrate. For example, when the harvest has been gathered in they hold great celebrations in the grounds of The Hall. I was very fortunate to attend one of these gatherings and I have never eaten so much as I did on that day, but when these parties take place I am usually on the way to my Romany friends, so there is no great point in requesting my presence. I know that the family in The Hall attend the chapel, which is situated just off the Bath Waye, it is the same chapel where Ruth now attends for worship, this is why it's easy for us to say thank you to her on a Sunday morning. The house itself is very grand, although it must be almost a hundred years old, and the grounds, especially the farm, are extensive."

"A little further up the lane is the Blue Bowl," continued Ding, "again this is another building which has stood the test of time and is very much a going concern. It serves as a coaching inn, being a convenient stop between the cities of Bristowe and Bath, but it can also be the habitation of some very unsavoury characters that gather there, often with ill intent. The position of the inn provides an ideal situation for such men to plan and execute their forays, and then simply let the forest swallow them up. I feel this is getting harder for them to achieve, as the forest is far less dense now and there are many more treeless areas, some of which are being enclosed to contain the livestock. At the rear of the inn is your beloved sawpit where the sawyers slave to earn a living, but I have a strong feeling you could probably supply me with a far more accurate account of such an establishment than the one I can furnish."

Ding sat back and awaited a reply from his fascinated listener. Sam required several moments to digest the knowledge imparted to him, but finally collecting his thoughts, he replied. "I am inclined to agree with your final remark, because, when my father was with us, it was his delight to seek out the sawyers, the wheelwrights and the coopers in the city and having done so we would stand and watch, captivated by their skill. I have a dream that one day I might be in such a situation myself, the satisfaction afforded to these craftsmen must be of far greater value than pursuing some of the more mundane jobs that are the mainstay for many families. I have the same feeling for timber and the way it is worked, especially with a tool like the drawknife, as an artist has for his brushes. Somehow I know my future will be spent with the shavings and sawdust created by working as a sawyer or a wheelwright. I just hope that I am justified in feeling this way."

"I hope you will see the realisation of your dreams Sam, because I can tell by the expression on your face that you are speaking with a great deal of sincerity. My Romany friends would say you are speaking from the heart and by so doing you are revealing your true self, but I would add a warning with regard to the sawpit," Ding had launched himself into another session of the blarney. "The pit is very close to the inn, and as I have already indicated, there are some very strange characters who gather there. To make matters worse there have been a number of accidents within the confines of the premises, none of which have been fatal, but serious enough to cause injuries which have resulted in the men involved being unable to continue in the positions they were holding at the time. I have no real details on these matters and perhaps I have taken too much notice of some of the local gossip, but feel I must give you the benefit of the knowledge I have."

Sam remained quiet for a little while, he had hoped that he would have much more encouragement from Ding but then he reflected as he replied, "There is danger in many of the trades that are carried out in the forest and the city, when my father was down the pit there were many accidents, some of them fatal. The strange thing is, when he was employed as a lighterman, he was not involved in any kind of ill fortune, yet he was snatched from the riverside and now we have no idea as to his whereabouts. I do not know if we shall ever meet again. With a little good fortune I certainly hope to meet my mother and sister at some future date. Do you have hopes and fears for the future Ding, or are you content to take life as it comes, day by day?"

Ding was not unprepared for the question posed by Sam and quickly replied, "Some of the ladies who live with us in the caravans earn a good living by telling personal fortunes and endeavouring to look into the future. When we travel to the various fairs in the country they are always ready to read your palm, provided you have already crossed theirs with a coin or two. They are not very happy about returning to the same venue too often, for there have been incidents where a client has been told to expect good fortune and this has not come to pass. He or she is therefore in no frame of mind to endorse the claims made by the ladies who read the palms, so the signs are not good. I have an open mind about their claims, I do know of several prophesies that did actually materialise, but I have a feeling this was a shot in the dark that found its mark. Several years ago one of the ladies read my palm and she informed me I would at some time in the future travel to a far away land. I am not too sure this will ever happen, because she indicated on my palm the line that told her this, and that particular line is a scar. I did not have the grace to tell her the line was a result of an injury, which became infected and took a long time to heal. If it is my destiny, or kismet as she called it, then so be it, time will tell, I am of the opinion we cannot change the future. We have sat here for some time Sam and my backside is getting sore, shall we take a stroll before we bed down for the night?"

Sam readily agreed and they set off between the trees in the opposite direction to The Hall. In front of them and over the right-hand side of the track a scattering of cottages could be clearly seen through the trees, the yellow candlelight giving a glow of comfort. "It would appear it is later in the day than we imagined," said Sam, "let us turn up across the meadow, then we can wander through the little wood that leads to the opening by the palace."

Sam suddenly stopped in his tracks motioning Ding to do the same. In a low whisper he pointed out to Ding that there was a nice fat hen roosting on a low branch over to their left. "If we leave it there, the fox will take it, we do not know who owns it so I feel this is a gift from the gods."

Ding looked at Sam and simply said; "If you want it for our larder, you catch it, I will help you eat it."

Sam accepted the challenge, in his head he could hear the voice of the 'sparrow': 'now boy, you do it this way'.

With Ding as a silent witness, he stepped carefully forward moving towards the unsuspecting bird. As soon as he was close enough, he reached forward taking the bird by the feet. What followed would have pleased his tutor in the hothouse, for in no time at all and without any noise the bird lay dead in his grasp, dispatched the way the 'sparrow' had taught him.

Ding was speechless. Suddenly he blurted out, "If I had attempted to capture that bird, the whole forest would have heard the rumpus, there would be a line of feathers from here to the palace, I probably would not have caught it and regarding the silent kill, as far as I am concerned there is no such thing. They squeak to high heaven when I try to twist their necks and on at least one occasion the bird has been spared simply because of my inability to kill it. Sam you are a genius and I will honour your skill by plucking and drawing the fowl ready for cooking."

It was now Sam's turn to puff out his chest, and passing the bird to Ding he quoted the 'sparrow', 'it is much easier to accomplish this while the bird is still warm, so you must carry out your promise before you turn in for the night.'

Between them they became quite expert at catching small game such as rabbits and there were rare opportunities for collecting woodcock from the forest. The birds would become entangled in the nets stretched across a road in the trees, causing injuries which prevented them from flying or, in some cases, their necks would be broken. Ding would linger for some time before he decided they could pick up the stricken creature, knowing the nets were set by some of the rougher element of the district and he had no desire to cross swords with them, or to argue the case as to the ownership of their find. Their experiments with tapered fishing baskets, made from the withies which grow near the towpath and which Ding called a creel, were fairly successful as were the fishing spears they fashioned from a stout, straight piece of timber. As a Romany, Ding possessed a sound knowledge of how to weave the baskets from the young willow and he was also aware of the intricate rules governing the use of the spear. "These items are used in the north of the forest," said Ding, "especially the tapered baskets when the salmon are running. The salmon are large fish, they put up a tremendous fight if you happen to catch one with a rod and line but they are extremely good to eat, I sincerely hope there will be some on the table during my stay with the Romanies."

The friendship became a solid bond between the young men, they would sit and talk well into the night, and especially when the weather was too wet to venture out into the forest. Sitting at the mouth of the cave they could watch the nearby brook swell with the falling rain and become a substantial stream during even a short summer deluge. It was during such a spell they recounted to each other the experiences shared at the fairs they had attended. They told of bloody, bare fist fighting between hard men, the cock fights, the tumblers, the jugglers and Ding could add the horse trading invariably sealed with strange hand signs which he could not fathom. He could also tell of seasonal employment in Somerset and other places to the south, "The withies grown there are first class for basket making and we also harvest young hazel to make the hurdles used on the farms. The women look after the children, keep their caravans spick and span and, as I have already explained, they look into the future." Ding concluded their reflections with these words and as the rain had ceased and they looked out towards the river they resolved to wander along in the direction of the quarry.

The men had left the workings, large pieces of pennant stone lay ready for dressing, cutting into smaller sections, or loading on to one of the forms of transport to carry it to its destination.

"Look over there," Ding said, "there is a large stone being carved into a headstone for one of the graves in the churchyard and if your observation is good, Sam, you will notice some strange wooden wedges driven in the natural fissures of the rock. This is an uncanny way of removing quite large sections of stone. The wedges are driven home then soaked with water and of course weather like this helps to further swell the wood, until the pressure exerted on the rock is such that it simply breaks away from the face. It is as though an unseen hand is applying an enormous force, which finally separates the stone, and I think this is a very clever way of letting nature work for you.

Talking of nature working for us, Sam, we will make our way back to the rear of The Hall, inspect our hiding place to see if our little angel has left us a gift and then we can have a final glance at the sawpit."

Sam endorsed the suggestion and they were delighted to find that Ruth had placed a parcel out for them, especially as she now managed to find sufficient for two hungry mouths. "We must give her a special wave this Sunday," said Sam, "because I feel that without her help we would be in some distress. I know we catch and cook a good deal of our own food and you are very clever at making the cows in the meadow part with their milk, thus providing a very welcome change to the cold spring water, but we are indebted to Ruth for what I would term the luxuries of life."

They were across the lane from the inn as two large draught-horses rounded the bend in the road. Chains from their harness were fastened to a large trunk of oak, which had been trimmed of its branches so only the bole remained. Sam stood watching as the horses were constrained to manoeuvre their load over the sawpit and into the position required by the sawyer.

"We can start work on the log first thing in the morning," one of the sawyers said as they moved away from the pit, and as the men turned to leave the two companions followed their example. Returning to the palace they kindled a fire then cooked and ate their evening meal. The parcel from Ruth lived up to expectations and as Ding congratulated her he endorsed the previous remark, which Sam had made concerning the luxuries of life. They planned that on the morrow they would wander up to the top of the hills that overlooked The Hall and the village.

The following morning the weather was bright and clear and having climbed the hill they used this vantage point to survey the scene. Looking down across the meadows of the farm attached to The Hall, it was possible to see portions of the road as it twisted between the trees, a highway which would lead him to his mother. In the far distance he realised the city of Bristowe was established around the mouth of the river, how far away, he was not certain, and Ding could not reassure him on the issue. His mind wandered back to the tenement and as he pondered over the happenings of past days he saw the coach and heard the noise of the horse's hooves as it travelled along the Bath Waye. His mind was in turmoil as they made their way back to the palace but the sight of a majestic stag with several hinds brought him back to reality and the confidence of youth.

"Before I leave we will make every preparation possible for you Sam, so whilst I am away and you are here in the summer palace we shall both be safe during the winter, then we shall meet again next year." The confident tones of Ding's voice had a reassuring effect on Sam and over the next few weeks he was as good as his word in putting them into practice. They had experienced the late spring and summer together, watched the green mantle overhead thicken and now begin to change colour, delighted in the bird life near the palace where blackbirds, thrushes and tits had built their nests, and fed their young which were now free within the safety of the forest. The amazing sight of the small blue tits bouncing on the air, then darting into the hole of an old tree trunk made their happiest memory. They envied the complete confidence of the little creature, its industry when feeding, and the way the parent birds shepherded their wayward brood when they finally tumbled from the safety of the nest on uncertain wings.

"If only life was as easy for us," remarked Sam, "we could spread our wings and fly to any destination of our choice, stay as long as we liked and then, if we so desired, return here to the palace."

Ding was not quite so moved by the apparent ease of the bird life, which was a new experience for Sam. "What we have seen, Sam, has been the idyllic period in the lives of just a few birds in the vicinity of the cave, but there are many other features which we have not seen and on which my Romany friends are well informed. They can tell of the swallows, the swifts, the cuckoo all flying hundreds, if not thousands of miles to return to warmer climates, some of them going as far as Africa. But there are many dangers on the way and a great number of birds die, driven off course by rough weather. They also perish from hunger following

69

a long flight over the sea, or desert, and of course there is always the possibility of being killed and eaten by predators such as larger birds, and other animals. Even human beings enjoy dining on the succulent flesh of some of our wild birds. It is fairly certain only one or two of our little family of blue tits will survive to raise their own brood, but that is the way nature works and we have to accept it, and if possible, learn from it. So my friend, we will get your supplies in for the winter months and I shall migrate, but will return to the nest next year."

Sam knew this blarney was one of the aspects of their friendship he would really miss and as they made preparation for Ding's departure he began to wonder how he would employ himself during the long, dark nights. He looked at the corner of the cave where the kindling was stored together with a reasonable stack of coal they had scavenged and he was fairly confident of keeping himself warm, the big question was; could he feed himself? He now sensed Ding was getting restless and that his departure was imminent, so it was no surprise when his friend informed him one evening that if the weather was fair he would commence his journey to the north on the following day. They spent that evening concerned for each other; sharing their belongings so one could travel safely and the other remain secure.

Chapter Five

The Trek

Sam watched as the forest swallowed up the dapper, springy figure of his companion, he had accompanied him as far as the Bath Waye, then he turned to walk as close to The Hall as possible. In his mind he thought a sighting of Ruth would ease the parting he had just experienced, but this was not to be. Returning to the summer palace he suddenly felt very much alone and rather vulnerable.

Meanwhile Ding had decided upon taking the same route as he had done on previous occasions but as he commenced his travels to the London Waye, he sensed that the atmosphere of the forest had changed and unfortunately not for the better. He knew from his previous experience the area which lay quite close to Annum, just a mile or so to the north, was one that was inhabited by groups of rough miners, thieves and robbers. Some of these were the men Sam had observed on the Downs collecting their protection money, and he had no desire to meet with any of them. Whether they were first or second generation, it was a case of like father; like son. In fact there was a tale of a son waylaying his father, or was it the other way round, in any case the story ended in fatality, and Ding required a quiet life with safe travelling. He had some thirty odd miles to go before he came to a large common near a busy little town and with luck, coupled with fair weather, he could reach his goal in three or four days. His priority was to head towards the track that led to Staple Hill from where he would strike a path slightly east to bring him on the Westerley and Sadbury Waye. There were several good farms in the district, one of which possessed a very comfortable barn. He had used this barn on one of his previous travels with no serious repercussions, there was no angel of mercy waiting with a parcel of food, but his one desire was to wake on the morrow with dry clothing. Even the dew would now soak his flimsy attire and to have wet clothing, gradually drying as he walked along, so the heat and the strength was sapped from his very being, did not appeal to Ding. As far as he was concerned dry clothing was one of life's necessities. With this philosophy fixed in his mind he made fair headway, only stopping to consume the contents of the parcel presented to him by Ruth, as a travelling present, and to carry out some temporary repairs to his footwear which was now sadly in need of replacing.

He noticed how the forest had been decimated over the three years of his travels, no new planting had taken place, the hollies and the furzes were now in control of many areas, or there was just rough pasture where wild pigs rooted and the deer were absent, a new sight was the increased number of rather scraggy sheep and the mushrooming of so many new dwellings. He refreshed himself from a nearby stream, looking out across the landscape he could see small fields of corn awaiting harvest and he thought to himself that this would be an opportunity to earn a little money if he had time to spare. It would add to the few pence he and Sam had managed to scrape together before he left the palace. Feeling in the pocket of his outer clothing he absent-mindedly fingered the few coins, which comprised his worldly wealth, as he did so he came across a metal object, which he did not immediately recognise. Bringing the mystery article into the cold light of day, he laughed at himself for his short memory and recalled the old lady in the Romany group who could remember in great detail the happenings of years past, but she could not recall what her daughter had given her for lunch that day. Looking at the two metal leaves of a small talisman given to him by one of his adopted mothers, he wondered if he would ever see the second part of the charm again. The other two leaves he had given to Sam before they parted. Together the two halves made up a four leaf clover which he had treasured for most of his life and he became fascinated by the thought Sam and he were now sharing whatever good fortune the leaves might bring. He hoped there would be more than enough for both of them during the coming days. The farm came into sight, at the turn of the lane he could see the barn was still standing. He cautiously crossed an open field to reach the back of the building, wormed his way inside, found some dry straw, then lay down and almost immediately fell asleep.

The early call of the farmer to his few cows brought him to his senses before he was ready to face the day, but having awakened he decided he must leave before he was discovered. He was soon back on the lane which ran by the side of the main farm buildings and to his delight he noticed in the brambles a plentiful supply of delicious blackberries, ripe and ready to eat. In the field, nestling in the darker grass of a fairy ring he picked a number of fresh mushrooms. These items became breakfast and satisfied his immediate hunger, he decided, having eaten his fill, to continue on his way. As he journeyed, the weather began to deteriorate and although he made as much haste as possible he could see ominous dark clouds gathering on the skyline. He resolved he would seek a lodging, the small sum of money he had would suffice for one night in a tavern and he would be refreshed for the final part of his journey.

Suddenly he realised that he was not alone on the roadway, a number of folk were dispersing as if they had attended a meeting of some kind. As they approached, Ding could hear snatches of intense conversation; it centred on the Pastor who had ridden on horseback from the city, to deliver the message of the gospel. They talked of his fervour, of the Saviour he presented to them, of the tough miners who had been moved to tears creating white channels down their blackened cheeks. He described the new life they could all possess if they would only have faith and believe, whether they were rich or poor was of no avail, this new life was for all. A rather rough voice in the crowd suggested with a laugh that Bert Stone would probably be presented with a new life as he had been apprehended for pick pocketing during the meeting. He would have no defence against the accusation because he had been caught in the act.

Ding moved away from the throng who now were suggesting the tortuous equipment in the city, the pillory, the stocks, the whipping post, free passage to the sugar plantations of the West Indies and even the gallows. The laughing voice continued, urging the folk around him to attend the next assizes so they could give Bert their moral support. The talk of the Saviour had ceased, Ding felt in his pocket and fingered the two leaves of clover and he was thankful the crowd were journeying in the opposite direction to him.

The sky was now black with what he knew were thunderclouds. In the distance he could see a collection of dwellings and amongst them, a small inn, he pressed on to reach the inn before the storm broke and even if he was not happy with it, he must rest there that night. The heavy, dark sky made him quicken his pace and to his great relief he reached the inn before the rain came. He entered the establishment and was not made welcome by the innkeeper.

There followed a lengthy argument as to his identity, where he had come from, his destination and his ability to pay for his food and lodging. Ding had passed the test and he almost cut his hand on the cloverleaf as he gave it an extra squeeze to show his pleasure.

His appetite was fierce as he had not eaten since the blackberry feast, but he restrained himself and made an effort to show the habits of a young gentleman, rather than those of a ravenous urchin. His hunger satisfied he decided to leave the confines of the smoky room and seek an early night so he would be thoroughly refreshed by the morning. The innkeeper directed a strange looking creature of rather frightening appearance, to show Ding to his room in the attic. Following this gaunt specimen of humanity, who limped badly and had one eye covered with a patch, he wondered what lay at the top of the narrow, creaking staircase and in such company he deemed it would be a miracle if he ever saw the light of day again. Finally the staircase completed its winding course and came to rest on a small landing. Ding was offered the candlestick, which had added to the eerie character of their journey.

"Secure your door firmly," said the man in a very gentle voice, "the people in the inn are honest enough but there are always individuals around who cannot be trusted and at the moment there are several French prisoners on the prowl, they have escaped from custody at a place just outside Bristowe. He hesitated and then as he departed he added, "I have the French to thank for the state that I am in."

Ding was grateful to the man for his concern, for some reason despite his appearance, he had endeared himself by this little conversation and as he departed Ding pondered over the adventures he might have had, what suffering he had seen and what pain he had endured.

Closing the door, Ding looked around the tiny room set high in the roof of the building, he had one small window and he assured himself that if he pushed the bed against the door, then he would be secure. The room was far from palatial, there was little furnishing and what was present was covered with the dust of ages. He eased himself under the blanket and was not impressed with the grubby mattress he discovered. Undismayed he finally secured a position of reasonable comfort between large lumps of straw and hard, dry stems protruding through the meagre covering. With a final wriggle of his young frame, a nervous glance at a rather menacing spider secure in the centre of its own creation, and a well-aimed gust of breath at the candle, plunging his surroundings into obscurity, he closed his eyes. His sleep was disturbed in the early hours of the morning by torrential rain, hammering on the roof not far above his head and he knew that his desire for a comfortable night had been fulfilled. He had used his few pence wisely and kept his clothing dry. Tomorrow was another day.

~*~

Morning dawned, the rain had cleared, and with a grubby hand he wiped the condensation from the window so that from his high vantage point he could look out over the scene. He almost froze in horror. The inn was not far from the crossroads and there on a small rise in the ground stood a gibbet. The little boy swinging by the neck at the end of the rope had not seen as many summers as he had and the ragged clothes, now soaking wet, made the pathetic figure even more grotesque. He left the inn in a hurry, not looking back, but on the way he gleaned the intelligence that the terrible price the lad had paid was for stealing a loaf of bread. In disbelief and utter revulsion he hurried away on the final leg of his journey. He thought he had experienced most of life's surprises because when he was in Somerset he had witnessed at least one public hanging, but this young, thin body partly covered with wet ragged clothes made him weep with rage. He quickened his pace to put space between himself and the ugly scene, leaping over the puddles, which were all too frequent in the surface of the road leading northward through the forest. His destination was a large open area of common land where he knew he would find friends and be made welcome.

His progress was suddenly accelerated when the familiar voice of the driver of a passing cart hailed him. A smiling, weather beaten countenance, combined with a gravel voice, endeared the carter to Ding as he climbed up beside him in response to a very welcome offer. Sitting in comparative comfort with the carter on the front of the open, flat cart, Ding was very appreciative of the wind in their faces as behind them the load of sheepskins offered a putrid smell like he had never experienced and he had no desire to repeat the discovery. Ding was extremely grateful for the ride, he knew most of this day's journey would be done without shoes and his feet were not as hard as they used to be. He had covered many miles since he left Sam and now he could rest his tired legs, besides he was now making faster progress and he felt certain he would reach his destination before darkness fell.

As they travelled the carter gave Ding news of happenings in the area since his last visit and he responded by informing the carter of his newly found friend. As he spoke he realised the bond he had created with Sam meant a great deal to him and he hoped they would renew their acquaintance in the following summer. He did not inform the carter they had a summer palace, because he thought he would be ridiculed, or worse still when they reached his destination he could be charged for the ride on the grounds he now belonged to the landed gentry. His final few pence were in the coffers of the innkeeper but for the immediate future he could rely on his Romany friends.

They warmed to each other's company as they enjoyed the autumn sunshine; the trees along the roadway were now displaying amazing colours as the foliage reached its dying glory, whilst the steady pace of the horse brought Ding ever closer to the common. The carter had agreed to take Ding as near to his destination as his own route allowed and he indicated they were not far from the parting of the ways. Ding could feel his spirits rising as he began to recognise the countryside, so when his attention was drawn towards some flashes of bright paint well over to their right-hand side, he made ready to jump. He did not even request the carter to slow down, he had seen the object of his desire and with a cheery thank you and good luck, he jumped, tumbling over into a mass of fallen leaves. He regained his feet, exchanged a final goodbye wave and set out on the way to a small copse on the edge of the common. Here amid the trees he could see the shape and bright colours of his favourite caravan.

He now began to run, his heart was light, he was a little boy again, kicking at the piles of fallen leaves, which the wind had scattered and then collected into uneven heaps. He noticed a large puffball and let fly with his right foot with all the force he could muster, the puffball remained but his right shoe, or what was left of it, sailed into the distance and rested where it landed. Briefly he thought of the sheep that had offered up their skins to provide protection for human kind, but the cart on which they were placed was travelling on. Under a tree, two piebald horses grazed quietly near the caravan, one raised its head, it whinnied a welcome, shaking its long white mane as if in disbelief.

The smell of the wood smoke was a joy and as he quickened his step, the barking of an approaching mongrel finally became quiet as it muzzled up to him. A figure appeared and called his name. He ran faster. He had arrived home.

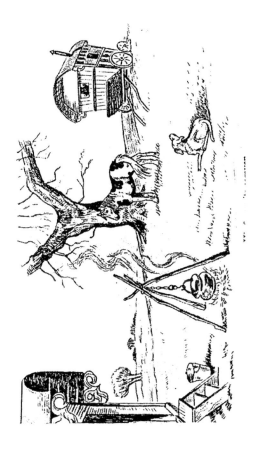

His Favourite Caravan

Chapter Six

The Good Samaritan

Sam had made a reasonable start in the palace, he had kept to the routine he had planned and Ruth had been most generous with her parcels of aid. Now the days were getting colder, there were sharp frosts at night and he was very reluctant to damp down the fire when he required the warmth and comfort of it. The alternative was to draw attention to the fact there was an occupant in the palace and he had no desire for unwanted guests. As he thought on these problems he finally came to the conclusion he would not be able to see the winter out if conditions became really bad. He knew the river meandered to the Spa city where his mother and sister were staying, it therefore seemed logical to suppose a possible solution would be to follow the river and endeavour to make contact with his kin. He possessed no real winter clothing, the cave could be cold if the wind was in the wrong direction and the long, dark nights spent alone were an alien feature to a young man who had known a happy family life and close friends.

Like Ding, he had a few pence which had been earned locally, mainly in the harvest field, but this would soon disappear if he had to buy his victuals locally he therefore deemed it necessary to retain his modest fortune for a real emergency. The forest had given him a reasonable diet if rather lacking in variety, it was good he had become proficient in fishing and snaring rabbits although at times his imagination wandered back to the butchers and Mrs

Streer's hot soup. He wondered if George was still happy in the slaughterhouse, and shuddered at the thought, but then he said to himself, "George was family and that made a world of difference."

It was pleasant to wander through the meadow situated behind the hall, a little exercise he did on a regular basis and there was always a possibility that a special hiding place would produce an offering from the angel of mercy. Tonight there was no such offering, so with a little ache in his stomach he turned to trace his way back to the palace. As he journeyed he suddenly became aware of a flapping of wings, it seemed as though an injured bird was trying to fly but could not make it. Then he saw it, there in the bushes a fine woodcock was endeavouring to become airborne but because of a broken wing was unable to do so. Realising the bird would be easy prey for foxes he decided to catch it, kill it and take it back to the palace. He had no trouble in carrying out either of these tasks and he was soon on his way carrying his trophy, head down, by his side. This good fortune had come just at the right time, his food stocks were low and he needed to build up his physical strength before he attempted to follow the river, or take the Bath Waye, in search of his mother and sister. His spirits were raised as he walked when he imagined a simple but joyous family reunion.

Emerging from the trees on to the narrow lane leading to the little clearing before the palace, he was abruptly confronted by the Ward brothers, they enquired of the woodcock which Sam was carrying and immediately accused him of taking the bird from a net they had tied across one of the roads through the forest. Sam pleaded his innocence, explaining how he had found the bird and that he desired to consume it. His efforts were in vain; they were lost in the night air as one of the brothers grabbed the bird, commenting it would make a tasty supper. The second brother then made his move, swinging his right fist with considerable force so that it landed on the side of Sam's head. Sam fell to the ground still pleading his innocence in the matter. He did all he could to protect his head whilst he endured a terrible kicking to his defenceless body by both brothers who were demanding the name of the recipient for the bird. The voices became muffled, they began to fade into the night, the kicking ceased when the brothers noted Sam was no longer conscious, they departed, mocking him by telling him to have a good night's sleep.

When he recovered his senses Sam found he could not move his battered body without enduring unspeakable pain. Very gradually he managed to sit up but to rise to his feet was an impossibility. Utterly dejected, with tears of rage and pain trickling down his cheeks, he sat in the fading light lost to the world. His mind raced over his predicament and as it rambled a picture of Ding came into vision. For a moment he thought Ding was there with him and then he knew, he had to work out what Ding would do if he were in this situation. Somehow he had to get back to the palace even if he crawled on all fours, because if he stayed where he was he would probably perish during the night. By some quirk of fate, some miracle, perhaps a pair of cloverleaves, he finally made the shelter of the cave and collapsed exhausted on to the damp straw mattress.

How long he lay there he could not remember, but when he awoke his limbs would not respond to the actions he desired, his head was aching, he was terribly cold and yet he felt he had a temperature or a slight fever. He was thirsty as well as hungry and the air in the cave felt raw and damp. Gingerly he turned his head to look out of the entrance to the cave and noticed the ground was soaking wet, the trees were dripping large droplets of rain from bare branches and the once lively leaves now lay in sodden piles. Was it possible for him to start a fire so he might warm his aching body? He was not sure, but he knew that he must make an attempt. He had one fish and some bread in his larder, after that; there was nothing. Gradually he moved his body to the pile of kindling and dry grass, every movement was accompanied by pain but he finally collected sufficient material to commence his labours. Several times he almost threw in the towel but his courage did not fail as he willed his fingers and arms to create fire. He recalled a simple instruction from Ding, 'talk to your body and it will respond to your wishes.' He told his fingers what he required of them, his arms to co-operate and his strength to hold fast. Finally the dry grass began to smoke and then smoulder, the thin dry twigs warmed and added to his joy when they burst into flame. After what seemed an age, the coals were aglow, he could rest, utterly exhausted but thankful and a little more confident in his ability to cope. The warmth of the fire renewed his spirits and as soon as the fish was ready, he consumed it eagerly with his final portion of bread. As he lay on the mattress, longing for company, someone to talk to, anyone, Ding with his blarney, any of his kin, even the 'sparrow', his world suddenly went blank.

~*~

Ruth peered through the misty rain as she followed her master to the little Baptist Chapel for she could see no sign of her young friend. This was the second Sunday without contact and she was now becoming concerned. She felt certain that if he was leaving as Ding had done, then she would have received some kind of indication this would happen, but there had been no word. Throughout the service she became distracted, pondering on possibilities and finally deciding as a first step she would check on the cache. This she would do as soon as an opportunity presented itself, she could then plan her next move.

The itinerant Pastor was lunching with her master at The Hall, so as they entered the grounds she watched the men stable their horses then retire to the long dining room where a huge, inviting log fire burned. Ruth rushed into the grounds and to her amazement and consternation she found the parcel she placed there several days ago had not been removed and that some little rodent had taken advantage of the situation. Her dilemma was real, being compounded by the fact she must inform someone as to the possible outcome of her worst fears; knowing full well this might lead to her dismissal, especially as she had to prove her misgivings by using the food parcel as evidence. The rain had cleared and following lunch, her master together with the Pastor wandered into the grounds, deep in conversation. Ruth, her mind in turmoil, watched the two men as they slowly paced the garden, the more she observed the less likely it seemed she would be able to approach either of them.

Her salvation was a call from Cook requesting her to go into the herb corner to collect a small trug of sage leaves. This she willingly agreed to do. Carefully she selected a path to the herb corner knowing it would lead her in the direction, which would produce a confrontation with her quarry. As the men and maid approached each other Ruth stumbled and fell resulting in the trug being thrown to the ground. The men stopped and as she retrieved the trug they inquired of her well-being. Ruth replied she was unhurt except for a slight graze that Cook would willingly bathe, but she was greatly concerned about a young friend of hers. The opening gambit had the desired effect and soon amid tears and muddled explanations, Ruth blurted out the full story and directed her master to the cache in the far corner of the grounds, above the ditch. Both men appeared puzzled, her master commenting that he was unaware he was feeding half of the local population, but there was no real reprimand for Ruth, but rather concern for the young lad she had brought to their notice.

As her story unfolded she mentioned the existence of the summer palace, but when asked its actual location her knowledge was sparse. She had visited it on one occasion, but it was over two years ago when Ding had first made contact. She could remember a small clearing, the sound of running water, a brook or something similar, and the fact that it was basically a small cave situated on a rise overlooking the river and a stone quarry. Ding, she added, had been coming to the cave for three summers now, but this year a companion had joined him and it was this young lad she was concerned about. Although the intelligence they had gleaned from Ruth was sparse, the two men decided to search the area. The Pastor indicated that on his return to the city he would endeavour to find the place called the summer palace and if successful, investigate its mysteries. Ruth's master agreed to join with the Pastor, and as there was not much daylight at their disposal, they would leave forthwith because if the young lad was in any distress then it would be incumbent upon them to find him.

Complying with Ruth's directions to proceed along the path known as the Annum Waye, the two men, now mounted, were soon lost in the trees leading in that direction. With a hopeful heart Ruth had watched as they left the grounds, then turned aside to be comforted by Cook and to quietly pray, in her simple way, that their mission would succeed.

They traversed the Annum Waye not really sure of the place where they should leave the track and search among the trees and scrub. They scrutinised the area for some time with several false alarms and gradually they realised the knowledge in their possession was insufficient, and soon it would be too dark to continue. They were also concerned for their own safety, particularly that of the Pastor, there were several factions who strongly disagreed with his actions and beliefs and would take advantage of the situation if they found him alone in the forest.

Pulling over to the edge of the track they were discussing their predicament when the Pastor thought he could hear running water. He urged his horse into the trees to find, on his right-hand side, a swift running brook rising from the forest floor, it then bubbled away down a stony bed into the forest towards the river. More by instinct than reason he turned away from the brook and as the ground was becoming stony, much of it like loose shingle, he decided to explore further on foot. He recalled Ruth had indicated she was of the opinion that in the area near the palace the ground fell away towards the river. He turned to regain a firmer foothold and as he did so a large holly bush caught his attention, to one side of it he noticed what appeared to be a wall of stone. Tethering his horse to a nearby branch he continued to investigate the scene, he stumbled upon a circle of stones, contained inside these were the ashes of extinct fires. He gently disturbed the pile of black ash, coming to the conclusion the fire had been extinguished some days since. As he stood pondering he heard a low moan coming from within the wall in front of him, he sharpened his senses and moved carefully towards the source of the sound. The cave suddenly became a reality and the noise he had heard was coming from that direction. Walking gingerly upon the loose, gravel surface and retrieving a useful branch as a weapon he approached the entrance to the cave. His instinct told him the branch would not be required; casting it aside he peered inside the gloomy cave and beheld a young man lying on a dirty blanket, which covered a thin, uncomfortable mattress. The person was obviously in great distress and running a fever for, as the Pastor made move to get closer, he turned on his side crying out that he could take no more and please would they leave him alone. The Pastor moved over to the young man assuring him he had not come to cause him harm, in fact if he could be of assistance in any way he would be pleased to help. Sam looked up, he beheld the large form of the Pastor bending over him, and behind him the figure of the Squire who had now come upon the scene, he made one exclamation of "No," then fell back unconscious.

The two men were of one mind, they could not leave the young man in the cave, they must remove him to a place of safety where he could receive attention and they must act quickly as darkness was falling and time was not on their side. Gathering up the ends of the blanket between them they gently raised the inert figure and carried it to the Pastor's waiting horse. There was no movement, resistance or sound of any kind; the body of Sam lay across the horse's back ready to be transported to any point the Pastor chose. Quickly he informed his companion he would take the young man to someone who lived a little further along the Annum Waye and if she could not help, then he would have to make inquiries nearer the city. The men parted company wishing each other God's speed and promising to meet again as soon as possible.

A pair of cottages nestled along the pathway some little distance from where they had found Sam and it was towards the larger of these that the Pastor headed. The cottage was neat in appearance, displaying a warm glow of candle light from one of its windows and the Pastor approached the door, knocking several times upon it before there was any reply. Finally, from inside the building a woman's voice enquired, "Who is there?"

The Pastor quietly informed her of his identity, adding they had already met earlier in the day when she attended morning service at the Baptist Chapel. Whereupon the door became slightly ajar and finally wide open as the lady confirmed the information she had been given.

"I am seeking your help, Widow Webb, I have with me a young man who has been badly injured of late, he is staying on his own in a cave in the forest further along the way, but he is in no condition to look after himself, do you think you could be of service in this matter?"

Leaving the protection of her dwelling the lady went over to the Pastor's horse to inspect the condition of the young man who was the concern of her visitor. When she saw the bruises, the congealed blood and the general condition of the body, she suddenly had great compassion for the individual. Lifting the blanket from Sam's face she declared that he appeared to be of an honest countenance, but had obviously fallen on hard times.

Yes, she would take the young man into her care for the present, on condition that the Squire or the Pastor, within the next few days, made a call to ascertain all was well. "I cannot understand Pastor, how anyone can do this to their fellow creature, if this young man had been left in the cave, on his own, I venture to say he would not have lived many more days. Come let us bring the lad into the warmth of the cottage and you must make haste back to the city, there are those around who have done this to Ruth's friend and I know given the opportunity, they would treat you likewise."

She was a lady of action and having said her piece she looked at the Pastor in an inquiring fashion which had such an effect that in no time at all, with the Pastor at one end of the blanket and herself at the other, Sam was gently transported into the cottage and with great restraint laid on a rug in front of the fire.

"I will attend to him now Pastor, he is in no condition to harm a soul and you must return to the city. God's speed and may he protect you always." She accompanied him to the door and returned to her patient.

Widow Webb was as good as her word, but then she was always reliable and took pride in the way she handled her life, especially her relationships with others. She was a lady of great faith, even though she had endured some very hard times, so this episode now thrust upon her, she viewed as a challenge, but like everything else in her life it would be tempered with compassion. The young man had been brought to her, he now relied upon her and she vowed she would not fail him. Looking down at Sam, she decided his present condition required some immediate nourishment and following this she would endeavour to clean up his wounds, wash him and replace his tattered clothing with some of her late husband's apparel. He could rest where he lay for the night, there was a straw mattress, which would relieve the hardness of the floor, and she felt certain she would be able to move him gently on to it.

Thus resolved she commenced the tasks she had outlined in her mind, knowing full well her labours would not allow her much rest through the night, she recognised the young man was seriously ill and if she was going to save his life, then certain things must be done. She did not fail; when morning dawned she had been keeping vigil throughout the night with only brief moments of sleep. Sam, the young man as she now knew him, had been hallucinating during many of the dark hours and his ravings gave her no rest. He was quieter now and was sleeping peacefully. As she sat and watched him she joined him in the land of nod.

~*~

Over the next few days Sam's fever began to wane, he was now taking more nourishment, the widow's beef tea being a particular favourite. As his strength returned, his ravings decreased and he could finally hold a conversation with the dear lady who had saved his life. She wondered why he was living in the cave and how he was hoping to survive the winter months when the really cold weather came. He explained the situation in terms of his family history and his association with Ding during the summer

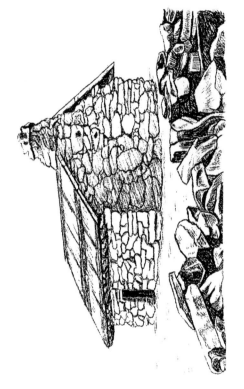

A Simple Dwelling

months, the role of a young kitchen maid who worked for the Squire and who supplied them with parcels of food, in particular bread and cake. He remembered being very disappointed when he had looked in their special hiding place one evening and found it empty, then on the way back to the summer palace he had had the good fortune to collect a fine woodcock which he knew would sustain him for several days. From this point his memory was rather hazy, he had been robbed of the bird then beaten unmercifully by two brothers. He had a notion that he had seen these individuals on the Downs, collecting their protection money, but he could not be absolutely certain of this. After that he had no idea of how he had been rescued, brought to his present situation, nursed back to health and now clothed in the garments of another.

Chapter Seven

The Widow's Tale

"I can answer some of your questions, Sam, but I will leave the majority of my story until you are stronger and we can talk more, for I know you will be in no hurry to return to the place you call the palace. I feel you have gained my trust; therefore, I am prepared to keep you here until you are fully recovered, and then you will have to decide what you will do in the future. You were quite correct in thinking the Ward brothers were responsible for your downfall, they appear to carry out this kind of action with impunity, in fact the night they punched and kicked you they were returning home having carried out a similar attack on a farmer who had not paid them his protection money and did not have the means to do so. You were fortunate in so far as the Pastor and the Squire managed to locate this summer palace of yours, find you and bring you here. They did so on the evidence of a young kitchen maid, although I understand that they came close to abandoning the search, in which case I am certain you would not be sat here now looking so resplendent in my husband's old clothing."

Sam looked at the attire he was now wearing and realised he had not seen his old clothes since he had regained consciousness. His intuition told him he could have lost the talisman given to him by Ding, but not wishing to destroy the relationship he was building with Widow Webb he decided to be very wary in endeavouring to ascertain the fate of his old clothes.

"I am more than grateful for the loan of your husband's

raiment," stammered Sam in a rather nervous fashion, "if the clothes I was wearing when you took me in, are now dry, I will change into them and you may have these returned. I feel sure you must cherish such grand attire, especially as you probably have special memories associated with them."

"What you have just stated is very true." replied his friend, "and for a young man with your experience of life to express such sentiments is admirable, but I have to acquaint you with the knowledge that the clothes you were wearing when you were brought to me, have been helping to keep you warm in another way. They were beyond repair Sam and I had no alternative but to burn them, they would not have kept you warm during the winter months, so it seemed common sense to dispose of them."

Sam was rather startled by this news and his face reflected his thoughts, so much so, that it prompted an immediate reply, "do not be disturbed, I have informed you it was the clothes I have burnt and that is the truth, the odds and ends in your pockets I still have. You were not carrying a fortune when you arrived here, all your worldly wealth is in a small box on the mantelpiece, including two funny little pieces of metal shaped like clover leaves. I will not be inquisitive Sam, but it seems to me they are of more value to you than the few pence which accompanied them, perhaps one day you may want to tell me about them."

As Sam grew stronger these conversations became an important part of his existence and they helped to develop a strong bond between the two friends. Gradually as his strength returned he began to take on the tasks appointed to him, he could now chop and stack the kindling required, collect the eggs from the little hen house behind the cottage, harvest a few root vegetables which grew in the small garden and be of general use in the home. He was always aware of the passage of time; the widow attended the little chapel every Sunday morning and one day in the middle of the week she would meet with the ladies of the fellowship for an hour or so, for prayer and Bible study. It was following one of the Sunday morning services that Sam received his first visitor. The Pastor had already fulfilled his promise and paid two visits to the cottage, then passed on the good news of his progress to the Squire, but Sam was unaware this was so and he was completely unprepared for the visitor who returned with Widow Webb. He had finished the odd jobs for the morning and was resting in front of a glorious fire when his friend entered the cottage accompanied by the 'guardian angel,' as Ding had called her. Sam was taken completely by surprise and when Widow Webb introduced Ruth to him and they politely shook hands, he was lost for words. Realising the young man was somewhat embarrassed by her sudden appearance, Ruth decided to break the ice by enquiring of his well-being since his fortuitous arrival at the cottage. Sam replied, "I am extremely grateful to Widow Webb for all she has done for me, I feel certain that I would not be alive now if she had not taken me in and cared for me. However, I also feel I am greatly indebted to you for your part in my deliverance. I understand it was your initiative, which was responsible for my rather dramatic rescue from the summer palace and for this act of kindness I shall be forever in your debt. I thank you from the bottom of my heart."

He had found it hard to start this little discourse, but as the words came tumbling out his confidence had returned and by the end of his speech it was Ruth who was now looking a little ill at ease. Recovering her composure, she explained how the Squire and the Pastor had volunteered to search for the summer palace relying on the very flimsy evidence and poor directions provided by her. "However I feel they were guided to you and if I am correct, then I hope and trust the guiding hand, which brought you, your deliverance will be with you in the days to come. I must be away now Widow Webb," she called into the kitchen, "the master will be wondering what is keeping me, and Cook will be fretting because she is missing a pair of hands. I wish you both good day and perhaps at some time in the future we shall see this young gentleman in chapel. From now on I will refer to you as Sam, because I was informed of your name by David not long after your arrival in the forest."

Before Sam could collect his thoughts, Ruth had left the cottage and with her bonnet ribbons flying in the wind she was making haste across the meadow towards The Hall.

Widow Webb came in from the kitchen to enquire of this David of whom she had heard mention and it took Sam a little while to give her the full details of how David and Ding, were but one and the same person.

"He would appear to be a bit of a young rascal, Sam, I hope one day in the future I shall have the pleasure of meeting him, he sounds an interesting character, meanwhile ponder on the invitation given to you by Ruth and should you be desirous of joining us one Sunday, you must tell me. Come now the meal is ready."

As soon as food was mentioned Sam realised he had made a great omission in his talk with Ruth, he had not mentioned the food parcels, which she had placed out for Ding and himself, one of them proving to be the catalyst precipitating his rescue. He told himself he must make a point of thanking her the next time they met. This raised a question in his mind and speaking out loud enough to be overheard, he said, "If I attend the service, it will provide me the best opportunity to talk with her again?"

His question was soon answered by his companion, "Sam, in a few weeks time we shall be rejoicing because it will be Christmas, what better way can you find of saying thank you, not only to Ruth, but to the One who looked after you when you were in need, and whose birthday we shall be celebrating."

Sam agreed to the suggestion and in the intervening weeks he hoped he would further improve in health and be physically stronger by the appointed time. In the period leading up to the festive season Sam and Widow Webb forged a strong relationship, they would sit near the fire, safe and secure in the cottage and in each other's company, talking through the lengthy dark evenings. It was through these discourses that Sam gleaned a picture of the life of his newfound companion; he no longer called her Widow Webb, but Sarah. As a mark of their growing friendship she had already invited Sam to remain in the cottage during the winter months mainly because she did not think he would survive if the winter proved to be severe, but also because the summer palace had been vandalised by persons unknown and all of their belongings stolen. If Ding did return in the following summer they would have to find an alternative place to stay, as the cave no longer existed. But for the moment he was content.

He learned that Sarah had been brought up in a comparatively wealthy family in the city. Her father had inherited a small family business, which concerned itself with the importing of exotic hardwoods and also the local trade in oak, ash, elm and beech. These timbers were stored and stacked on the wharf by the river. Trade was good and the reliable income gave the family a comfortable life, allowing Sarah to attend one of the oldest schools in the city. She described to Sam the red uniform and bonnet she wore, the celebrations in the city on a special day of the year when they honoured their founder by attending service in the large cathedral. Her teachers had instilled in her a love of literature and because of this she became a student of the Bible, she adored the psalms, together with many of the Old and New Testament stories. This interest was also shared by the foreman of her father's timber business, a nicety that brought them together when they attended a free church in the city. Edward was some years older than Sarah, but she told Sam the age difference was not noticeable when they were together. Her parents were not greatly in favour of the marriage, but marry they did, and although the union was childless they shared an extremely happy wedlock.

Her father was always looking for ways and means of expanding his business, so when the opportunity arose to purchase the yard behind the Blue Bowl, he bought it and gave Edward the job of running this new venture. The acquisition of these second premises stretched the family finances to the limit, especially when her father helped Edward to stock the seasoning sheds adjacent to the sawpit and helped buy the cottage in which she now lived.

"The cottage was fairly small and had none of the conveniences which we now enjoy," her tone and voice had changed as she explained the situation to Sam, "you see my husband was one of the kindest people I have ever met and he was very skilled with his hands. It was he who built on what we call the far back kitchen, beyond the original walls, all the furniture was made by him, the little out-house for the livestock and the wall surrounding the garden are all still standing as a living monument to his memory. In fact Sam, there is a task you might like to try your hand at during these winter months, when there is little we can accomplish outside. Over in the corner of the room by the side of the dresser you will find a board with a chequered, squared pattern on it; a chessboard. Edward made this from some of our local holly for the white squares and some beautiful rosewood for the darker ones."

Sam retrieved the board and sat admiring the workmanship as she continued, "of course the board requires a set of chessmen to make it possible to play; these have almost been completed but there remains a white queen, a white king, a white knight and some black pawns to be made. Do you think you could take on this task and complete what Edward commenced?"

"I am honoured to be asked to finish this task," Sam replied, "although the game itself means nothing to me and I have no notion of how to play it, but I will endeavour to be found worthy of the challenge you have set me. I assume that the pieces of timber and the necessary tools are available and, should I be successful in this venture, I suggest that you teach me how to play the game."

Sarah's face glowed with admiration as she anticipated seeing her husband's final work being completed, "Sam you will make me a very happy woman if you finalise this task. Edward commenced it some time before he had the accident at the sawpit. One of the hands had not erected the stack in the drying shed as it should have been done and when my husband saw that it was dangerous, he attempted to correct the situation without enough men to help him. The stack collapsed, the other two men who were present managed to jump clear, but unfortunately Edward was trapped under a number of heavy baulks of timber. We were aware he had injuries to his legs and arms and these took a long time to heal, however, his strong constitution brought him through and he was preparing to return to work. Unknown to us he had also suffered some internal damage and this proved to be far more serious, he was never able to work again and found great difficulty in walking. During the long months when I made every attempt to nurse him back to health, he would occupy his time with the carving of his chess pieces, but as you can see, he did not quite finish the task. It will mean a great deal to me Sam if you can make the remaining pieces, then I will do my best to show you how to play."

The bargain was sealed and finalised by Sarah giving the pieces of timber and the necessary tools to the new apprentice.

"To continue my narrative, Sam, you may be wondering how I managed to live here on my own during the years since Edward died, the simple answer is that I was not alone. My parents suffered a catastrophic time during the final year of Edward's life. First there was a fire in the timber yard in the city and although not a complete disaster, when it was coupled with the loss of the new stock being shipped in from the east, the two events drained my father of the will to live. The insurance claims on both calamities were meagre, the yard being under insured, whilst the boat on which the timber was being transported was little more than a hulk. It sunk off the coast of Africa with all hands. Following these events they deemed the time was ripe for them to review their business connections in the city. At the time both were in their sixties and it seemed prudent for them to sell the business and move to the forest to live with me. For the next three years we lived happily here in this cottage, during which time my parents and Edward settled their differences and became the best of friends; we were all one family.

As a result of this close relationship they were both broken hearted over his death and grieved for him night and day. Because he was like a son to them, they could not readily console each other, but he was also my husband and I found it very difficult to alleviate their pain, as well as bearing the burden of his death. I think they both died of broken hearts and I have been alone until the day you were brought to me. In some ways I feel it was the hand of providence that guided you here, for, had I borne a son, I would like to think he might have been in your image. You have most of my story now Sam and you also have the explanation of my attending to the grave in the churchyard of the little Baptist Chapel where we worship."

The autumn progressed; the deciduous trees gave up their leaves to the forest floor presenting it with a many-coloured carpet. Large chestnut leaves, spread out like huge hands, tumbled down from the overhead canopy. The horse and sweet chestnuts together with the shining acorns fresh from their cups, lay awaiting the warm snout of some rooting pig, or to be transported to an unknown destination by an industrious squirrel, there to be stored as an appeasement to its hunger later in the year, or to germinate into a life of its own and become a pillar of the forest. The tall birches looked down on the scene, bestowing everything with a fall of confetti like leaves, these appeared reluctant to leave the parent plant in singular mode. There was a change in the behaviour and colouring of the wild animals in the forest, all ensuring their survival for the following spring. Inside the cottage the untrained fingers of a young man were coercing a piece of holly to become the likeness of the black queen, which possessed the touch of a craftsman. He would struggle with the knight and pawns later, not knowing why, he reasoned that if he could fashion the queen the rest would follow. Peace reigned inside the cottage as the two worked together, talked together and planned together, as his first visit to the little chapel came ever nearer.

Chapter Eight

The Chapel

Prior to their visit Sarah decided she would impart to Sam the background knowledge which she had concerning the witness of the Baptists in Annum and the surrounding area. She had informed him that during the second half of the seventeenth century evangelists came from the city bringing the gospel to the people of the forest. Because of religious persecution they held secret meetings in the woods where the Pastors from the city churches, notable the Pithay Chapel and Broadmead, came as missioners to a lawless and hostile population. Continuing her story on the eve of their visit she said, "Such was the situation before the chapel was built, Sam, and it was to their eternal credit that they did not give up. There were several Pastors who were imprisoned because of their witness, at least one died in Gloucester gaol, one drowned in the Avon when he attempted to swim across the river to escape from the troopers, who I understand did nothing to help the poor man. But the greatest escape story concerned one of our very early Pastors. He was apprehended in the woods at Annum because the person acting as his lookout became frozen to a stone, on which he was resting. It was said the frost was so severe, that the cloak of the lookout was firmly attached to the stone and by the time he had freed himself, the Pastor had been apprehended. Despite the time of day he was transported to Gloucester gaol, where he was admitted a few minutes before midnight. The law demanded that an inmate remain in custody for six months, if after that time there had been no trial or sentence passed, then he or she would be given his or her freedom. No such trial or sentence came to light in the time allowed, so on the final day marking the end of his incarceration he demanded an audience with the governor. This gentleman was greatly annoyed to think any prisoner could be demanding his freedom just a few minutes before midnight. The Pastor must have presented a very strong case, pointing out he had been willing to open up the gates to let him in at this 'unearthly hour,' so why could he not open them now to let him out. The governor finally relented and our beloved Pastor was freed and returned to his people. Back at the gaol on the morning following his release, a summons was delivered, post haste from London, confining our Pastor to prison for the rest of his days. We have talked of your deliverance being guided by the hand of providence, but I firmly believe this is one of the greatest escape stories you are likely to hear, and these are the people who had the vision to build this chapel which we are attending today."

They had reached the main road running through the village and as they passed the sawpit, Sam made reference to the fact he would like to seek a position at the yard if ever one became available. Sarah responded to the request by assuring Sam that should a vacancy occur she would speak for him, she still maintained an interest in the yard although she no longer had any financial involvement in it. Even in its deserted silence the yard held a fascination for Sam, he looked at the stockpile of local timbers in the seasoning sheds and wondered into what marvels these baulks would be transformed. Perhaps their destination would be on the high seas, protecting brave mariners exploring the unknown, or in the shape of a high-speed coach drawn by four magnificent black horses, travelling through the forest along the Bath Waye linking the Spa city with the large port to the west. He

The Chapel

was aware these pictures in his mind were recognition of the ties he had with his family.

He then noticed a farm cart that was standing at the back of the yard awaiting repair and realised there were many other uses for the timbers demanding the attention of the sawyers and the wheelwrights. It was certain the life of the lady walking by his side had been enriched by the wealth of the forest, which had given her husband the means to make a living. He made a quiet resolve to finish the chess pieces to perfection. Whatever the need, the forest with its natural wealth could fulfil it. In his mind he could hear the 'sparrow' extolling the products of her husband's labours and laughing to himself he thought, 'the populace will always require timber, whether on land or at sea and the forest can supply the need'; as he dodged a non-existent, wet cloth.

Sarah had noticed on previous occasions the slightest reference to the yard, or the merest glimpse of any form of craftsmanship had the effect of transporting Sam into a world of his own. She was not surprised therefore, to find that as she approached the wrought iron gates leading into the churchyard, her companion was several yards behind her. As she awaited the arrival of Sam, members of the congregation invoked her with a greeting and wished her a Merry Christmas. They finally climbed the two steps together and moved up the pathway towards the porch of the chapel, cleaning their footwear on the metal scraper set in the porch wall. Inside they were greeted by a member of the Fellowship who shook hands, wishing them the Season's Greetings as he did so. Sam felt he was welcome although he was not aware he knew many of those present, in what he thought was an impressive building.

He had been fascinated by the clean lines of the chapel when he had first seen it some time ago, now from the inside he looked up at the high ceiling, the thick walls, the long windows reaching almost to the eaves as they finished in a graceful arch. Sam looked at the windows in amazement, the panels of glass which formed an inner, parallel line were not clear like the rest of the window, but were a marvellous blue colour and in the morning sunlight they appeared unreal, almost a part of the sky. In front of him in the middle of the east wall, a sturdy platform rose up from the floor whilst a small flight of steps gave access to the pulpit where a huge Bible rested on the reading lectern, this formed an integral part of the whole. Covering the lectern a deep purple cloth created a drop front, which displayed to the congregation the letters 'IHS'. These were gold in colour, intertwined with each other and stood out boldly between the simple Christmas decorations of holly and ivy. Sarah and Sam settled themselves on one of the bare, wooden seats, acknowledging the glances of friendly, inquiring eyes and whilst Sarah bowed her head in prayer Sam surveyed the rest of the assembled folk looking for a particular individual. There was a whinny from a horse and the little porch of the chapel was suddenly alive with people. The Squire, together with his family and various servants had arrived. They seated themselves several rows in front of Sam and Sarah and as they did so the young man looked with inquiring eyes at the row of bonnets worn by the ladies in the party. He found that from the position he was in, it was impossible to distinguish one young lass from another and as all the bonnets were identical in shape and colour, he had no idea of the identity of the wearers. He took a quick glance behind him to espy the Squire's horse tethered to a little hitch rail in the churchyard, but he was soon brought to book by the elbow of his companion, as the congregation stood to welcome the Pastor emerging from the vestry door on the far side.

In a deep, resonant voice the Pastor gave a welcome to everyone and hoped they would all enjoy a very happy Christmas in the name of the Saviour whose birth they would be celebrating in a few days from now. There was a chorus of 'amen' from the assembled group of villagers and a sense of expectation as the little pedal organ struck up the tune for the first hymn announced by the Pastor. Sam was fascinated by the words of the carol as they sang about shepherds watching over their sheep, then being told by an angel to go to a stable where they would find a newborn king. Ding had called Ruth an angel, and for a moment he wondered if he would be aware of all the intricacies concerning angels, shepherds and sheep. It was inevitable; his first thoughts always reverted back to the meat wagon and the sheep that he had to leave to the mercy of the Streers and George.

The Pastor read from the Bible and still the sheep were there, someone was led as a lamb to the slaughter and became dumb before the shearers. He explained this passage from the scriptures was a prophesy which would be fulfilled with the birth of Jesus, who was the lamb of God and that 'He' had come to earth to bring salvation to every living soul. There were long prayers which the Pastor said with great fervour, petitioning God to bless the folk gathered in the chapel, together with their loved ones some of whom were unwell in body and in spirit, and to guide the church through the dark days in which they were living. His hope rested in the Lord and he prayed sincerely for the revival which had started some years previously and which he desired to continue. There were other hymns, some of which Sam had heard Sarah singing from time to time, but he could not fully participate in the lusty rendition of these.

Throughout a lengthy sermon Sam found his mind wandered over many aspects of his own life. He scrutinised the folk gathered in the chapel, none of them were rich, except perhaps the Squire, but most of them displayed a peace and calm which he had not noticed with the majority of the village mortals. He was somewhat surprised when two of the gentlemen in the chapel passed baskets amongst the congregation and was even more startled when he noticed gifts being placed in them by folk who had very little in the way of worldly wealth. Sam was somewhat mystified by all the proceedings and he could not see how Sarah had derived her simple, almost childlike faith from what he had seen and heard during the service; he was not sorry when the proceedings came to a close. He could now see Ruth was with the Squire and his party, for as the heads turned the auburn curls, the fresh complexion and the blue eyes came into view.

The last 'amen' was said and folk began to wander out into the winter sunshine, standing in the churchyard and relating experiences and news of the village folk, together with their expectations for Christmas day. Sarah was joined by the Squire and at this juncture Sam found sufficient nerve to talk to him and thank him for his part in his rescue, the gentleman was gracious in his response but pointed out to Sam that the Pastor and the young lady on the edge of the group to their left were more instrumental than he was. Sam moved towards the Pastor and once again found enough reserved strength to express his thanks, only to be given the news that it was the intelligence which they received from Ruth that made the whole venture possible. He now recalled he had much to thank Ruth for, as during their previous conversation he had omitted to say anything about the parcels of food which she had passed on to Ding and himself. Moving across to the group of servants awaiting the Squire, he noticed Ruth was deep in conversation with one of the lads who worked as general hand at The Hall. When she saw Sam she welcomed him, but the sight of the young lad had robbed him of his confidence and had stirred within his being a strange jealousy. Gradually, he managed to regain his self control and impart to Ruth his deepest thanks for all that she had done for Ding and himself during their time in the summer palace. He wanted to remain and talk, especially now that he felt he had captured the high ground, but Sarah had already gestured she was ready to go home. Sam joined her and as they strolled down through the churchyard to get to the Annum Waye, Sarah intimated the Squire had given them an invitation to attend The Hall on Christmas day to dine with him and his family.

"You may prefer to eat and have fellowship with the younger members of the household staff, rather than remain with me and feel out of place with the Squire and his friends. You are quite at liberty to do so Sam, there will be nothing to stop you from being with those who will make you feel at home and give you most pleasure. You must make the decision and the Squire will fully understand whatever you desire, however, there are a few days for you to cogitate before we acquaint him with your wishes."

They had reached the cottage and enjoyed its welcoming

warmth, together they tackled the tasks that had to be done and settled more like mother and son than two strangers who had only been aware of each others existence for a few months.

Christmas morning dawned and Sam was ready with the special gift he had made ready for Sarah. He had worked day and night to complete the chess pieces by the time this special day arrived and although they were not carved to the same standard of perfection as the ones he had used as patterns, they displayed a very competent quality which Sarah admired.

"You have done extremely well to complete the set by this time and especially to such a high standard, I will always regard this set as being singularly private, my treasure, for they will bring me more pleasure than jewels. Now I wish to surprise you with a gift Sam."

She left the room for a time, returning with clothes she had fashioned for Sam's use. He was overjoyed with the gift, to the point where he readily agreed to wear them to the chapel that very morning and then later to The Hall, where, he said, "I will be the envy of all the young men and the desire of all the young ladies."

Sarah greeted this final remark by saying, "You look fine Sam in your new attire and I am glad that the fit is good, but inside the clothes is the same young man who came to me and I agreed to take you in because I recognised there was something about you which demanded saving. So far I have not been proved wrong. Come we will attend the service and then dine in style at The Hall, although I am fully aware your preference is to be with the younger element, no doubt in the hope you will be able to contact the maid called Ruth."

Sam covered his blushes, knowing in his heart Sarah's reasoning was correct and his one desire, whether in the chapel, in The Hall, or anywhere, was to see Ruth again. For some reason, which he could not explain, Ding came into his thoughts and he wondered where he would be spending his Christmas day. For himself he was more than thankful that he was not alone in the summer palace.

The service was well attended, full of joy and praise. The sheep were still present, although Sam now noticed that there was also an ox and an ass in the stable. Of much greater importance, the auburn curls and the blue eyes were present. To Sam's relief, after a fairly short service they departed from the chapel together with the Squire, his family and the Pastor. As they made their way to The Hall a few snowflakes fluttered through the thin air.

Cook and her kitchen staff were congratulated by the Squire for the wonderful meal, which they had prepared for the day. In the large dining room, the guests of the Squire and his family all dined on venison from the forest, served with vegetables from the garden, followed by Cook's own special pudding and fruit which had been picked earlier in the year. The humbler beings had fared almost as well, with a large piece of pork bearing plenty of scrumpy crackling which was shared out by Cook. During the autumn months they had gathered a collection of nuts and some of these, in particular the sweet chestnuts, were roasted over the fire causing much amusement as they exploded. Sam had never eaten like this before, he remembered that Ding had told him of the huge meal he had devoured at a harvest celebration in the same place and came to the conclusion that the Squire was a very generous soul. He was not the only one to hold this opinion, the folk in the dining room thanked the Squire for his kindness and hospitality as they raised their glasses to toast his health, then added Season's Greetings to everyone.

Sarah, when asked by her host how the young man called Sam was progressing, gave a glowing report of his physical recovery and his advancement in the social skills which we all require in order to live in harmony. She added her heartfelt thanks for his skilful completion of the chess pieces, which she had given him as a challenge, declaring she was of the opinion Sam would probably make a first class craftsman. One of the gentlemen present commented he had an interest in the sawpit and wheelwrights near the Blue Bowl and he was fairly certain that a position for a trainee sawyer and wheelwright would be available in the late spring. He, therefore, suggested to Sarah she keep in touch and when the position became vacant, they would interview this young man. Meanwhile it was imperative Sam should get as strong as possible, regaining his full health in order to combat the rigours he would encounter should he fill the vacancy.

The evening progressed with polite chatter; the progress being made in the chapel, the disappearance of the deer from the forest, the general degeneration of the area as the mines and the quarries were taking precedence and their workers built more cottages. All these were topics of a lively conversation and others followed. There was disquiet at the robberies being made on the Bath Waye as well as the London Waye, but as one of the informed gentlemen pointed out, there would soon be another place on the far side of the world to house these miscreants. He continued, "the West Indies is not the place for the white man, there is too much for him to bear, it is therefore hardly worth sending our criminals there, because of disease, they do not last long enough to make it worthwhile. Far better that we populate this new land discovered by Captain Cook and keep them in custody on the other side of the world."

In the kitchen the talk was rather different, the latest news on personal relationships was much to the fore, with Sam completely unaware of many of the characters under scrutiny. He had noticed the eyes of the Cook were upon him and he was not unprepared when she began to question him on his life in the forest and also in the city. The jovial lady was not unkind in her desire to gain more knowledge of this young man, who she felt had an interest in her adopted daughter and who she had been feeding through the summer months. As they conversed Sam felt he had made a new friend, a good ally but a formidable foe. He liked the Cook and he understood why Ruth possessed the qualities which he admired. There were times when their conversation was overshadowed by the raucous laughter of some of the other servants, but they persevered until one of the stable hands produced a fiddle and began to play. The music prompted the company to rise to their feet and to dance around the kitchen with great glee, this inspired Cook to issue a solemn warning as to the fate of anyone who might wreck any part of her domain. Before he knew what was happening Sam had been dragged to his feet and was being whirled around with the rest of the young guests, being passed from one partner to another. They finally came together in each other's arms and as they danced, Sam thought that he would never let her go again, but the music continued and he was holding another. Ruth was renewing the sequence of the dance in the arms of the groom, but the memory she had left with Sam was etched on his heart.

There was a call from the Squire to the effect that Sarah was about to depart and several of the young men would, together with Sam, form a bodyguard to escort her home. The light dusting of snow was enhanced by the moonlight, producing a special glow, as they walked back to the cottage in the safe keeping of some of the tougher characters employed by the Squire. Sarah expressed her thanks to the young men who had escorted them home and agreed with Sam when he stated it was one of the best Christmas days he had experienced. It was impossible to compare it with a day alone in the inhospitable summer palace.

~*~

Time quickly passed, the effort required to keep the cottage clean and warm, produce enough food for the table, give sufficient attention to the livestock and the upkeep of the out buildings was as much as they could manage. Life was hard as it was for all the villagers, but Sarah somehow succeeded in keeping everything spotlessly clean and reasonably tidy. The dark winter evenings found them huddled by the fireside with the chessboard placed between them and Sam endeavouring to master the intricacies of the movements of the various pieces. Sarah found it was a losing battle and although not a great player herself, she wondered if Sam would ever have any standard of proficiency. Later in the springtime, when Sam was interviewed for the vacancy at the sawpit behind the Blue Bowl, she was able to speak on his behalf and, to the delight of them both, he secured the situation. The immediate effect upon their life style was not apparent, but during the next few years as Sam progressed they began to enjoy a much better standard of living.

As the weeks passed Sam paid several visits to the summer palace to ascertain if there was any sign of Ding's return. To his dismay, he found that on every occasion there was nothing to indicate that anyone had made any endeavour to rectify the initial damage, or the subsequent depreciation caused by the ravages of time. He knew, had there been any visit from his friend, there would be some sign to indicate his presence. Leaving the site, which was now becoming overgrown, Sam would finger the talisman given to him by Ding and in so doing his thoughts would range over the possibilities of his whereabouts. However, with the Romany families travelling the countryside and Ding's constant desire for adventure and variety, there was no answer to any of the questions raised in his mind. Sarah could not offer any solution, only the simple fact that if he stated that he would return to the summer palace, then he would probably, at some time, fulfil that promise. Ruth too, thought it was very unlikely Ding would disappear without trace. His previous three visits to the palace were all expected and each year he had promised to return, usually in the early summer or late spring, but this time she had no contact of any kind. No grass whistles, no smiling thanks given with a wave as she walked to the chapel. Nothing. Even Cook had passed comments about the provisions, not being depleted by parcels being secreted in the special hideout. Perhaps one day they would know the answers to their questions and theories, or he would walk into their lives again as bright and as cheeky as ever. Sam found it very difficult to accept this negative situation and he was more than grateful for the company of Sarah and the growing friendship of Ruth. These factors allied with his work at the sawpit more than occupied his time and his mind. Gradually, Ding was becoming a misty memory until the clover leaves nestled in the palm of his hand or were lightly caressed by his fingers, releasing recollections.

Sam was now attending the chapel more frequently, he would accompany Sarah on most Sunday mornings and to his delight he found the great majority of folk in the congregation became acquainted with him. Not only did this make him feel at home in their company, but it helped to secure business contacts with the local farmers and merchants, as well as the ordinary villagers who from time to time desired a small favour or two. It was at one of the services in the summertime when a certain announcement by the Pastor startled him. He was unaware of the term 'believer's baptism' and the situation was made more complicated when the Pastor gave the names of three candidates for baptism and Ruth's was one of them.

Sam had a great desire to know the full implications of what would be happening in the service, at the same time he did not want to intrude into what might be a very private part of Ruth's life. He therefore decided to attend and see for himself what took place in this very special service.

When the time came Sam was surprised at the increase in numbers in the congregation, he and Sarah could not seat themselves in their normal places, they had to be content with seats that were much further back. This did not deter them in any way, because the atmosphere in the building was expectant, the singing was jubilant and Sam could see a head of auburn curls in the front row with the other two candidates. Each of them wore a long white gown and was accompanied by a friend or relative. Ruth protected by her mother by adoption; the cook, looked radiant, safe and secure. The service continued in much the same way as for any Sunday morning, but the Pastor was carried along as if on the crest of a wave. He mentioned the baptism of Christ in the River Jordan by John, as an example to us all, saying the Lord was pleased to witness the obedience of his only Son in this way, and the candidates were following in the Master's footsteps as 'He' directed.

He illustrated his sermon with other baptismal references, pointing out that these were adult baptisms made by the persons concerned as an act of faith and because they desired to follow the preaching of Christ. The sermon continued for rather longer than Sam thought necessary, but there were frequent 'amens' from the appreciative congregation and these acted as a spur giving the Pastor a new lease of life and greater zest to continue. Finally, he announced a hymn and left the pulpit to enter the little vestry at the side of the chapel emerging a short while later dressed in a long black cloak.

The Pastor was helped down the steps leading into the baptismal pool by one of the elders, who then joined him in the water, the two men standing side-by-side awaiting the arrival of the first candidate. Each of the three ladies quietly rose, in turn, from their seats, faced the congregation and gave a short testimony of faith explaining why they were taking this great step in their lives. As Ruth gave her simple exposition in a quiet, confident voice, Cook was seen to bow her head and wipe away the tears, as she recalled a similar day in her own life which took place in this very chapel not long after it was opened. At the conclusion of each testimony, the candidate was led down the steps into the pool and baptised by the Pastor. Complete immersion symbolised the death of Christ, whilst rising from the water celebrated 'His' resurrection and the candidate's rebirth into a new life. As each lady came up from the water the congregation spontaneously sang a short chorus, the words of which Sam could not clearly hear. Arising from the pool, soaking wet and looking rather chilled each person was guided by their companion to the little vestry to change into dry clothes. At the conclusion of the service Ruth stood talking to Cook and several other ladies from the congregation, many of them embracing her and enquiring if the water was very cold. Ruth replied, "The cloaks we were wearing are made of a substantial cloth, weighted in the hem with lead so that you do not feel the full impact of the cold water. Besides, throughout the service and the baptism itself my heart was strangely warm."

She stood in front of her friends, red in the cheeks, her eyes ablaze with happiness and her auburn curls drying in the mid-day sun. Sam was speechless as he looked on and realised he had held this young lady in his arms, albeit only for a short while, and he had not fully recognised her beauty. His mind was in a whirl.

~*~

In the weeks following the baptismal service Sam saw little of Ruth. She became caught up in the work of the chapel and her spare time was occupied by visits to the sick, helping to clean the sanctuary, attending the mid-week service and taking under her wing the well-being of a family who were the victims of a very tragic accident. The parents were distraught; their little daughter was killed in a terrible mishap whilst she was playing with her friends near the quarry. A large, rectangular piece of stone had been cut and was propped against a cart awaiting loading before transportation to the mason's yard, to be inscribed as a headstone for an interment in the little churchyard. Something startled the horse and this triggered sufficient movement to disturb the stone, causing it to fall from its upright position. In so doing it crushed the little girl, killing her instantly. The whole episode was a tragedy that touched the heart of many of the folk in the village, and in particular that of Ruth. She could not come to terms with the death of a young girl who at one moment was laughing, playing, and so full of life, then without warning was suddenly crushed beneath the huge headstone.

Sam was required to supply the elm boards for the little coffin and he stood with Ruth throughout the service in the chapel and in the churchyard where she was interred. The stone erected over her grave was the very same that had caused her demise and the mason had carved on it, in verse, the story of the accident. They stood together offering their condolences to the relatives and in particular the father and mother. As they made their way to leave, the mother gripped Ruth closely to her and simply said, "I pray that you will never have this experience of loosing a little one, especially one that you love so much, I cannot face the future without her smile and all her funny little ways."

Ruth was lost for words, how could she console the despairing mother? She did not know and although she felt inadequate, she made it her duty to visit the parents as often as she could.

Chapter Nine

Contact

It was some months later, Ruth had taken charge of a delivery of New Testaments and began to unpack the parcel in the chapel. In order to keep the books clean and separate, odd pieces of paper were wrapped around them and also placed between them. One of these pieces caught Ruth's attention, it was part of a broadsheet which although crumpled was in fairly pristine condition but she was unable to find a date on the publication, however, she calculated it could not be more than a few weeks old. Scanning the news on a particular report she noticed the name Bell and decided to investigate further. The article gave an account of a disturbance at a fair in Somerset. Seeing the headline: *'Murder Committed During Fracas,'* Ruth felt compelled to read the following:

At the Annual Fair held recently in Somerset, a group of Romanies were involved in a bruising confrontation with several ruffians who, we understand, originate from the Kingswood forest area. It would appear two brothers by the name of Stone were collecting protection money from a farmer who was on the legitimate business of endeavouring to sell several horses. Having sealed the transaction with two of the Romanies he was then set upon by the Stone brothers who demanded that he pay them his debts from the proceeds. The farmer refused to do so and was quickly informed by one of the brothers what would happen to him if he did not comply.

One of the younger members of the Romany group overheard the conversation and immediately informed his colleagues, a general fracas ensued during which the farmer made his escape taking his hard earned cash with him. It was only when the belligerents were restrained and a measure of peace was restored that it was noticed one of the brothers was lying in a large pool of blood. In his chest a gaping wound indicated the savagery of the attack made upon him and the once proud, boastful bully now lay motionless on the floor. He had been stabbed through the heart and was pronounced dead at the scene of the crime. As a result of this confrontation that had ended in murder, three Romanies, one by the name of Bell who is the young man mentioned above, the Kelly cousins and the surviving Stone brother have been taken into custody. They will be transported to Bristowe gaol where they will await the next assizes to hear their fate.

Ruth was completely captivated by the article she had inadvertently found, she read it, then re-read it many times and always the same question came into her mind. Could this Romany named Bell be the young man she had befriended in the summer palace, the one Sam had stayed with some three years back? If the answer to this puzzle was in the affirmative then she needed to inform Sam, so together they could make a combined effort to establish some form of contact. She knew nothing about the prison in Bristowe where they were being held, but she was aware of the fact that one of the visiting Pastors to the chapel had made reference to giving sustenance to some poor wretch who was incarcerated within its walls. Furthermore, she was fairly certain the same Pastor had contacts in the city called Quakers, who made regular visits to offer help and comfort to the prisoners.

She had completed the unpacking, placed the precious testaments in a secure cupboard and began to clear the odd pieces of paper that remained. Suddenly a second headline jumped from the page, *'Prisoners' Cart In Crash,'* she read. To her dismay there was nothing more on the paper she had retrieved and despite a diligent search she discovered no further information on this particular subject. She knew these two incidents had occurred but there was nothing to indicate which had taken place first and she could not fix either of them in time because the part pages contained no dates or day of reporting. She must seek out Sam and talk with him and perhaps together they could possibly establish the truth of the matter.

At the close of his working day at the sawpit, Sam was making his way to Widow Webb's cottage. As he wandered down the lane he was pleasantly surprised when he met Ruth, who told him very briefly of the broadsheet articles which she had found, whilst unpacking the testaments in the chapel. As soon as Sam heard her story and recognised the possibilities presented by what she had found, he readily agreed they seek co-operation in order to establish the facts. The merest glimmer of hope that he might see Ding again filled him with pleasure, so much so he was willing to agree to any plan Ruth had in mind. They therefore decided to call at The Hall in order to acquaint the Squire with the intelligence gathered by Ruth and now shared by Sam.

The Squire was intrigued with the story unfolded to him, and taking the pieces of paper in his hand he scrutinised them for several minutes. Suddenly he left the room, returning a little later bearing a copy of a complete broadsheet. Carefully he examined all the text, but could find nothing to shed any light on the subject. After a while he looked at Ruth and Sam and said, "I have a strong suspicion these reports have not been recorded in the broadsheet which I purchase. The layout and print are a little different and I am of the opinion they may originate from the same area as the testaments delivered to the chapel, in fact, it is possible they could have been produced by the same printer. Ruth excitedly agreed and stated she was certain that the testaments had been printed by a Bath concern.

"Should that prove to be the case," the Squire remarked, "we must make inquiries in that city and endeavour to trace the printer, or better still, the broadsheet editor. It would seem there have been events happening under our very noses and we have no knowledge of them. This would indicate," continued the Squire, "that a visit to Bath might shed more light on the situation and provide us with a clearer picture of what has taken place. It would also help to put your young minds at rest regarding the fate of your Romany friend, should this prove to be the same Mr Bell known to us. As it happens I do have a business appointment in that very city a few days from now and if my business commitments can be concluded in time, I will make every endeavour to follow up the leads which you have provided, either at the printers or at the broadsheet offices. Perhaps between you, you could prepare a synopsis of what you know concerning your Mr Bell and also pick out the salient points of the reports which Ruth found, this will help me to remember the direct line of inquiry and I shall not have to rely on my failing memory."

Some days later Ruth eagerly awaited the return of her master from the Spa city. On his arrival at The Hall, he dispatched Ruth to the sawpit bearing a message for Sam. "I would like to speak with both of you concerning my visit to Bath," he said, "therefore please impart to Sam that I desire his presence, here with you, tomorrow evening in order that we may speak together. I wish to impart to both of you the facts of the case as they are unfolding and you may be able to add to the intelligence which I have gleaned during my stay in Bath. Tell him Cook will have some sustenance ready for him, so there will be no need to inconvenience Widow

Webb and we will excuse his working attire on this occasion. I would have spoken with you this very evening but my business commitments need to be completed so we must wait until the morrow."

Ruth hastened to carry out her master's wishes returning to tell him Sam would be delighted to participate in any discussion relating to his friend Ding, especially if it resulted in making some form of contact with the lad with whom he had shared the fish and who had given him the two clover leaves which he now secretly fingered.

The following evening, the Squire, the kitchen maid and the sawyer settled to see it they could piece together the various fragments of information in their possession and from them unravel the mystery they had discovered. Sensing the fact that the younger members might feel a little ill at ease, the Squire took the initiative saying he would impart to them the complete story as he knew it and then they could add their comments. From his time spent with the printers, who were very helpful, and also his examination of the broadsheet records, he had learned the following:

"It would appear," he said, "that several incidents have occurred of late, some of them here in the village and we have not realised the significance of them or even thought they were connected. The headline you found Ruth which concerned the crash, was the very one which Sam attended near the mill-clack brook bridge. Do you remember the day we received a message requesting Sam to attend to a broken cartwheel, brought to him from an accident that had happened near the bridge? You repaired the wheel Sam, it needed two new spokes, a new felloe, and a new tyre and you worked into the night to complete the task. The following morning you took the wheel to the hollow in the hill where the cart, which had been damaged, was resting on the roadside. Following the completion of all repair work you were told by the carter, who by the way left in haste, that payment would come from the magistrate's court. That cart was the very one in which the prisoners were being transported, but when it finally departed into the city the only passengers were two, muddle headed troopers and a dead Romany. The dead man I hasten to add was not Ding; from the description given he was too old and too large in stature. His demise was brought about in the following manner.

The accident was caused by the cart running away down the hill and because of brake failure and the inability of the carter to restrain the horses it hit the side of the bridge with a good deal of force. The carter managed to jump clear and in so doing, he escaped without injury but the unfortunate prisoners were thrown out on to the side of the road. Hindered by their fetters they were unable to save themselves and all suffered some injuries including concussion. The troopers on their own mounts were unhurt and one came to the village requesting your help, Sam, but at the time you were not available and it was only when you returned from your other duties you were made aware of the task set before you. The second trooper commanded the gentleman now farming at Londonderry to take the prisoners to the Blue Bowl, where they could be safely kept in custody during the hours of darkness. The farmer grudgingly obliged, so later that day all four were unceremoniously dumped in one of the stables at the rear of the inn and the door secured. There now follows a little twist in the narrative. The news of the accident reached certain individuals in the Kingswood area of the forest, in particular some associates of the Stone brothers and they did not intend to stand by without making an attempt to rescue their friend from the Blue Bowl. They therefore came to the inn later in the evening and struck up a conversation with the troopers, plying them with cheap ale until they were unable to stand. At this point the troopers were bound and gagged, then removed to an upper room where they were relieved of the keys for the fetters. Going to the stables the men soon located the unfortunate prisoners and, after freeing all of them from their shackles, they departed in haste on their own horses taking the Stone brother with them. The three Romanies left behind were not in great shape, one of them had several gashes in his head and upper body, as a result he had lost a great deal of blood and unfortunately he expired during the night. This must have been the man taken to Bristowe by the troopers. The two remaining Romanies, despite cuts and bruises, had recovered sufficiently to escape from the inn using the trooper's horses. The saddles and harness are still in the stable so it is assumed both rode bareback, this indicates a rare riding skill, especially on strange horses; but these are desperate men. A little later a very interesting sighting was made of these two horsemen by a quarryman who was on an early morning inspection of some cut stone. He stated the men rode down towards the river but, as they emerged from the meadow and began to head for the trees, one of them slowed his mount and he had a very cursory look at the little clearing where the brook rises and bubbles away to the river. As you are aware the summer palace was in that area, but the site is now very different to when you sought refuge there. However, I firmly believe the rider who made the very quick inspection could be none other than your friend Ding. Both riders were last seen making for the Bath Waye and on into Somerset to the south."

The Squire sat back in his chair, he had felt a great deal of emotion as he related his story and this was apparent in his countenance; he looked at his young guests and he could see they were lost for words. Sam in particular was shaking his head in disbelief.

"To think," he finally spluttered, "Ding could have been as near to us as that and we had no notion of his presence. He certainly is a very accomplished horseman and he would be quite able to ride bareback on a strange horse. It must have been him, who else would stop to look at the summer palace especially when trying to escape from the law? Do you know, Sir, if the riders were very badly bruised, or injured in such a way that their progress would be severely hindered?"

The Squire shook his head, "The story I have related to you has been built up on the facts I managed to glean from various sources, some of them are more trustworthy than others and in particular the printer, who apparently had a keen interest in the whole story. It was he who provided me with the major part of my narrative and the landlord at the Blue Bowl, although not willing to say a great deal, agreed with the facts relating to the happenings on his premises. As I have already intimated, there is no doubt in my mind one of the horsemen was Ding and in all probability it was he who sought out the summer palace. Should this not be the case I find it very difficult to find a logical explanation as to why one of the riders made an inspection of the area."

His young friends concurred it was the kind of behaviour they would expect of Ding and furthermore the area was now so desolate and overgrown that even a very quick glance by an observer like Ding would indicate there was no longer a summer palace. They both felt elated to have news of their friend, however there were a number of questions requiring answers and Ruth was the first to put her thoughts into words. Looking at her master, her bright eyes full of life she asked, "Have we any idea as to what may have happened to the two Romanies who were last seen riding away and do we know when these events actually occurred?"

The Squire hesitated a little before he answered the points made by Ruth. "To give you an answer in a word, Ruth, I can say yes, we found the newsprint items were a little older than we

The Blue Bowl

calculated and the payment to Sam for the repairs fitted into the time scale. The accident happened some two months ago, it is simply amazing how the time has passed since then, and your young friend is safe for the time being. This coming spring there is a special gathering in Ireland when all the Romanies will be celebrating the wedding of their leader's son. As you may know they look upon their leader as a king, so every Romany from far and wide will gather for the wedding of the man who will one day replace his father. I have it on good authority, but please do not ask me to betray a trust, that Ding, who is now fit and well again, will be at this very important gathering, in fact he could already have crossed the sea into Ireland."

Sam was overjoyed, he'd expected news that would have made him extremely sad but to know Ding had survived the crash, had escaped in the way he did and had briefly looked upon the scene of their meeting, made his heart sing.

"I sincerely thank you Sir for the time and energy you have spent on our behalf. If you have no further need of my company here with you I will be away to Widow Webb and let her share in our good tidings. I thank you once again, and Ruth would you please pass on to Cook my admiration for the sustenance she provided."

Ruth was quick to reply, "You may fulfil that obligation yourself, Sam, I am sure Cook is still in the kitchen, so you may pay your respects as you leave and I will see you to the side entrance of The Hall."

They were both walking on air as they bid farewell to the Squire, Sam made his speech to Cook with such fervour that he embarrassed himself and her, but it was near the side door of The Hall that he was carried away by his feelings. It was as Ruth turned to bid him goodbye he lost all reason, sweeping her up in his arms and without warning he tenderly kissed the rosebud mouth he had been admiring for months. Turning quickly on his heels he was away down the lane leaving Ruth flushed, surprised and elated.

Chapter Ten

Haberdashery

Sarah had taken on the task of inscribing the words Annum Baptist Chapel on to the flyleaf of the testaments recently delivered. To this end she would take home with her a number of the books in order to carry out the task she had set herself. It was while one of the testaments was lying on the table in the cottage that Sam picked it up and began to turn its pages. He stopped at the fourth chapter of the gospel of Mark, recognising the reading, which had been the subject of the Pastor's discourse a few weeks ago. The passage described how Jesus and his disciples were crossing the lake by boat, when a fierce storm arose. Jesus was asleep at the hind part of the vessel but this did not prevent the frightened disciples from awakening him and in their panic accuse him of not caring about their fate. When he awoke Jesus stilled the storm, but he also rebuked his followers for their lack of faith. Sam recalled the Pastor making the comment that when they set out on their journey they must have selected a fairly large boat to accommodate all of them, and therefore they were comparatively safe compared to the other smaller boats which also set sail. A further point had been established when the Pastor stated it was only Mark who mentioned the little boats, the remaining gospels describe the stilling of the tempest, but made no mention of any other craft. "Do you not think," the Pastor said, "that these other small ships were not affected by the storm? And did they not share in the calm, which Jesus created? Mark shows us we can be close to our Saviour, but like the disciples we can be very selfish in our attitude to others, for did they not say to him when he awoke; 'carest thou not that we perish?'"

Sam thumbed through the pages of the other gospels and found that he could find no further references to the other 'little ships', but he had thought on the fact that all of the craft on the lake at the time of the storm must have been affected by it. So the Pastor applied the reading to the daily life in the village. "When the little girl was accidentally killed by the stone, the whole village mourned. When three young folk from our fellowship here were baptised in 'His' name, the Church rejoiced. When we have all laboured long and hard to cut and store the harvest, everyone has a happy heart and there are times when all the villagers share in the good fortune of one family."

Sam found his mind wandering back to the small boat owned by his father, the times when they had stood on the Downs and gazed out to the estuary at the larger craft. Craft with mighty sails and many crew, craft that would sail to the far corners of the globe. It was on one of those craft his beloved father had been taken away, against his will and now no one knew of his whereabouts. His mother and sister had departed by coach when he was left behind with the butcher, but they were not very far away, it would not require a mighty storm to get him to the Spa city. He stopped thumbing the pages, he had come to the back cover of the book, 'printed by Manpitt and Son, Bath,' he read. He had seen or heard the name before, could it be the printer who had taken his mother and sister under his wing? He must find out, he had made plans to walk to Bath when he was living alone in the summer palace, but things had changed, and although he had not forgotten them, he had been busy trying to organise his life so other events and thoughts had crowded them out. He would seek advice from Sarah and if she thought the Squire might offer assistance then he would follow that course of action. This he did and a few weeks later he was on the way to the city of his desire, travelling in style with the Squire who had promised to take him to the printer's office near the Abbey.

When they arrived Sam endeavoured to enter the premises of Manpitt and Son but he found to his horror, the shop was closed until later in the day. The notice on the door indicated that the printer would not be there until after one o'clock in the afternoon. With time on his hands Sam began to explore the fascinating maze of small streets in and around the Abbey precincts. Almost without warning heavy rain began to fall and he was in danger of getting soaked when he noticed a small shop with a window display of silks, ribbons, pins and all the requirements for a good seamstress. He was not penniless, the cash in his pocket would be sufficient to purchase a present for Ruth and he fingered his two clover leaves as he entered the shop, leaving the storm behind him.

It was some time since Sam had entered any establishment, apart from the sawyer's yard, but here he sensed a warmth and homeliness, surely in this place he would not encounter anything, or anyone to remind him of the 'sparrow'. His reasoning was more than correct, for as a young lady entered from a back room and asked what his requirements were, she stopped and gazed in utter disbelief at her customer.

"Sam," the shopkeeper uttered, she then quickly placed her hand to her mouth as if to retrieve the very words she had just spoken and return them to the comfort of her vocal chords. "My sincere apologies sir for my forwardness, but you are so much like my brother of that name, who sadly I have not set eyes upon these past four years or more and who I greatly miss. May I be of service to you, please tell me your requirements."

Sam was dumbfounded, he stood and gazed at the young lady who had spoken to him, he recognised the voice, the face had the same determined set of the jaw it always had, but it was the laughing, gentle eyes that finally sharpened his reason and gave him the insight to understand the situation. "May I be so bold madam as to suggest we are possibly brother and sister, for indeed my name is Sam and the lapse of time between our last meeting is in the region of what you have just stated. Should my reasoning be correct then you are Emma and you came to this city with our mother to reside with and work for a printer by the name of Manpitt."

The bond was sealed. Emma ran to Sam and embraced him with a joy that almost squeezed the breath out of his body. For several minutes they stood together in disbelief and admiration of each other, finally Emma suggested she would put her assistant in charge of the shop and they could then repair to her private room to talk about their miraculous re-union.

Seated in comparative comfort at the rear of the little shop they began to talk. Question and answer, more questions more answers. Emma learned of the time Sam spent with the butcher, his sojourn with Ding in the summer palace and his rescue by the Pastor. Now he was with Widow Webb, he hesitated to give her name to Emma in case he gave the wrong impression, mainly because somehow he had to fit Ruth into the picture. This he finally managed to do, making it all too obvious to his discerning sister that his feelings for Ruth were stronger than for an acquaintance, or even a good friend. Sam waited upon every word to hear the news concerning his mother and Emma was pleased to tell him all he desired to know. He was aware she had visited the butcher's from time to time, but he had no notion as to when her visits would take place, only that they had already happened. Emma explained that their mother recognised the butcher and his wife were a very devious pair and their sole interest was in the money they collected month by month to pay for training and lodging.

"Mother and I were of the opinion you were purposely given no prior knowledge of her visits to prevent you imparting the knowledge all was not well, especially after the arrival of George. We were glad to hear of your escape, although the butcher still collected money for keeping your bed, in the hope you would one day return to the fold. He and his wife were of the opinion you had run away to sea in search of father, but we knew this was not the case. Mother was definite in the knowledge her son was a landlubber at heart and he would find more satisfaction in building a boat, rather than sailing away in one. You have proved her correct and I am sure she will be overjoyed to hear of your visit here today and to learn of your employment in the sawyers."

The time had flown as they talked and Sam found, when Emma informed him of the correct hour, it meant he would have to go directly to the meeting place he had arranged with the Squire. Somehow he must offer his apologies to the printer and also make arrangements to hold a simple family gathering. Emma promised to be of service on the first count as she would be seeing the printer that very evening, but she hesitated on the second as there could be difficulties in finding a suitable place to meet. Mrs Manpitt was still alive, mainly because of the care their mother had bestowed upon her, but her health despite all the special Spa treatment, was definitely failing. The main issue with the Manpitt family at the moment was the alliance being forged between their family and a publisher within the city. The daughter of the publisher, a fine girl by the name of Rebecca Harding, was being courted by Richard and it was desirable the two would be joined in matrimony whilst Mrs Manpitt was still alive. Although very frail, she still possessed a strong will and she ruled the household from her Bath chair. They promised to talk further when hopefully all the family would be present and Sam indicated he would be able to contact the shop, or the printers when he had been able to arrange a family gathering. How he wished his father could also be present, with this thought running through his mind he bade goodbye to his sister and walked briskly through the wet, mucky streets to the arranged meeting place with the Squire.

Seated together in the chaise, Sam informed the Squire of his fortuitous shelter from the storm during the afternoon and the consequences that followed his entry into the little shop. Gradually the complete story was unravelled as, at a steady pace, they made their way back to the village. The response from the Squire filled Sam with pleasure, he stated he was more than willing to host a family gathering at The Hall and Cook and Ruth would be most welcome.

Hence a few weeks later the family was once again united as they seated themselves around the table for a sumptuous meal prepared by Cook. They sat and ate and talked, they complimented Cook on her culinary skills, they thanked the Squire for his hospitality and they thanked the Lord for his goodness in bringing them together and for the food set out before them. Emma related she still had not recovered from the unexpected surprise of finding the young man who had entered her shop that day proved to be none other than her brother; Sam. Furthermore, as she was still not spoken for, she felt a little disappointment to find such a handsome being was a close relative and not a suitor. Rather embarrassed by the situation he found himself in, Sam turned to his mother and asked her if she would tell the present company of her life in the Spa city with the printer and his family.

"Yes," said the Squire, "I do not wish to be unkind at this time but we are fully aware of what has happened to Sam and he has already imparted the intelligence to Emma. We can therefore safely assume Mrs Stafford has been appraised of her son's adventures since they parted in Bristowe, I would suggest it is her story, coupled with that of Emma's, we are waiting to hear."

Hannah, with a cultured, soft voice which Sam knew she had developed whilst residing with the printer, replied she wished the present company would refer to her as Hannah and she would certainly tell them of all the happenings since the suspected capture of her husband Tom by the press gang.

"Following that fateful night and the meeting with Mr Manpitt, we were at our wits end to find a suitable position for Sam. We were not happy with the butcher's offer but it served its purpose at the time, whereas the situation proposed to Emma and myself offered us a tremendous opportunity, one we could not forfeit." She turned to Sam. "We were greatly concerned over your welfare Sam, especially when during my visits I never managed to catch a glimpse of you and I was instinctively aware your employer was not telling me the truth. Emma and I, since we arrived at the Manpitt home have been extremely busy, but we have also been very happy, of course we have had each others company and this has helped a great deal. The lady of the house as you know is in poor health, although I feel that sometimes she could do more to help with the smooth running of the household and refrain from the sharp tongued criticism meted out to her staff. This is one of the major reasons why we embarked on the shop for Emma, a venture in which she has made good headway and wonder of wonders it has proved to be instrumental in bringing the family back together again.

Mr Manpitt has been extremely cordial, always having our interests at heart and he has made many inquiries, Sam, concerning your well being and stating he would keep a lookout for you on his travels to Bristowe. We certainly have no regrets about taking up the positions, I have managed to maintain my authority with the servant staff without making enemies of them and Emma received a good grounding in her trade before she left the family in order to take up her responsibilities elsewhere. Since Richard has become engaged we have both been given extra responsibilities connected with the very special day. Mr Manpitt has asked me to oversee all the arrangements for the wedding, this means I will be performing tasks of which, at the moment, I have very little knowledge. Emma has been asked, and she has accepted, the task of helping to create the bridal gown and several other garments. We have a daunting but very interesting time ahead. I now know why we could not get news of your whereabouts Sam, but I am so grateful to all the kind folk who had your welfare at heart and cared for you at the time of your need and it is so gratifying to meet some of them here today."

Turning to the Squire she said; "Would you please accept my very sincere thanks for saving my son?" Then looking to Sam, "I wish with all my being I could pass on to you some news concerning your father, nothing has come to light to alleviate my sorrow and despite all the inquiries made by Mr Manpitt both in Bristowe and in Bath, we are still no wiser than on the day he was abducted. He has left a void in our lives which is impossible to fill. During the years we have been residing in Bath the printer's business has gone from strength to strength and now there is a possible amalgamation with the bookbinder. When this materialises, of course that will be after the wedding takes place, the new business will be a major concern in the city. Added to this is the fact that the broadsheet, which at the moment is being printed once a week, could become a very popular, but a demanding feature. There is every possibility of Richard becoming a very rich man."

She had held the interest of her audience during her discourse and left Sam wondering what luxuries he might have encountered had there been a position at the printers for him. Then he mused he would not have met Ding or Sarah, and most importantly, he would not have set eyes on Ruth. As his dear friend explained to him during their stay in the summer palace, you have to endure some of life's privations in order to appreciate its luxuries. He was pondering this in his mind as it applied to his father and to Ding, wondering if they were enduring privations or enjoying luxuries, when his thoughts were re-focused by the Squire. "May we enquire Hannah, when this wedding is taking place," he said, "it seems to me the burden you and your daughter are sharing is quite considerable and the tasks you have to perform cannot be completed in just weeks."

Hannah reassured him with the following answer, "We have time to finalise all that has to be done, as the wedding is planned for the summer of next year, but we have to be diligent and not let the grass grow under our feet, I feel Emma will be under more pressure than myself, but I have every confidence in her and the ladies who work with her."

They have given all they could give at this stage. The evening had been emotional for all of them, their happiness at being united exceeded all limits, and even Sam declared it was wonderful to be a 'family' again but their despair was unfathomable when they thought of Tom. Now links had been forged and with the help of their two benefactors it would be comparatively easy to keep in touch and this they promised to do.

Chapter Eleven

The Weddings

The months leading up to the special day produced a buzz of activity for both mother and daughter. Hannah spent many hours planning the sequence of events, going hither and thither to make certain all would be in order for the big occasion. Emma, with her two assistants, was pushed to the limits to ensure the garments they were creating fitted perfectly, with the design and needlecraft being a delight to behold. When the day dawned, the weather was perfect and the driveway to the Manpitt dwelling became alive with the comings and goings of gleaming carriages pulled by glistening horses transporting the many important guests attending the occasion. The large church was filled to capacity and as the bells sent their message across the city, Richard Manpitt and Rebecca Harding were joined in matrimony and their families were united in business.

Hannah watched with pride as the young gentleman who she had first seen as a lad, now grown and mature, walked down the aisle of the church with his beautiful bride clutching his arm. Both families were so proud of their offspring and they had so many hopes to be realised that even Mrs Manpitt gloried in the moment. Everything Hannah had planned had been brought to fruition, the reception and the dancing for the evening were to follow and she had double-checked on all the arrangements to ensure all was well. The dresses made by Emma were pure perfection, the sight of them today had drawn gasps from certain ladies in the congregation and would certainly guarantee a full order book for her in the immediate future. Even the printing business had played its part in producing special invitations, which were sent to those fortunate enough to be asked to share in the proceedings. Sam and Ruth were the recipients of such and were now seated in the church watching with awe the events taking place. Ruth found she was inadvertently comparing her surroundings with the little chapel in the village and the grandeur of the occasion with the simple wedding service she had attended there some months previous.

The service being concluded, the wedding party together with their guests retired to the Pump rooms to a wedding feast fit for a king, plenty of fine wine and speeches which congratulated everyone concerned in the planning of the day, and also looking to the future with great hope. Later when the trio commenced their music, the guests danced with great delight and Sam, partnering Ruth, joined in the merriment. From her Bath chair the mother of the groom watched with growing admiration and pride as her son and his wife took centre stage to commence many of the dances. Hannah was in close attendance with her mistress and as the evening wore on she was called to her side to be informed that she was feeling very tired and desired to be accompanied back to their residence. Emma too had had a full day and the three ladies retired to the Abbey precincts where a chaise was waiting to convey them home. In the bright moonlight the front of the Abbey displayed all its glory with the stone carvings standing out in relief against their own shadows. As they sat awaiting the coachman to complete his preparations for the journey Hannah looked at the two ladders, one each side of the main entrance to the Abbey, they were rising heavenwards and depicted the biblical scene from Jacob's dream. She was enthralled with the sight of the ladders with angels ascending, marvelling at the work of the stonemasons who had created it. She looked again, rubbing her eyes in disbelief, was it a trick of the bright moonlight? Had she taken a little more wine than she should have done? These questions came into her mind for as she viewed the scene she was certain one of the angels was no longer climbing the ladder but had fallen from it, fallen from grace. She indicated to the coachman Mrs Manpitt was physically weary as well as being mentally exhausted and they should be leaving without any further hesitation. Leaving the sound of the music behind them they drew away into the moonlit streets to return to the Manpitt home where the lady of the household could rest and relive the glories of the day.

Throughout the preparations for the wedding and the service itself, Sam and Ruth had been caught up in the excitement of the occasion. The experience boosted Sam's confidence and the relationship with Ruth entered new boundaries, it was therefore no great surprise when, on one of their walks along the riverbank, Sam asked Ruth to marry him. Before she could respond he explained he now had a good position at the sawpit, that Sarah was more than willing to share her cottage with them, in fact she would welcome a female companion. He also pointed out he had been busy during the light evenings when they were unable to be together, using the time to create a number of articles of furniture to ensure a fairly comfortable existence. Ruth hesitated over her response, she loved Sam and she knew he loved her although neither of them was demonstrative with their feelings; they just felt safe and happy in each other's company. Finally, as she sealed her answer with a big kiss, she told him of her love for him, of her desire to share her life with him; as long as Cook agreed to their union. Sam was elated and then brought down to earth again with the realisation he must win over Cook in order to gain the love of his life.

"I cannot just forsake my mother by adoption, Sam, she has

The Hall

been my sole protection since my early childhood when my natural parents were taken from me. I have her to thank for everything that is good in my life. I am aware the Squire has also played his part in allowing us to remain in The Hall, but it is by Cook's good council and industry I am here with you now. I know she looks upon you with great favour and she is wise enough to understand how we feel about each other, but I could not enter into marriage with you, my love, without her blessing. We must talk with her when the time is right, also with your mother and perhaps the Squire for he will have to make changes within the staff."

They ambled along the towpath, arms around each other, experiencing a new closeness, then they began to climb the hill leading to The Hall but Ruth could not constrain herself. She launched forth into the details of the marriage ceremony, which would take place within the little chapel, her dress for the occasion, the flowers for her hair, the wedding feast in the garden of The Hall, by kind permission of the Squire who would also loan her a carriage for the day. Sam questioned the suggestion of the carriage and was politely told it was not very far to walk, so no-one would be too exhausted to dance to the music of the groom's fiddle during the evening. They were still discussing possible arrangements for the day, their special day, when they reached The Hall.

It was not often Cook wandered in the gardens taking a breather from her duties, but today she had been baking bread and the heat in the kitchen was too much for her. So Sam and Ruth inadvertently met her in the grounds of The Hall and both parties were taken somewhat by surprise. Cook had an uncanny insight into most situations and this particular one did not leave her guessing, she could tell by the colour of Ruth's cheeks, the way they were looking at each other, and their general deportment that love was in the air.

"Have you two decided upon the date you are to wed?" she asked.

Ruth and Sam were quite unprepared for this sudden plunge into the deep end and stopped dead in their tracks. "Well am I to be informed or kept guessing, young lady?" Cook sounded a little belligerent, which made Sam spring into action.

"This very day Cook, I have asked Ruth if she will be my wife and she has made me the happiest of men by agreeing to my proposal, as long as we have your blessing. We both realise, especially Ruth, how much we are indebted to you for bringing us to this moment and we know that without your approval we could not be happy together and if I follow the dictates of my trade and strike whilst the iron is hot, then I would ask for your blessing at this very moment."

Cook sensed she had stirred the emotions of the young man who was seeking to become her son-in-law and she decided to test his mettle with a little teasing. She plied him with questions of every kind, twisting his answers so they in turn became more questions, until Sam felt he was in the dock for first-degree murder rather than asking for the hand of his prosecutor's daughter. Finally she relented, telling Sam that to endorse the marriage of the two people standing close to her, would make her the happiest lady in all Christendom and she would do her utmost to ensure it would be the most wonderful wedding ever witnessed in Annum. She clung to both of them, "I give you my blessing," she said, "and may your union be blessed by the Lord and I pray you share much happiness together over many years in the future. Come, we must go indoors and invite the Squire to the kitchen to share the good tidings and perhaps drink a little celebration."

They wandered into the warmth of the kitchen and it was not long before the Squire was adding his congratulations and best wishes whilst Cook replenished their glasses for the second time.

"I will do all I can to make your special day a day of rejoicing," said the Squire, "but you must prod me into action should I need it. I am now an old man, my memory is not what it was, and although I feel well in myself I am mindful of the fact we mortals do not live forever. May God spare me to witness this marriage for I have been informed I may have the honour of giving the young lady away to the one she loves, a duty which will give me great delight, as much as if Ruth were my own daughter."

There were no grand plans as there were for the Spa wedding, the various factions concerned in making the arrangements acted on instinct and on the goodwill of many of the villagers. Emma delighted Ruth by producing a simple wedding dress, which she thought may be of service after the wedding, and as the date fixed was in the early summer there would be plenty of wild flowers for decorations of every kind. The Pastor had agreed to conduct the service in the little chapel and the Squire gladly gave his blessing for a meal to be set out in the garden and for dancing to take place in the meadow immediately outside the confines of The Hall. For this purpose he promised the area could be roped off and the sheep would be allowed into the enclosure in order to crop the grass ready for the response to the groom's fiddle. "All we want is sunshine," commented Sam.

And it was sunshine for a whole week, so when the day dawned, the garden, the meadow, it seemed the whole of creation was at its best and just waiting to honour the happy couple.

The little chapel was filled to overflowing; the bridegroom nervously awaited his future wife whilst there was an expectant buzz in the congregation, which flavoured the atmosphere with cordiality. One of the stewards stood like a friendly sentry in the confines of the porch and to his right-hand side the Pastor also kept vigil; they were both focusing their attention on the gates at the bottom of the churchyard. Many of the village children were also near the gates eagerly awaiting the site of the chaise rounding the corner near the Blue Bowl. They knew the carriage would be bearing the Squire and the bride to where they were standing, and as soon as it made its appearance they would send a cheer to the heavens so that all would know Ruth was arriving. The cheer came and what a cheer, it echoed along the Bath Waye, through the trees alerting the Pastor, the congregation and Sam.

The cheer died and the sound changed to one of breathless appreciation as the Squire helped the princess of the village to alight from the carriage and, clutching his arm, walk majestically up through the graveyard towards the waiting Pastor, followed by a bevy of ragged village children. Inside the Chapel the congregation stood in wonder as the young lass, whom they all held dear, entered the building with a radiance which encaptured everyone. Sam was moved to his very soul as he realised this vision of beauty standing by his side was not only in love with him but had agreed to share the future as his wife. He suddenly felt humble and very thankful and to his surprise a prayer to the almighty welled up in his very being. The Pastor took charge and the singing almost raised the roof, the vows were made, the Squire gave Ruth to Sam to nurture through all their future days together and Sam proudly placed a plain gold ring upon the finger of the new Mrs Stafford.

Emerging from the porch of the chapel into the bright sunlight, the bride and groom were cheered by a crowd of well wishers of such numbers that it would appear the whole village had crowded into the churchyard to share in their happiness. As the newly weds stood in admiration and appreciation of their friends, the village children threw handfuls of flower petals of every hue, covering them with a myriad of colours and scents from garden and meadow. Gradually they made their way to the gate leading on to the Bath Waye where the carriage awaited, looking in the direction of the

Squire, Sam said, "Sir, as it is such a beautiful day do you mind if we walk?"

"Not in the least," came the reply, "in fact, if you will allow me I will walk with you, we will leave the chaise for Sarah, Hannah, Cook and anyone else who would like to ride with them."

Having said this the Squire accompanied the bridal couple along the Bath Waye, passing the quiet sawpit on route to The Hall further down the lane. Behind them the villagers, the children and the wedding guests straggled along as an uneven, good-natured crowd whether invited or not, it did not seem to matter.

As the gates of The Hall came into view the folk behind the leading group split into the various factions representing those who were attending the wedding feast and the rest. These were composed of those who were simply inquisitive, older folk who never missed a wedding or a funeral, and lively urchins hoping to gain a little free food. The guests filtered into the garden of The Hall where Cook and her helpers had prepared a feast that rivalled the one created for the Manpitt wedding. All agreed there never was such a banquet and that there would never be such a one again, the spread was magnificent, the appetites were immense, or fussy to a degree, but whatever the situation, Cook had somehow catered for it.

There were speeches, short pithy tales of happenings in days gone by, votes of thanks to those who had made the day such a resounding success and a declaration of love from the groom which brought a tear to the eyes of many of the ladies present.

"Let's dance," came the cry from the younger members of the guests, whereupon the groom began to play upon his fiddle leading them to the dancing area of the meadow cropped short by the sheep. They danced, they ate, they drank, then danced again and more than one grubby little hand belonging to a cheeky urchin from the village was given a share of the remnants of the feast.

As the sun dropped lower in the sky, Sam took Ruth by the hand and together they slipped away unnoticed towards the little wood on the top of the hill. It was from this vantage point that Ding had helped him get his bearings and now as he explained this to Ruth their eyes met, it was a long searching look, they knew now they belonged to each other. Ding faded into the background and in a passionate embrace, amid the shelter of the trees, oblivious to the party down in the meadow, and to the rest of the world they consummated their love. Having satisfied their burning desire they fell back into each other's arms gazing heavenwards at the evening sunset.

Some time later as they returned to Widow Webb's cottage, they passed the late revellers near The Hall. A light in the window informed them Sarah was safely home and as she welcomed them in she exchanged a glance with Ruth. Nothing was said, no indication was given, but Ruth knew that Sarah knew and they were both glad.

Chapter Twelve

Sons

Mr Matthew Manpitt was overjoyed to print in his broad sheet the announcement of the birth of his grandson. Richard and his wife Rebecca were delighted to tell the world that a son had been born to them, blessing their union and presenting to the combined business of publisher and printer an heir apparent who would secure the future. Hannah was pleased to act as a nursemaid until a younger and more able-bodied person could fill the position. The years caring for Mrs Manpitt had taken their toll and although she had stayed on in the household following the death of her mistress, her position was now questionable despite the fact Mr Manpitt required her to carry on with her household duties. This she had agreed to do for the foreseeable future.

The new addition to the family was a joy and Hannah found great pleasure in nursing the young child. It was whilst she was caring for him on one occasion she noticed a slight imperfection to one of the toes on his right foot. The toe nearest the big toe was bent back on itself. She had seen the deformity before and had heard it described as a hammer-toe, because gradually the end of the toe together with the nail thickened to a hammer shape. She also understood the condition to be hereditary but not serious and of no real problem to the person concerned. She decided to hold her counsel and not to inquire, or suggest treatment by qualified doctors, she would just keep her eyes and ears alert to any developments in the matter. Thus, apart from this small blemish, the printers were going from strength to strength in the Spa city as well as the large port to the west.

In Sarah's cottage Ruth's figure had changed shape, she now could no longer work for the Squire as her time was approaching and Sam was reluctant to leave her despite the fact Sarah was nearly always at hand and Cook could be available at quite short notice. He would hurry home in the evening and also make sure he had some news of his wife's well being delivered to him during the day. When the day came it proved to be long, for many hours Ruth had a difficult labour before her first-born son was safely delivered. Both parents were overjoyed to see this tiny baby nestling in his mother's arms, or tucked up in the cradle, which his proud father had created. Sarah and Cook shared their delight although the situation was tinged with a hint of sadness. The midwife in the village, who had stayed with Ruth during that difficult time, was of the opinion that, because of the prolonged labour, Ruth would probably not be able to bear any further children. When she informed her husband of the situation he replied, "This makes our son doubly precious," as he lifted little Luke from the cot and presented him to his mother to be fed.

The summer days gave way to autumn and the two new arrivals had survived their first six months of life, this according to Sarah was a good sign and proved they were healthy offspring. The Manpitt parents had decided upon a course of action with regard to the deformity of their son's toe. One evening when he arrived home from business Richard imparted the news to his wife that a certain medical gentleman, of very high standing, was visiting Bristowe in early December and had agreed to inspect the foot of their little one. He was of the opinion it would be worth a visit to the city to see if anything could be done to correct the deformity, and to make the visit easier the friends they had in the city were willing to offer overnight accommodation if they so desired.

Rebecca was not sure, she did not want little Mark to undergo treatment that might not be successful or even make the situation worse. For a while they had reached deadlock and neither would give way in the matter. Finally, Rebecca compromised in so far as she agreed her son could be examined by this gentleman but they would make no decision as to any form of treatment until the matter had been thoroughly discussed. Accordingly, the visit to Bristowe was arranged and the young family would travel during the second week of December.

Meanwhile, Luke had been taken to the chapel and had been blessed by the Pastor. His parents had given thanks for this wonderful gift of new life, which was now entrusted to their care, and together with the members of the congregation they had made their promise to bring him up in the knowledge of the Lord.

There was now an established coach service between the two cities, some of the runs being part of a longer trip to the city of London. Rebecca and Richard discussed the timing of these public services and found they were not suitable for their requirements, it was therefore decided they would travel in a smaller, lighter coach owned by Mr Manpitt. Because of the nearness of the festive season Rebecca persuaded her husband to make the visit to Bristowe an opportune holiday, she reasoned they could take advantage of the offer made by their friends combining it with a little shopping, as well as taking Mark to see the medical practitioner. This programme proved to be a great success, especially as the doctor's opinion was to leave well alone for the immediate future, allowing Mark to grow into his teenage years before seeking a second consultation. The situation was such that should the toe give him any real problems or pain during his boyhood years, then he would willingly examine him again and comply with their wishes in the matter. Rebecca was delighted to think her son would be saved the horrors of any kind of medical quackery, and as she placed her shopping parcels in the rear of the chaise then climbed into the seat beside her husband, she felt a heavy burden had been lifted from her shoulders. Her friend handed Mark to her, well wrapped in several blankets which covered his whole being so that only his small, neat face was showing. Looking down she could see the likeness of his grandfather and as they set out, with a final farewell wave to their friends, she remarked to her husband; if their son resembled his grandfather in other ways then the printing business was secure.

They moved off in bright sunshine, on the same road taken by Sam when he absconded from the butcher. But today no one was looking for an escape route and the family journeyed happily away from the city and into the forest area. They passed through the hilly terrain leading to the Annum village and as they approached the village itself Rebecca informed her husband she felt faint and ill.

"We can rest awhile at the Blue Bowl Inn my dear," said her husband, "or we can proceed down the lane to The Hall where the Squire lives and prevail on his kindness for a few hours. In point of fact if you feel you are not strong enough to continue the journey today, I am certain he will give us lodging for the night and then we may depart at our leisure in the morning."

Rebecca indicated she preferred to visit the Squire, as there were many tales of ruffians residing at the inn and as they had young Mark with them she would feel far more secure if the Squire would shelter them for the night. Richard could find no fault with his wife's reasoning and as they approached the lane he turned the horse down towards The Hall passing the sawpit on the way.

He was in sight of The Hall itself when a young deer came out from the shelter of the trees and ran across the lane, startling the horses. As they reared high in the air the chaise turned on its side with sufficient momentum to unseat Rebecca, she tumbled on to the grassy bank still clutching her son. Richard did well to restrain the horses and bring the chaise to a gentle halt and in next to no time he was comforting his wife and endeavouring to find the extent of any injuries she and their son may have suffered. The noise created by the accident alerted some of the staff in The Hall and immediately Cook was on the scene followed by her master. The Squire took charge of the situation, calling to two young lads working in the grounds; they quickly contrived a stretcher from some timbers and a blanket given to them by Cook. Recognising the gentleman in the party he invited them into The Hall and the young lads carried Rebecca on the stretcher under the direction of Cook.

"We were coming to see you and seek your permission to stay the night," said Richard, "but this unfortunate accident caused by a deer running across the path of the horses has left me at a loss as to what action to take. I feel providence has placed us in your hands and I would be forever in your debt if you can arrange to get medical advice on my wife's injuries."

The Squire quickly responded, "You know any of your family are welcome to The Hall at any time, especially when you are in difficulties as you are at the moment, so please make yourself comfortable and I will get Cook to take care of Rebecca. If in the opinion of Cook we need to contact a medical practitioner to attend to her, then we will make every effort to see this is done, but at this time of the day it may not be possible and we may have to wait until the morrow. What we can do, and I suggest we do so as soon as possible, is to pay a call on Sam and Ruth. Sam will give a professional look at the chaise to make certain it has not

150

suffered any serious damage and I am well aware Ruth would gladly take your son into her charge whilst his own mother is unable to care for him. Cook would be more than pleased to attend to the little one but she will have enough to do if she is catering for extra guests and one of them is not well. Come I will put these arrangements in hand before darkness falls."

Ruth accepted the extra responsibility of young Mark with pleasure and it was quite noticeable that Sarah was more than willing to have a third gentleman under her roof. When approached about the chaise, Sam agreed to examine it first thing in the morning and as it presented a priority, any repairs that were required he would treat as an emergency. Sarah also offered her services if she was required to help with Rebecca. This kindly gesture made the Squire think back to the time when Sarah had nursed her sick husband after his accident in the sawpit and what skill and patience she had shown over several years. He also deduced, the experience gave her an increased knowledge of nursing, which although self-taught, must have increased her caring capacity considerably, and he had the evidence of Sam's recovery to underline his reasoning.

"Your offer of help could be a great blessing Sarah, for the hour is late and we do not think we shall be able to get medical help this night. Cook is keeping an eye on Rebecca and if her knowledge was as great as her compassion, we would have to look no further, but if you could join with her for a time then we may well prove that two heads are better than one. Would you care to accompany us back to The Hall and if the situation warrants it we can arrange for you to stay the night."

Sarah was quite honoured to think that the Squire held her in such high regard and willingly accepted the proposal he had put to her. Wishing Ruth, Sam and the two young gentlemen God's blessing and a sound sleep, she left her cottage and accompanied the Squire back to The Hall.

The Squire's strategy worked well, Cook had examined Rebecca for any obvious injuries and found apart from a few superficial cuts and bruises, the fall from the chaise had caused no real harm. The soft, grassy bank on to which mother and son fell had proved to be their salvation, whilst all the blankets wrapped around Mark had given him extra protection. As they drew away from their first joint examination of the patient, Sarah asked Cook if Rebecca had complained of feeling unwell prior to the accident. Cook informed her that they were on their way to the Hall hoping they could stay the night because Rebecca had complained to her husband, whilst they were approaching the village, that she had a terrible feeling of nausea.

"It is not for me to make a hasty judgement," said Sarah, "but I am of the opinion there is something radically wrong with our guest. I have seen this very pale, listless look before and I understand she has been complaining of a complete lack of energy and loss of appetite. I am wondering if she is suffering from consumption because these were some of the signs manifested by a group of miners some years ago. They lived near the river and became so ill that two of them died. We will have to wait for the medical practitioner to examine her before we come to any conclusions." Cook agreed and added, "If your feelings have any substance in them we must, as soon as possible, get her back to her family, this Hall can be very draughty in the winter and I do not wish to expose Rebecca, or any of my staff to the slightest form of infection. Sam will inspect the chaise in the morning and effect any repairs he deems necessary, sleep well Sarah I think we may have a busy day tomorrow."

Sam reported the chaise had not suffered serious damage, a small crack was apparent on part of the bodywork and if he placed a metal strap across it and bolted it in place, then the rest of the journey to Bath could be accomplished without mishap. Medical opinion could not be obtained until later in the day, it was therefore arranged for Richard and his wife to return to Bath in a carriage belonging to the Squire and the chaise would follow later. Rebecca assured everyone she felt much better after a good night's sleep and a special breakfast supplied by Cook. She also thought it advisable not to wait for medical attention because when they arrived home her own doctor could visit her. Ruth prevailed on the parents to leave their son in her care for a few days until they established what would happen in the immediate future, she explained, with the help of Sarah, that the little lad was not a burden, in fact it was a pleasure to have him.

Chapter Thirteen

Dark Days

The medical opinion given to Richard confirmed the uncanny diagnosis supplied by Sarah and it was decided that the best treatment available was in a special hospital in Somerset. The patients were treated with kindness, good food and kept in the fresh clean air coming in from the sea. Richard was assured this simple way of combating a terrible disease had already proved to be successful, but it was a slow process and his wife would be separated from her family for some time, it could be several years. They had to accept the situation, the fees for the treatment could easily be paid by the printing firm, and Ruth was willing to look after Mark rather than let the lad return to his father where only elderly folk were on hand to help.

Richard found he could not adapt to his new way of life, his work was important and the firm was prospering but he desired more. As a young, fit, intelligent being he began to find new outlets for his energies but unfortunately these did not always lead in the right direction. Hannah noticed the change in his moods but his father would not, or could not agree with her views on the matter. Hannah, on her part, deemed that Mr Manpitt was too set in his ways to even criticise his son, let alone seek a remedy for his waywardness. Thus Richard was left to his own devices and although he acted the part of a faithful husband and father, the visits to his wife and also to his son were now burdensome and therefore became less frequent. He became a regular visitor to the gambling games held at private parties, his drinking habits grew worse and he was easily recognisable in the city as a playboy. It was inevitable that he began to get into debt, sometimes taken as a good loser, if not a fool, he was never short of invitations where the clever rogues in the city would fleece him of hundreds of pounds. His debts grew to the point where they became the concern of his father, but despite all the stern, paternal warnings given on a regular basis, his habits did not change.

One evening following a particularly heavy loss at dice, the fact that he could not meet his debts, plus the refusal of his victor to accept an I.O.U., all contributed to a violent brawl. A special paper knife with a diamond inset in the handle was used by one of the combatants and although sustaining a minor cut himself, Richard was charged with seriously wounding his opponent on the grounds that the knife was his; it even had his initials engraved on it. Strong representations were made concerning the knife as being a part payment of a gambling debt some months previous, but these were of no avail and he was removed to Bristowe gaol to await trial on an attempted murder charge, this became more serious when the man died. When this news reached his wife, she began to lose the little interest in life that had been sustaining her and her decline began to deepen. Ruth and Sarah offered a ray of hope; they knew Quaker visitors to the city gaol and through various contacts would, in all probability, be able to get some information on Richard's well being. Meanwhile, his dear wife was losing the will to live.

The merchantman sailing from Ireland to Liverpool had many passengers who were travelling light and travelling cheap. They were Romanies returning from the land of their birth to the lands of their adoption. All were looking in need of the fresh air they were inhaling as the boat ploughed its cumbersome furrow across the choppy sea. The wedding of the son of the king of the Romanies had attracted fellow believers from all points of the compass and this comparatively short sea journey was the beginning of many miles of travelling for the great majority of them, but not so with one particular individual. He was towards the stern, looking out to sea so the wind was not in his face, he would never be a sailor by any stretch of the imagination, and he was the first to admit he would rather be on a horse than trying to keep his feet on this rolling deck. Over the past weeks they had all eaten far too much, drunk whatever was at hand and had not escaped a headache for days. It was one of those celebrations that happen once in a lifetime and as he looked down at the white wake and further out to sea at the white horses, Ding felt his stomach was no longer part of his anatomy.

He had enjoyed the celebrations, meeting up with so many of his adopted family and reminiscing for hours on end. Now he was travelling back again to his favourite caravan and his special mother, she had been unable to attend the wedding and would therefore be waiting to hear all the details at first hand. A tedious journey lay before him, he had accomplished it once before and fortunately he would have a companion for the major part of his travels; therefore as soon as they disembarked the two friends set out to the south. They travelled well in good weather and within the week, having taken leave of his friend, he had the common in view. He thought he would run as fast as he could and surprise everyone, but before he had made a start he stopped dead in his tracks and the colour drained from his face. There flying from the front of the caravan was the danger signal, a little red duster fluttering in the breeze like a piece of washing put out to dry. Ding dropped to the ground in disbelief, the signal could only mean one thing, somehow the troopers had traced his movements from his escape in Annum to his caravan home. He would have to keep out of sight and wait until dark before he could attempt the final part of his journey.

As dusk was falling, he was alerted by movement on the far side of the caravan and, as he strained his eyes in the half-light, he saw a trooper arrive, dismount, and enter his home to emerge some moments later with a colleague. Together they rode off into the gloom and still afraid to breath Ding was finally relieved to see a figure emerge to retrieve the red duster. After a while, when the common was dark and with only a glimmer of light emerging from the caravan window he approached his home with great caution. Sliding between the wheels he pushed upwards on a section of the floor that gradually opened up for him, quickly he was pulled inside to the warmth of an embrace from his adoptive parents.

"We were hoping and praying you would arrive before dark so you would be able to observe the danger signal. The troopers have been hanging around for several days and we feel certain they have a good deal of information on your movements since you stole their horse. But here you are safe and sound," and concluding her welcoming speech his adoptive mother gave Ding such a hug that he was breathless for a few moments. There followed questions and answers, explanations, opinions and warnings, the conversation advancing well into the night until Ding was hoarse and began to show signs of falling asleep on the spot.

A few days later Ding informed his adoptive parents he had decided his presence with them posed something of a threat to their liberty.

"If the troopers are aware I come here to stay and they also know the Romanies from Ireland are now dispersing from the wedding party, it is fairly certain they will return and begin to ask questions again. I love you both dearly and trust you with my life, and you are aware there is nowhere else in the whole world I would rather be, but I fear for your safety and if you do not know of my movements it will be better for all of us. It is my intention to travel back south, I think the community there will protect me, they are always on the move and this will help in keeping me safe. One morning you will awake and find I have left, it maybe tomorrow, it could be the day after so I will take this opportunity of thanking you with all my heart, for everything you have done for me. We shall meet again one day when this cloud which is hanging over me has been lifted and I shall be free." Ding knew in his soul he must make a move and the morning would find him away to the south, but he had neither the heart nor the stomach to tell them the blunt truth. He had to escape before the troopers returned.

The dawn found him several miles to the south keeping to the forest area away from the road and endeavouring to restrain his hunger, hoping the food he had brought with him from the caravan would last for several days. The further south he travelled the forest became thinner, there was very little cover in some areas and he was uncertain as to the best time of day for his journey. The night offered cover but could be dangerous as he was alone, the day gave little chance of obscurity as the population had grown since his last visit to the area and many of the cottage dwellers looked rough and untrustworthy. There were also countless numbers of dirty, unkempt children roaming free and Ding was firmly of the opinion any of them would betray you to the authorities for a few pence. He would have to rely on his own good counsel and keep alert, watching for signs of danger during the day and finding a safe haven for a good night's sleep. Day three of his travels had passed without mishap and he was pleased with his progress, in the distance he could see the winding of the river as it caught the evening sun and his heart became lighter as he recognised the terrain and he knew that he must soon start looking for caravans and wood smoke. In a small copse on a piece of rising ground, overlooking the river, he settled for the night hoping his friends might satisfy his hunger and his desire for company when the morrow dawned. For some reason he fingered the two clover leaves, now hanging round his neck on a special wire he had been given in Ireland, in so doing he was reminded of Sam and his first experience in the forest. He lay wondering about the fate of the summer palace, his little angel and the guardian of the other two clover leaves, and he fell asleep.

A bright morning sun brought him to his senses and as he stirred he sensed a presence. Turning away from the bright light he noticed only yards from him, the brown and white fetlocks of a horse. If only he could have had the same vision as Sam; the delicate legs of the deer, but these were heavier, stronger legs, the legs of the trooper's horse. He knew trying to escape would only make matters worse, besides what match would he be for a mounted trooper. Give me a horse so we are on equal terms he thought and I will outride you, but it was not to be. The trooper's mate was not far away and between them they manhandled Ding to a collection point on the Bath Waye where two other prisoners lay be the roadside manacled together.

"We have reason to believe you are a partner with these other ruffians and you have all been inciting the population with the intention of stirring up trouble against the authorities," the trooper was addressing all the prisoners including Ding, he continued, "this is a very serious charge and will be dealt with severely by the magistrate, you can all expect a prison sentence."

Calling to one of the other troopers standing near he enquired if the cart coming to collect the miscreants had arrived. The trooper came closer to the three men huddled together on the grass verge and made some comment to the effect that the cart was on its way, but, if by some misfortune it did not arrive, they all appeared fit enough to walk. He then came closer and peered down at Ding with evil in his eyes, "Not you, you young varmint, we meet again but on different terms, I am sober and awake, you my fine friend are in manacles. This time you will not be able to steal my horse and escape as you did at the Blue Bowl the last time we met, however well you ride, saddle or bareback."

Ding felt his anger rise and staring at the trooper with a gaze that made the redcoat withdraw a little, he said in a sarcastic voice, "The horse you have today is a fine one, but you would never catch me if I could be mounted once again on the roan I borrowed from the stable at the Blue Bowl. We made a great team and I could tell the way he responded to me he had never been ridden kindly before. You do not deserve the mounts that come into your possession, your horse should be your greatest friend, but you do not see the relationship in the same way as I do and so you do not get the best from them, I pity the mounts given to you they deserve a better horseman."

This final jibe released a torrent of threats from the trooper to the point where his fellow soldier intervened and in all probability saved Ding from a good kicking.

Ding looked at the trooper who was obviously enjoying the position of authority he held over the prisoners and gloating in the abuse he was throwing at them. The other prisoners looked at the young man who had joined them without any sign of recognition, just a hint of admiration that underlined the speech they had just heard. The trooper's voice rang out, "The cart is approaching, get the prisoners to their feet and make sure there is no last minute mishaps." Within minutes all three men had been bungled into the cart and the sorry procession was on the road bound for Bristowe.

Chapter Fourteen

News From Afar

It had taken over three years for the explorers to reach the far shores of a new continent and for the return of some of the men to their homeland. During the long voyage, which was punctuated with a great many surveys of land and chartings of the sea, several sailors had paid with their lives during the horrific storms encountered in the southern ocean. Back in the confines of the aptly named Botany Bay, Tom Stafford was applying his new found skill at helping to draw and catalogue the fauna and flora which grew around them in abundance. There were species of wild life never seen before and these held his attention, even if some of them defied his ability to describe them without copious sketches. This was work he had never envisaged because he did not realise he was capable of carrying out such intricate studies, compared with underground mining back in the forest, this was paradise. He just wished with all his soul he could have his family around him. Seated under a tree, which gave him some protection from the scorching sun, he was enjoying his labours and looking forward to the next sailing back to England when he would be returning with the work he and several others like him had accomplished. A colony was gradually being established, but life was hard and if the rumours proved to be correct then for some of the unfortunates yet to arrive the privations would be far worse than anything he had endured. As he later finalised his skills in a wooden shack set up in the bay, he would look out over the clear blue sea, breaking gently on the shore of the inlet. Tom gazed at the rippling surge and ebb of the tide and then reminded himself of how a good 'southerner' could raise the level of the surf to a point where in some bays along the coast the breakers were taller than the buildings back in Bristowe.

He was leaner now, but for his age he was fit and the sunshine had given him a bronzed body, which emphasised his white hair. There were daily swims in the creek or from the beach, but dangers lay hidden in the small blue bodies of certain jellyfish and Tom had seen the effects of a sting by one of these creatures. He had no desire to be left in a sandy grave, three thousand miles from the city to which he would be returning in a few months time. He had sent a message with a comrade whom he trusted. Delivery would be made to anyone who knew of the whereabouts of his wife, or any members of his family, therefore with a reasonable amount of good fortune they would have some inkling of his homecoming next year. After almost a decade away, this was his second visit to these far away shores, he longed to be united with his folks, especially his dear wife.

Back home in the Spa city Mr Manpitt was arranging the various articles for his broadsheet and wondering what the lead story might be, it was unlike him to be undecided, he usually thought and planned with decisive ideas but the forthcoming trial of his son seemed to take precedence over everything else. Suddenly one of his assistants rushed into the office with the information that the vessels that had sailed to Australia had been sighted in the Channel last week and two days ago had docked at Plymouth. These proud ships and those who sailed in them had been away for three years and the printer decided it might be a wise move to hold the publication until more news on this particular story could be gathered. As he sat mulling over the situation he thought to himself three years was a fairly long time and therefore another day or so would not be amiss. He would shut up shop and have an early exit from the premises on what was usually his longest day. He would surprise Hannah by his unexpected arrival and also with the news that had just come to his notice.

When he gave Hannah the information concerning the return of the ships, she was overjoyed and required to know as much as Mr Manpitt could tell her. Trying to be optimistic, yet cautious, he explained there was nothing to indicate whether Tom had returned with the vessels or not.

"In point of fact," his manner and voice were very business like, "we have no proof Tom was taken on board such a vessel and furthermore, during the time he has been away, many things could have happened. We have to face the possibility that he may never come home. There are indications Tom was with the explorers, but we are only surmising, however they give us hope. Firstly the timing of his abduction fits the period of preparation for sailing, and secondly we have never been able to gather any information concerning what might have happened to him had he not sailed to Australia. My guess is he is with them but whether he has returned is another matter, if he has then we will do all in our power to unite you with dearest Tom. We may find in this kind of situation the broadsheet I produce could be of service in establishing a contact, we shall have to wait for a few days for news to seep through." Hannah was content to be guided by the printer and simply added that it would be wonderful to see Tom and the family re-united.

~*~

Daniel Amos Matthew Norris held his head high as he disembarked from the Man-Of-War at Plymouth. He had been press ganged the same night as Tom and they had spent their days together serving on the same ships. A Welshman, built like a mountain, and given the initials of his name because that is what his mother exclaimed when she found she was making her family into the round dozen; he and Tom had been inseparable. Now he was bearing a message for his best mate and he would do all in his power to make sure it reached its correct destination. Between them they had the brawn and the brains to deal with most of the eventualities that assailed them, and their enforced comradeship had blossomed and matured during the years they were together. He had been granted release from the ship once they had docked back in England, but now he and Tom were parted for the first time because the work on which Tom was engaged needed to be done at its source. His mate would not be back for some months when the next voyage was planned. His priority was to reach the West Country port of Bristowe and make every effort to deliver the message he had been entrusted with before he finally made for his hometown in South Wales.

With his size, his cheeky approach to all situations, and a voice that seemed to reverberate for miles, he was not an easy character to ignore; it was therefore not surprising to find him on a small merchantman sailing from Plymouth and bound for Bristowe. He had been accustomed to the bright sunshine and the blue waters around Australia, even if they had sailed through rough seas and icy conditions on the way, it was the final destination which had enthralled him and in some ways he envied Tom's protracted stay. Now in the mist and damp of an autumn morning he wondered if he would have travelled safer by road, but he had joined the crew for this short voyage and the moderate wind was beginning to fill the sails. Within days the Severn estuary came into sight and with the tide in her favour the little merchantman was being tugged almost to the heart of the city, where Dan decided to quench his thirst before starting his inquiries. In the tavern he listened to the chatter of the men around him hoping to hear a name, a happening, any clue to start the trail on which he might travel. There was a great deal of talk concerning the coming assizes, it was generally known the presiding judge was not kindly disposed to any miscreants, he especially despised little sneak thieves and at the other end of the scale the dandy cheat. One individual was quick to comment, "in that case Dewdrop", who would be in the dock on the first day, "may get a stiffer sentence this time than he did for his first attempt at robbery with violence". A river man who was sitting close to the speaker looked a little puzzled then said, "Dewdrop, the name rings a bell, although it is some years since I have had knowledge of the varmint. Am I correct in thinking it was he who informed on our good friend Tom when he was taken by the press gang, the evening the big Man-Of-War was anchored in the estuary?"

The first man replied, "Dewdrop was certainly suspected of doing what you have said, there were good grounds for this, but nothing was ever really proved, although Dewdrop was supposed to have made a confession after being rather roughly handled."

Dan had overheard this conversation and was more than intrigued by the possibilities it promised. Towering over the two talkers he made it known he was more than a little interested in a friend of his by the name of Tom, and as he hailed from this city he wondered if there could be a connection with the man they had been discussing. "If I have been eavesdropping, then I am glad that I chose this time and place to do so, for I too was press ganged around the time of which you speak, and I am hoping the Tom you have mentioned is none other than the one who has been my shipmate these last ten years or so."

A small group had now gathered around the stranger all endeavouring to add their particular piece to the puzzle. One stated he knew the family when Tom and his father were plying their trow on the river, then added; "there were three children, a girl and twin boys. I have a feeling Tom's father and one of the boys died on the night of the terrible snowstorm, and the family moved away after Tom had been snatched."

"Ah, I remember," someone else took up the story, "the surviving son had an apprenticeship with the butcher by the market, but he ran away into the forest and we have not heard anything of him since."

Dan felt this news was good news and he might well be on the right track, "Does anyone recall the name of the butcher," he interjected, "and where can I find the shop he owns?"

The remark caused a number of the listeners to collapse in laughter and Dan smiled too when he was informed that the butcher was now dead and whether he had gone 'up' or 'down' he had not taken the shop with him. The shop he was told is still in the same place, his wife is now in charge and she has the help of a young male relative named George. Folk were not absolutely certain of the name of the butcher but the consensus of opinion finalised a name that sounded like Steer.

"You are not quite correct," a new voice joined the chorus of opinion, "the name is Streer, and the shop is not too far away," Jack the carter puffed out his chest and continued, "that young lad, Sam they called him, gave me the slip after we had collected two sheep from Annum. While I was watching the horse toil up the hill, he slid off the cart, he did, and just vanished. No-one seems to have had any contact with the little devil since that day."

Sensing he now had the attention of the stranger and perhaps there was an easy picking, he suggested he could travel back the way that led past the butchers and give the stranger a lift if he so desired. By this time Dan had made up his mind the butcher would be his first contact, and therefore he welcomed the suggestion he could be taken there forthwith, making it plain to the carter he was ready and willing to travel with him.

A little while later Dan was standing in the front of the shop, the carter had reduced his fare after the attempt to swindle the stranger had failed, and this little episode had put Dan on his guard. The man who was swilling down the frontage to the premises looked up as Dan arrived.

"Sorry," he said, "we have just closed for the day you will have to return in the morning."

The 'sparrow' could hardly believe her ears when she realised George was turning away good trade and rushed out to the front of the shop, "You look like a steak man to me, sir," was the opening gambit as she eyed the stranger's physical frame, "can I be of service?"

Dan replied, "I am hoping you can supply me with information concerning an apprentice who was in your employment at one time. A young lad named Sam, I understand he ran away into the forest and nothing has been heard of him since." At the name of Sam, George dropped the besom he was using and the 'sparrow' sidled up to the stranger and beckoned him inside the shop.

"Now sir what exactly do you require to know concerning our little run away? I think I may be able to help; if you can help me. The truth is my dear departed husband was giving the lad full training, and me? I was keeping him in victuals, and looking after the little rogue better than a mother, and he's done the dirty on us and scarpered. My dear husband would turn in his grave if he knew something terrible has happened to the lad, having no children of our own he looked upon Sam as a son. Of course Sam put a great financial strain on the business so I feel he could repay us a little if I make so bold as to ask for a little return for the information I am about to impart."

Dan was overjoyed to think his inquiries had progressed so far in such a little while and was willing to part with every penny he had if it meant he could find Sam and, through him; his mother.

"I feel we can come to some arrangement if I gain the intelligence for which I am seeking. My concern is to locate the family of my dear shipmate who at this moment is in Australia, and to acquaint them with the news concerning his homecoming some time next year. I understand Sam and his mother are not the only members of the family, there is also a daughter and if you can help me contact any of Tom's kin, I am sure I can find some reward for you."

The butcher's widow was hesitant, she knew how, together with her husband, they had fleeced Sam's mother and even after he had run away they still collected a token rent for keeping the bed warm. Was this man mountain here to exact justice, or was he what he said he was, she wished the butcher was still with her, he would not be much of a match for this hulk of a man but his voice would demand respect. If only he had not attempted to match his strength against the frisky steer that 'smelt the blood' and turned on him, gouging out most of his stomach with its horns. She mourned him then, until George decided to stay on and help with the business; but this arrangement with Sam's mother was no concern of George, even though he was family. She would have to deal with this matter herself and she decided to take the man at his word.

"As far as I am aware," the voice was as sweet as she could make it, "Sam's mother and sister took up residence with a printer who has an office here in this city but his main concern is in the city of Bath. The name is unusual but I have it written down somewhere. The mother gave it to me in case Sam returned and we would therefore have to make contact with her again, I cannot be sure where the premises are in Bath but I have been given to understand his printing works are in the vicinity of the Abbey."

She departed rather abruptly saying she would seek out the name of the printer and that was as much as she could do for him. Some minutes later Dan stood holding a piece of crumpled paper with a very strange name written upon it in even stranger writing.

"That's it" she gloated triumphantly, "the name is Manpitt."

Dan folded the piece of paper, placed if firmly in his inside pocket, and was about to depart, when he was sharply reminded he had promised to pay a fee for services rendered. He thanked the butcher's wife for her help, then without any haggling, he gave her what he thought her information was worth, knowing full well she had not told him her complete story. However he had enough intelligence to commence his search and his first objective was to reach the city of Bath in order to find the printer.

~*~

The following morning found him travelling on a coach from the city of Bristowe to the city of Bath on the same road used by Sam and also Richard Manpitt and his family. Later in the day, somewhat bruised by the movement of the coach over a very rough surface he had his first glimpse of the beautiful spa city. He wandered around, oblivious to his immediate mission, there were so many things that caught his eye and held his interest until he finally came into the vicinity of the Abbey. Standing in awe of the building and admiring the massive structure with its curved buttresses and wonderful stonework, he pondered on how such a holy place had been visualised and then created. Would anything akin to it ever be built on the virgin land, three thousand miles away where his shipmate awaited his home voyage?

These thoughts brought him back to reality and the purpose of his visit. Tom had always called him a nomad in mind and spirit and he suddenly realised he was proving the point. With renewed purpose he set out to find the premises of the printer knowing it could not be too far away as the butcher's wife had stated it was in the vicinity of this magnificent building. To his delight he saw in the window of some premises, a small stand and on it a broadsheet was displayed. The large print at the top of the page made him stop and make use of his meagre reading ability. Realising the words he was now trying to decipher contained information he was already aware of he glanced up above the window to see the name of the establishment, which had gathered this news. To his great delight he recognised the name of the printer, or was it? Quickly he retrieved his crumpled piece of paper and began to compare the names, one on the paper, one on the shop, he examined them both letter-by-letter, not once but several times until he was quite certain this was the place he was seeking.

It was a little while before Dan mustered the mental courage to enter the premises, when he was ready he manoeuvred his rather large frame through a somewhat small entrance to the printers. Once inside he felt more secure, partly because he filled most of the little anteroom, which served as a reception office. He certainly towered over the young lad who was seated behind a desk and who was now regarding him with fear and trembling. Dan inquired of Mr Manpitt and before he had completed his request for an interview with him, the lad had disappeared into a room to the rear of the premises only to return a few minutes later accompanied by a smart, if ageing gentleman who introduced himself as the proprietor of the business. Dan was at the cross roads as to how to approach this kindly looking newcomer, he was certainly not seeking a business deal although he had the feeling he was being observed as a potential customer. Finally he plunged in with both feet in the manner to which he was accustomed, "My name is Daniel Norris, I am a friend of Tom Stafford, in fact we have been mates for the last decade or so and

I am searching for any of his family, in particular his wife Hannah. I have news concerning Tom, whom I have promised to deliver to his nearest and dearest, and I understand from the butcher widow in Bristowe you may be able to aid me in my mission. Please assure me I have been given trustworthy information and my journey here, to find you, has not been in vain. I am hoping to deliver to his dear wife intelligence which will gladden her heart."

Mr Manpitt was somewhat overcome by this sudden rush of news, being delivered to him with great passion by an unknown voice. He was, for a little while, carried away by an accent he had not heard before imparted by the individual towering above him. With the good tidings still ringing in his ears he thought to himself, this man must be genuine otherwise why is he here, there is nothing to be gained by making false representation of this kind, I must take him at his word and grant him an interview with Hannah. He recovered his composure and wishing to keep the matter private he dismissed his assistant and invited Dan to accompany him to his home in order to see Hannah and give her the special information he knew she would treasure.

Hannah was surprised to welcome her master and a rather large stranger of whom she had no knowledge.

"Today, this gentleman" said Mr Manpitt, "arrived un-announced in my office and introduced himself as Daniel Norris. He tells me he is a friend of Tom's, in fact he states he was press-ganged the very same evening as your husband and they have been together until quite recently. I see no reason to doubt his word and as he insists he has special good tidings for you, I have brought him here for you to hear his story. You may use my little study to keep your conversation private and then you may inform me of any details which you feel I should know."

Walking in Dan's shadow Hannah led the way into the study and closed the door behind them. Dan stood and looked at the neat figure in front of him, her face indicated she had endured a good deal of hardship, but there were little crow's feet around the eyes advertising the fact there had been good times too. The eyes now danced with expectancy and when she suddenly blurted out, "Is my Tom safe?" he knew the love Tom had expressed for his wife, was the same love which had lay dormant in this charming lady standing before him and he was lost for words. He had no idea why he did what he did next, but Tom would have understood, he walked gently over to Hannah and picking her up in his arms as though she were a little child, he warmly said, "Your Tom is safe, at the moment he is on the other side of the world in Australia, he is in good health and God willing he will be coming home some time next year."

Realising he was still nursing his best mate's wife he placed her gently down on the floor. It was now Hannah's turn to act on impulse and looking at Dan she replied with great fervour, "Thank you! Oh! Thank you for bringing me such wondrous news," and in so saying she flung her arms around his neck and together they spun in a circle like a carousel. "Come we must tell Mr Manpitt my wondrous news, I will prepare supper and you can then impart to both of us the details of your adventures and give me more information of my love."

When Mr Manpitt saw the couple emerge from the study he could see at a glance Hannah was elated, her cheeks were flushed, her eyes were sparkling and she burst forth with the news that Tom was alive and was hoping to return to England in the summer of next year. Over supper the conversation did not cease, with Dan answering all the questions being thrown at him. Mr Manpitt listened with interest and realised this man seated at his table was not only a mountain in build, but he also had a colossal story to tell. A story, which would look good in print, read well and hopefully sell even better. He was about to make a business proposition to

Dan when he remembered Tom would be arriving home in the summer of next year, and perhaps a combined story might have a greater impact. He decided to hold his peace and await the arrival of Tom. At that point in time he would propose the two men put their story into print, to the advantage of all concerned.

They had relished all the intriguing anecdotes supplied by Dan, the battling of the ships against the wildness of the sea, the extreme cold when sailing in icy waters in the far south, the glorious Christmas sunshine in Botany Bay where the seasons were the reverse of summer and winter at home. He did not dwell on the hard times although it was obvious they were legion, instead he endeavoured to describe the strange animals and colourful birds they had seen, the wonderful fish they had caught and eaten, the miles of white sandy beaches and the crashing surf. It was a land that offered great opportunities as long as you were prepared to work hard and endure certain privations. It was almost morning when the conversation drew to a close and three tired, but elated folk decided to call it a day.

The following morning, fortified with some of Hannah's home cooking and accepting a ride with Mr Manpitt as far as Bristowe, Dan, his mission accomplished, turned his thoughts to his own family and his hometown in South Wales. Before they parted Mr Manpitt gave Dan the address of his premises in Bristowe, assuring him he would do all in his power to unite the Stafford family. He therefore requested any intelligence that came to Dan's notice, be passed on to him so he could take appropriate action. Back in the Manpitt establishment Hannah was living on rekindled hope. The day was not too distant when her Tom would once again be home, by her side.

Chapter Fifteen

The Assizes

The day Mr Manpitt had been dreading had finally arrived. He had made representations to all those in authority who he thought might be able to wield some influence on the outcome of the case against his son, but he had a negative result. It would seem Richard would be gaoled for his part in the fracas, during which one man lost his life. He knew his son was not a murderer, but he was at a loss as to how to prove his innocence, and he hoped and prayed the court would show understanding in their proceedings and be lenient in the sentence imposed upon him. He must attend the court, and at least give his only child the moral support he deserved, he felt in his heart that, had Rebecca not taken ill, none of this would have happened.

Rather conspicuous in his neat, clean attire he sat and gazed at the riff raff in the public gallery. In all aspects the onlookers appeared as bad, if not worse, than the miserable citizens being brought to the dock and sent away again, the majority of them being given sentences which had little or no relevance to their crimes. Mr Manpitt sat and could now see the human tragedies behind the unfeeling words of the presiding judge, who appeared to show little or no interest in the families he was tearing apart. The young lives being committed to penal servitude in far away places, or the sudden draining of the blood from the red face on an individual condemned to the scaffold. He realised that many times in the past, he had printed the accounts of these court proceedings and on every occasion he regarded them as a list of names, with just punishment meted out to the individuals concerned.

A poor specimen of humanity stood before the court, he was slight in build, shifty in appearance with a large hooked nose from which hung the reason for his nickname; Dewdrop. Accused of a variety of offences, from robbery with violence, to inciting a crowd to break down a tollgate, he seemed incapable of committing any of them. He had his supporters in the crowd as well as those who wished him to be sent far away. It was the latter group who cheered when Dewdrop was sentenced to seven years penal servitude in Australia.

The same sentence was passed on a Mr David Bell, there was no reaction from the crowd, no one seemed to know this young man, but when someone remarked he might find it more difficult to steal the redcoat's horses in Australia, rather than in Annum, he was given a rousing cheer. This was the charge on which he was convicted, there being no proof of his involvement in the fatal fight at the fair in Somerset.

A tall, young man stepped into the dock and as he did so Mr Manpitt felt his heart sink. This place was not for the likes of Richard or any other members of his family. He steeled himself to watch his own flesh and blood standing there, being ridiculed by the riff raff of the streets. He was completely oblivious to everything being said and done, all he could see was the ashen face and the stooping figure of the man he hardly recognised as his son, it was very obvious he had already suffered much by being incarcerated whilst awaiting trial. There was no evidence, no witnesses, no proof that it was Richard's hand which dealt the mortal blow, although it appeared his paper knife was the cause of the fatal wound, and it was this fact that sealed his fate. There was little sympathy for the murdered man, his memory did not rouse any affection, in fact there were murmurs in the crowd that it was a case of good riddance and a tide of toleration flowed in Richard's favour. This did not in any way affect the judge, who deemed it necessary to mete out justice to rich and poor alike, he therefore pronounced a sentence of deportation for a period of ten years. Richard paled, steadied himself on the side of the dock and looked up to catch his father's eye, but he was not there, he had collapsed on the floor of the court and was being helped to his feet as his son was being led away.

Mr Manpitt was taken to his Bristowe office; here his staff and a Quaker gentleman, who had witnessed his collapse, comforted him. This kindly man had visited the prisoners during the time they had been held in custody, and his interest extended to learning of their fate at the assizes. He informed Mr Manpitt if his son was to be transported it was very doubtful if he would see him again until his sentence was finished. "These convicts, that is, the name describing these unfortunate beings, are held in custody on the coast until transport can be arranged to ship them away to the other side of the world." He further stated if there was any possibility of securing a contact of any kind between father and son then he would endeavour to make it, but from previous experience he had little hope. Mr Manpitt, somewhat recovered physically, was heard to mutter this was the saddest day of his life and he was glad his wife was not present to witness what he had seen and heard. He simply wanted to return home, and this wish was granted.

Chapter Sixteen

A Story To Tell

Tom was homeward bound, together with several other sailors now released, mainly because of their advancing years, all part of a crew bound for Bristowe where they would become free men. They were bringing with them the detailed work they had carried out under the supervision of learned men during their stay in Botany Bay. As the days passed and the ship made good headway, he wondered if his mate had been successful in his inquiries and if he had passed on the message of his homecoming to any of his family. He had high hopes as far as Dan was concerned, during their years together they had established a bond, which brought them as close as brothers and he would do all in his power to maintain the situation. He finally disembarked and endeavoured to regain his 'land legs' by seeking out the places he could remember, wandering through the dockside areas and further away from the river into streets which he could not recall. During his time away a number of changes had taken place, the city appeared to be extremely busy with much hustle and bustle and so many folk. It was with some relief that he finally found his way back to the quayside where he stood watching the river traffic and letting the memories of happier days renew his spirits. While thus employed he was suddenly hailed by a passing river man who seemed to take more than a casual interest in him. The man pulled his small craft to the jetty, where he secured it and stepping on to the bank he mounted the flight of steps leading up to the quayside. As he came closer to Tom he lost the delight of recognition and began to apologise for the intrusion he had made, stating that looking up from the river he felt sure Tom was indeed a certain gentleman he was acquainted with. The mistake served as an introduction and a little later the two men, now seated in the tavern, were recounting to each other stories of life on the river and the way in which the city population had expanded. The river man became interested in Tom's story and wondered if he could be of help in tracing his family.

Their conversation became intense when the river man recalled a situation, which took place here in this tavern some months ago. "I did not take part in the discussion that evening, there were several men here who managed to produce sufficient information for the gentleman concerned to make his first contact. I remember it well, the man making the inquiries spoke with a strong accent in a voice which although not loud, seemed to fill the tavern, added to this was the sheer size of the fellow, he was huge and towered over everyone present. Finally, he left with Jack the carter who gave him a lift to a butcher's shop of all places. That is Jack the carter sitting over there by the window, he may remember the conversation and what happened to the gentleman concerned, he can usually be persuaded to impart the gossip he collects on his various trips."

For a moment Tom was undecided as to his next move, he did not want to lose the contact which had just been established, but he had no desire to frighten Jack the carter by confronting him here in the tavern with his request for information. He decided to thank the river man for his help and to wait outside the tavern until Jack emerged. When he did so Tom found the carter was not quite sober and was therefore amiable to a degree, willing and able to impart the name of the butchers and to add other information concerning a printer who had interest here in this city and also in

Bath. On being offered the money for another drinking session the carter remembered the printer's name was Manpitt, and his son had quite recently been given a transportation sentence at the local assizes. Ignoring the carter, Tom rushed back into the tavern to enquire further from the river man the details concerning the big man with the big voice. He had to know if it was Dan.

The river man was pleased to hear Tom had succeeded in obtaining the information for which he was seeking and he added the printer's office was close to the market. "If you so desire I can direct you to the street and point out the premises to you, but firstly we must endeavour to establish the identity of the big man with the big voice. You have stated his name is Dan, I cannot recall anyone using that name, but I do recall the stranger's huge stature, his reverberating voice and the fact he was searching for the family of his friend. Evidently they were press ganged on the same evening and spent a number of years together and although I am not aware of the friend's name, the facts of the case seem to fit the description of the man you have called Dan. Should this be so then I feel the printer will be able to confirm it. You have nothing to loose by approaching him, and everything to gain. Come, I will direct you to the street in which you will find his office."

~*~

Tom was a little surprised by the appearance of the printer, who seemed aged and broken. There were obvious signs of the business being a success, there was a pleasant, confident atmosphere within the office but Mr Manpitt, despite his refined features and his grey hair, manifested the appearance of a man with a broken heart. Tom had seen this same aimless look coming from the first convicts he encountered working under atrocious conditions in Port Jackson; they were lost souls, shadows of men

179

labouring under the harsh control of the military. He suddenly recalled Jack the carter had informed him Mr Manpitt's son had been sentenced to transportation, so he could possibly be in the area in the future. He dismissed the pictures from his mind and tried to conjure up images of his wife and children. The mental process produced a friendly smile, which Mr Manpitt could not mirror, although the handshake was firm and warm.

"I will not beat about the bush, Sir, my name is Tom Stafford and I have come to seek your aid in tracing members of my family with whom I understand you may have had contact. If you can be of service in this matter then I shall be eternally grateful to you." Tom had not finished his little speech before the countenance facing him underwent a complete metamorphosis. A smile returned to the lips, the cheeks now becoming red as body posture changed.

"Tom, Tom Stafford, not the Tom we have been waiting for all these years. Come, whatever business remains for the day will be still there tomorrow; your dear wife awaits you at my house and we cannot keep her in suspense any longer. We heard the good tidings from your friend Dan, and now those tidings have reached fruition, without any more ado we will journey to Bath in order that you and Hannah can be re-united.

Tom seated himself beside his newfound companion in the comfort of the chaise. As he settled he admired the horses, commenting to the printer that they were of fine stock.

"You are truly blessed Tom, to have such a close and loving family awaiting your return. I could not have found a more suitable lady to take on the responsibilities that your dear wife shouldered. She has been a rock, someone on whom I could always depend and a more able individual I could not have found in the whole of Christendom; she has been completely honest in all her dealings and the compassion she has shown towards my wife during her long illness was beyond the call of duty.

Emma has grown into a young lady of high standing within the community, with a gift for creating fine needlecraft and her mother's ability for dealing with people. We have only known each other for a short while Tom, but I venture to suggest that she possesses some of her father's grit and determination. I have come to this conclusion simply on the grounds that she has applied herself in her business with a great deal of fervour and with admirable results. As a businessman myself, I realise I was given a wonderful start by my father, I can therefore only admire the way Emma has created her present position when I realise that she started with virtually nothing."

Tom listened to the printer extolling the virtues of his wife and daughter, it was music to his ears. The loving nature of Hannah he had enjoyed during their years of marriage, and this reminder, coming from a complete stranger, helped to enrich his longing to be with her again. With regard to Emma, he always had a special feeling towards his first born and as they journeyed he realised with growing pleasure that he would soon be in the company of their little girl, now a mature young lady, and he would be able to behold her together with all that she had achieved.

They were travelling on a rough road that made its way between the trees and continued down a fairly steep hill.

"We are approaching the village of Annum," observed the printer, "there are several places of interest which have a bearing on the events which occurred during your absence, but we cannot interrupt our journey today as time is against us."

"In that case," Tom interjected. "I must visit again sometime so that I may explore the area at my leisure."

"That you must do," replied the printer, and without further ado he urged the horses forward, at the same time informing Tom to be aware of the chapel set back in the trees on the left hand side of the road. It appeared quite suddenly and the printer now had to restrain his charges so that Tom could view the chapel where his son and Ruth had been betrothed. Before he could make any real comment on the scene his attention was directed to the opposite side of the roadway where he observed the inn with its Blue Bowl sign. It stood almost at the junction with another road which seemed to curve round to the right to become lost in the trees.

"The sawpit is directly behind the inn and situated further down the lane is The Hall and the farm where the Squire resides," said Mr Manpitt.

Tom was somewhat in awe of the scene, having endeavoured to observe so much in such a short space of time. Sitting back as though he was digesting the information received by his ears and eyes he absentmindedly remarked; "We seem to have lost the river."

"Not so," came the reply from the smiling printer who continued. "For the remainder of our journey Tom, you will see how the river meanders, there are occasions when the waters are very close to the road so they flood in wet weather, then again they can be several hundred yards away and the intervening land is lush and much favoured by wildlife and cattle."

Tom's reaction to the landscape he was now observing was that he preferred to see sleepy cattle and sheep to the amazing bounding of the kangaroos through the dry scrubland, or dodging the ghostly gum trees, or moving at great speed over an endless plain.

"You must tell us more of these wonders when you have settled into your new life here Tom. You realise your son, like my son, is now married and both have sons of their own."

With a good deal of joy and feeling in his voice, Tom replied. "I have gleaned some news concerning the family whilst on my travels and I trust you share my delight in knowing that a new generation is established. I simply hope and pray that their journey through life will have less hazards than I have encountered."

The printer remained silent for some time, knowing in his heart that he had not endured the privations which Tom had encountered and he wondered how each of them would have prospered had they exchanged birthrights.

There were now more dwellings on each side of the road, many of them quite grand, the sight of which brought comments and exclamations of surprise from Tom.

"My abode is this side of the city Tom, we live a little further along the way, you will notice a moderate building standing in its own grounds."

Tom's heart missed a beat when he saw the house to his right hand side with the gates opened ready to admit the master as he slowed the horses wheeling them round between the large pillars and down the drive. The groom held the horses and the two men descended from the chaise, stretching their bodies as they approached the main door.

"Hannah, I have a visitor to stay for a while, can you cope with the extra duties this entails?" Mr Manpitt called through the partly opened door. They were yards apart but unaware of each other's presence, as they drew closer there was a flash of recognition. Unbelieving, yet wanting to believe, they stood rooted to the spot until the magnetism of their love took control.

Without hesitation they ran joyfully into each other's arms, the only words audible were 'Tom' and 'Hannah', two names repeated several times on bated breath as they clung to each other in a close embrace for minutes on end. They finally parted, with tears of joy running down their cheeks, they stood looking at each other in utter disbelief, at last they were together again. There and then they decided the rest of the family should share in this glorious homecoming. With the co-operation of the printer it was agreed this could be arranged.

Chapter Seventeen

Where Now?

The foggy rain was tinged with smoke from the chimneys and the dust of the mines, it contaminated the surfaces on which it fell and Dan was mindful of the sun, the clean air, the white sand and the foaming surf he knew existed on the other side of the world. But here in the valley he would find something the rest of the world could not supply, here lived his family, and he thought nothing could replace the loved ones he was longing to see again. As he drew closer to the row of miners' cottages nestling under the hillside, he came into contact with several folk whom he thought he recognised, but there was no friendly greeting, so sign of familiarity, just a curt hello.

He drew closer to the cottage he called home and as he did so he wondered with mixed feelings and admiration about his parents, how they had managed to rear a family as large as theirs, beneath such a small roof. Childhood memories tumbled through his mind, memories of abject poverty, memories of happy days with other village children, boys chasing girls, girls chasing boys, memories of sunny days, memories of bitter cold, memories of mutton stew. He could see his father and three elder brothers coming home from the mine, dirty, dishevelled, hungry and very often bleeding. They would stop and greet him in the street with huge smiles, their white teeth gleaming through their black, dusted faces.

He stopped at the door of the cottage and stooped to knock upon it, had he grown or was the cottage always this size. He had not realised, or he had not remembered. Someone opened the door, but there was no familiar face, no 'welcome home Dan.' He stood in disbelief and for a moment did not know what to say, finally he peered down at the little woman standing in the doorway and blurted out the question, "This is the home of the Norris family, is it not, please tell me if they still live here?"

The woman looked up at Dan and he could tell by her expression all was not well. "I am so sorry to inform you the family with that name no longer reside here. Please come inside for a moment and we can tell you of all that has taken place during your absence, for I am assuming you are the youngest of the family. Mind your head, you are rather a big lad."

She spoke with the same accent as Dan, but with the persuasive authority of a mother who had demanded a lifetime of respect, coupled with obedience. Bending almost double Dan followed the little lady into a small, comfortable back room, displaying a glorious open fire; he knew the room had undergone many changes.

Dan introduced himself, and then explained he had only returned a little while ago from the other side of the world and therefore he had no knowledge of what had taken place during the years of his absence. He hastened to add the reason for his prolonged residence elsewhere, so the little lady and her husband were under no illusions concerning his character. He had gained their confidence and the lady began to recount the sorry tale of the demise of the Norris family.

"The accident in the mine took place not long after you went away, there were quite a number of men who lost their lives when the workings were hit by a flash flood following very heavy rain. It was disastrous for your mother to have four men taken from her on that terrible day, your father and your three elder brothers never had a chance, it was many days before their bodies were recovered. The whole valley mourned their loved ones, but your mother could not come to terms with the realisation she would never see her men again. Your two sisters, who were still at home, tried their hardest to comfort her but all in vain. Finally, after several years of real hardship and complete misery here in the valley, she decided to forsake the place, which held so many memories, so she left to make a new life with her sister somewhere in Kent. I am not sure how many of the family accompanied her as some of the children were already married and had moved away, but I do know there are no members of the family remaining here now. I never thought I would have to impart this knowledge to one of her children and I deeply regret having to inform you at such a time, your homecoming should be one of glorious joy, not one of great sadness. If it will help to ease the pain a little then we can arrange for you to stay the night and have a meal with us tomorrow. We live rather frugally but you are welcome to share with us."

Dan sat in complete silence, pictures in his mind showed him the panic in the mine, he could hear water rushing through the workings, the men's screams, he imagined the years of hardship endured by his mother, he visualised her travelling the long road to Kent, where he hoped she was now settled and happy. He thanked the couple for their kindness, knowing full well anything less than the truth would not do justice to his loved ones, but it was a bitter pill to swallow. He made an inquiry as to the location of the men's graves who were lost in the accident and stated his desire to pay his respects before his departure. Dan stood by the headstone erected in the corner of the little churchyard, he read and re-read the familiar names, which meant so much in terms of human love and companionship. He had never been alone, all his life he had enjoyed the affection and fellowship of family. There was always someone at home to welcome him, and as a child he could depend on the devoted presence of his mother, or the care of one of his older siblings. Later there was the different companionship of work mates, of shipmates, and one of the latter was very special. Somehow he knew this particular friend would hold the key to his future, and Tom's return to this country would be the realisation of a dream for both of them. He thought a return to the city of Bristowe was the first step along the road to contact those who would welcome him as a brother, in no time at all he had created a dream, the practical establishment of it would take a little longer.

He toyed with the idea of making his way east to try and establish contact with members of his family, but for the moment he was weary of travelling, he desired somewhere to lay his head and converse with friends. He could not remain here in the valley, he had no desire to shut out the sun in order to earn a meagre wage, he had the same feeling his mother must have experienced; that there were too many memories. He turned and left the valley, intent on seeking out the printer and hoping for Tom's safe return.

Chapter Eighteen

The Gathering Of The Clan

Tom and Hannah were inseparable; they walked, talked and shared each moment. There were countless memories of good times and bad, now they held the dream of all the family being together again. They had planned the day, Sam and Ruth with their young son Luke, were eagerly awaiting it and Emma had already stolen the limelight by making an unexpected visit to her mother without being aware of her father's return. It proved to be a very memorable day, Sam created much laughter when he described his time with the butcher, he shared stories of Ding, with help from Ruth, whilst together they praised the Squire, Cook and Sarah for all the wonderful help they had provided. Ruth told of her first contact with the printer through the packing paper she had found among the testaments in the chapel, pointing out that if Cook had not taught her to read, the opportunity would have been lost. Tom was very desirous of meeting Cook, Sarah and the Squire and all agreed that this could be arranged by a visit to Annum.

"And if you have no objection then I will accompany you and I can share in your pleasure, for with your permission my friend, your family will now be my family." Tom stood aghast as he recognised the voice, there was only one owner of such dulcet tones, and he swung round to focus on their origin, he saw with great pleasure the huge frame of Dan with the printer dwarfed by his side.

"It was very fortuitous," said the printer, "Dan and myself

met in Bristowe on this very day and therefore we have travelled here together. As he had been on the road for several days, Dan thought he was not dressed for such an occasion, but I felt certain you would not debar him on that count or for any other reason. So here we are."

The entry of the two gentlemen sparked new areas of discussion, topics which were of immense interest to Tom's son and daughter and when Mr Manpitt made the suggestion the two travellers should put their memoirs into print, Emma applauded the idea stating it would make absorbing reading. The printer continued, "We could make use of my broadsheet Tom, you and Dan are free to come to the office here, or in Bristowe, on a regular basis and relate to the clerk all you can recall. He will record what you recount to him, I can then publish a series of articles on a weekly basis and will monitor the interest of the readers, and it may well have the effect of increasing sales in which case both of you will have some financial interest in the project. For the immediate future, whilst we put wheels in motion, I intend to offer Dan a situation, which will ensure his presence here and give him a roof over his head. I now traverse the road between Bristowe and Bath at least once a week and it is becoming a hazardous trip, especially as I usually travel alone and during the winter months the light can be fading before I complete my journey. I noticed as we came here today, the presence of Dan beside me was greatly reassuring and I feel it also gave the horses confidence. It is therefore my intention to ask him to continue with this duty as payment for his board with us here. Furthermore, I also hope he will be willing to travel with Hannah and I when we pay our visits to Rebecca, who by the way, is making good progress following the initial shock of Richard's sentence."

The suggestions put forward by the printer received unanimous acclaim. Tom and Dan were already discussing news they might impart, but warning each other there could be pitfalls along the way, they had a number of good things to say, but some situations such as the fearful penal settlements established at Moreton Bay and Fort Denison could rouse deep feelings of unrest if folk knew that these places housed their kinsmen. They finally agreed the whole concept endeared itself to both of them and together they could look forward to a settled future. Tom made quiet inquiries concerning Dan's family only to find his friend was not very forthcoming and did not wish to discuss the matter at this juncture, he simply reiterated he now looked upon himself as a member of Tom's family and would do all in his power to enrich it. Tom found it perplexing to reply to Dan, he was deeply sorry for his misfortune but welcomed him as a brother, confirming the fact the bond they already shared would now be even stronger and never be broken.

When the suggestion for a meeting with the Squire, Cook and Sarah was made, Sam looked very thoughtful and somewhat concerned. "I do not think we can prevail on the good hospitality of the Squire, he is now in his nineties and although he will accept our suggestion with his usual aplomb, I feel it would be grossly unfair to ask him. He is not well and it would be a better solution if we make the arrangements for the day, and request his presence with us. As most of you are aware Ruth, Luke and myself will be taking up residence in the cottage next to Sarah and although it is a little smaller, together they offer sufficient space to make a very good alternative to The Hall. As yet we have not completed the move, but as soon as we are settled we will finalise the matter."

It thus transpired within the walls of the cottages where the atmosphere was warm and cosy, old friendships were cemented and new ones created. Mr Manpitt had already emphasised how the forest area was becoming quite lawless, hence his employment of Dan to travel on the coach with him. He continued his argument by saying, "This form of intimidation, I will not call it enterprise, is carried out with impunity by a gang of ruffians. They rob and steal, quite openly collect their protection money at the Lansdown Fair and the authorities do not, or cannot, control them. I understand the large house near the Bath Waye, the one called The Grange, has recently been burgled but on this occasion the miscreants have been apprehended and will be placed in the stocks near the village Pound."

The Squire, who had arrived in time to hear the discourse given by Mr Manpitt took up the theme saying, "The folk who are being intimidated in this way are endeavouring to form some kind of association to present a solid stand against this gang, I hope to witness the fruition of such a scheme." He paused for a while and continued, "It is now almost impossible to fulfil the conditions which one is constrained to comply with concerning the liberties within the area. Much of the standing timber has been felled, but trees have not been replaced because there is no replanting programme. It is the same with the deer, more than once they have been re-stocked but all to no avail, these have also been taken by the poachers. There are a number of illegal coal workings, one can trace a line of bell pits following a seam and I am certain the owner of the land is unaware of these operations taking place. With the clearance of the forest, open spaces are being enclosed and claimed by new folk, so now there is confusion as to rightful ownership. The number of cottages is on the increase indicating a rise in the population, hence in the future we may find it difficult to support the people who live within the village, and at the same time have sufficient produce to sell in the city, we certainly do not require a repeat of the corn troubles. There is less employment in the forest and with the cessation of the spelter industry the demand for coal has fallen; also the allied trades such as pin making have suffered greatly. Unless some form of employment, other than the mine, the farm and the quarry, becomes available to the common man, I can visualise a situation where the younger members of our community will be leaving to seek their livelihood elsewhere, perhaps in the city. We could experience quite a change in the village in the years to come. Sometimes I am glad my days are numbered, for I have enjoyed the fellowship I have shared during my life's span and although times have been hard we have weathered the storms together."

"You paint a troubled picture Squire," said Sarah, "although you are not the only one to express these sentiments, several of the older folk in the chapel hold much the same views, however their outlook is optimistically coloured by the upsurge in the things of the Lord and they look forward with hope. Unfortunately, you have not been able to attend service of late; otherwise you would have been much uplifted by the new hymns we have sung recently, some from the pen of Mr Wesley. I understand he has, together with Mr Whitefield, made many converts in and around the Kingswood area. These have included a number of miners who we thought were beyond redemption. We all have been especially moved by a hymn called 'Amazing Grace', written by the captain of a slave ship and to me it shows how 'His' love can shine in the darkest of places and bring hope. We must give these young folk something tangible to grasp, in order that they can face the future."

"There are a number of settlers in Australia who are also searching for a way of life and the necessary ingredients to sustain it," said Tom, "before I left, nine merchantmen escorted by two naval vessels sailed between the Heads and landed at Farm Cove. In the party were a large number of convicts, and in the final weeks of my stay I observed these men working on several projects. The civilians who accompanied them, some of them with young families, were endeavouring to find shelter for their loved ones and assessing the situation with regard to the future. I am assuming the vessels anchored in the cove have supplies for some months to come as, apart from a plentiful supply of good fish, there are no crops as we know them."

Cook with a puzzled look at Tom, asked, "What do you call the Heads? And if there are no crops to sustain these folk, how will they survive? In some ways we enjoy a more secure way of life here in Annum despite the doubts expressed by the Squire, and the lack of all the glorious sunshine. It seems to me only the young and foolish would undertake such a perilous journey with no guarantee of a decent welcome at the end. I think I will finish my days here in the village, where I can rely on a few vegetables and some meat on special occasions."

"I sympathise with your point of view Cook," replied Tom, "Dan and I have emphasised the positive side concerning our stay there and doubtless crops will be established and cattle and sheep reared, but it will take time and a good deal of hard labour. The latter will mainly be supplied by the convicts, they were starting to clear the land in the cove before I left, and to answer your first question the Heads are large headlands, hence Heads, on each side of the entrance to the bay, so they provide good shelter to a massive, natural harbour."

During part of this discussion Ruth had absented herself to check on the boys, she found them climbing over Dan and thoroughly enjoying the experience. "I wonder what life has in store for these young lads?" said Dan as he managed to free himself from a combined hug which was akin to a half nelson.

"I wish I knew," replied Ruth, "but on a different subject, Sam and I have been intrigued by the articles on your experiences in Australia, which you and Tom have written for Mr Manpitt. We have read every word so far, and the idea of making a new life there is becoming more appealing to both of us. We are somewhat apprehensive of the journey and wondered how you and Tom could re-assure us. It seems that unless new industry of some form is introduced and flourishes, the future here does not hold great opportunities for any of our young folk. This could be a wonderful chance to make a fresh start in a new country and from what we have heard from you and Tom there is much in its favour."

Ruth observed Dan closely as she finished speaking, on occasions he could be a man of few words and would communicate more by facial expression than by word of mouth. For several moments he searched Ruth's face with a kindly look in his eyes, and then simply said, "I am very thankful I had the insight into the situation, which I did have. Fortune favoured Tom and I, we had no one to care for but each other, and because we possessed the skills required at the time we therefore fitted into a routine rather than having to create our own future. However, when we were pressed ganged we had no idea where our final destination would be. It appears you young people may have the opportunity to emigrate at very little financial cost, to a country of your own choice. I calculate that in a year or two it would be well worth considering and I feel you and Sam could prosper should you decide to go. It is an interesting situation and you would do well to look at all aspects before you reach a conclusion. Together with Tom and Sam we must talk on the subject again." Without any more ado he picked up the boys, one under each arm and, closely followed by Ruth, they rejoined the others.

Sarah had picked up the point concerning the convicts who were being transported and inquired of Tom what would become of these poor creatures once they had completed their sentence.

"I have no authority for giving you this answer, Sarah, but I am of the persuasion a good number of them are basically good citizens, unfortunately they have fallen foul of the law at a time when we are endeavouring to populate a new continent and consequently they have been given this sentence of transportation. Dan and I are of the opinion that many of them will elect to stay in Australia once they have completed their sentence. It is a new land, a big land, we cannot say it is flowing with milk and honey but during our stay there we gained a firm impression the area around Port Jackson will, in due time, become the foundation of a new nation. The port is basically a large cove, a natural harbour and has very good deep water moorings, this together with the advantage of having fresh water available from the Tank Stream, which runs into it, makes it an ideal situation for the creation of a large city. We could talk for many hours on the wild life, the wide opens spaces, the wonderful beaches, the crystal clear sea water and the great variety of trees, many of them providing excellent timber; but the overriding difference is the clean air and the warm climate. You cannot compare the filth of our cities, which have muddy tidal waters and a horrid, putrid atmosphere with the conditions which we enjoyed. We did not fully realise it at the time but the situation is akin to paradise, which presents a difficult riddle, I understand that the intention is to call the area New South Wales. Perhaps Dan can tell me the reason for this, I shall have to remember to ask him."

Sam had listened with a keen interest to all the conversations and arguments put forward by the members of the group. He admitted he did not fully share the enthusiasm displayed by Ruth and tended to be swayed one way, then the other. Cook was not fully in favour, she did not want to be deprived of contact with her grandson but desired to watch him grow and mature, at the same time she agreed the trade in the sawpit had dropped to a disturbing level and would not be increased in the foreseeable future. Sarah was much of the same persuasion, realising perhaps more than anyone present that once the trade had gone from the sawpit it would never return. Furthermore, Sam was now in competition with a second wheelwright and blacksmith who was situated at the far end of the village and therefore tended to have first call on the trade from there. It was Ruth who expressed the strongest desire to emigrate but Sam had some misgivings, he could not fully share in Ruth's confidence in relying on divine guidance for making the final decision. He could not suppress his practical intuition, with a prayer of faith and a belief they would be guided in all they decided to undertake. The boys played together oblivious to the fact their future was in the hands of concerned adults endeavouring to reach the correct conclusion.

When they finally split up to go to their various homes, opinions were divided, the scales could be tipped either way, but no-one visualised the deciding factor would be outside of their immediate jurisdiction.

Chapter Nineteen

Life Is Full Of Surprises

Several weeks after the group discussion at the cottages, Mr Manpitt advised Dan the time was ripe for a visit to Rebecca. During her time in Somerset he had been seeing her on a monthly basis, watched her general improvement and of late had been very encouraged by her condition. The medical opinion was optimistic, if she continued making progress there was every possibility she could be home within the year, but she would require more time to regain her full strength. There was certainly more sparkle in her eyes and when they strolled in the grounds her steps were sure and she did not fight for breath as she had done on some previous visits. Conversation flowed and part of it was related to the articles on Australia which Rebecca had found in the hospital rest room and read with great interest. Dan thanked her for her comments and added it was Ruth's desire to emigrate to this new continent. To their complete surprise Rebecca said, "If the conditions in this new land are so much cleaner and healthier than here at home, it could be to my advantage to be travelling with her to a place where the climate would be very suitable for me. The doctors have imparted the good news that my illness has almost cleared and now all I want is to be with my son, and if going to Australia offers me a chance to be re-united with Richard, then we could start afresh and be a family again. Since I have been here in the peace of the countryside I have had plenty of time to think. I have come to the conclusion that I have nothing to lose by taking some kind of risk in the future, therefore should the opportunity to travel with Sam and Ruth be presented to me, I know I must take it. The worst thing that could befall me is that I die on the voyage, should such an event come to pass I would leave this earth in the knowledge I had endeavoured to redress the balance of our marriage. If I stay here in the West Country the doctors have warned me my illness, in all probability, will return, thus I have gained nothing and there is a very real danger the disease could be passed on to Mark. The other situation which presents a much happier picture, is where the three of us are united and all these problems are behind us. Richard is a good man, he has many qualities that endear him to me, and I know he loves both Mark and I dearly. What is more, despite everything, I still love him."

Dan was amazed at the strength and courage shown by this young lady who had gained so much vigour since their first meeting. Without trying to persuade her, or to suppress the spirit she had just shown, he informed her of the conditions that existed in the small colony when, together with Tom, he'd spent some time there. Selecting his words as he had never done before he painted a picture which was realistic, honest, and in some ways comforting, especially when he looked forward to a much larger settlement being established which he hoped would result in the living conditions being far more amenable. He concluded his narrative by adding; "it also follows you will only travel down this road if Sam and Ruth decide in its favour, you will therefore be in good company and the friendship between Mark and Luke will flourish."

Mr Manpitt admired Dan for the way in which he handled the situation and made a solemn promise that as soon as the doctors gave their permission he, together with Dan, would come and collect her. He would take her back to Bath where she could stay in the house with Tom, Sarah, Dan and himself, but the alternative solution of going to Annum and seeking accommodation with the younger elements of the family might have a greater appeal, it would ensure the boys staying together. He concluded, "You have some months before you are forced to make the final decision and I am prepared to honour that decision whatever it might be."

During the return journey the two men deliberated as to the next course of action. It was possible a visit to Annum would be preferable to going straightaway to Bath, however the weather decided against prolonging their journey and as there was no compulsion in the matter they hit upon the notion of letting Emma be the bearer of good tidings. She had established a sound relationship with Ruth and this would help to cement their friendship, Dan wondered if Emma was also toying with the idea of travelling with her brother and sister-in-law to the far side of the world.

When the ladies met again, Rebecca's desire was made known. The only dissenting voices were those of Cook and Sarah, they did so because they were not convinced Rebecca would be strong enough to face the dangers of the journey, or the possible privations on arrival. They all admired her spirit and supported her argument, which had brought her to the conclusion she had expressed. Emma and Ruth were happy to include her in the group realising the intervening period would give everyone extra time to prepare and both boys would be under the care and guidance of at least one parent. As regards what may happen on arrival no one really knew, it seemed Rebecca had the same chance of creating a successful future as the rest.

Sam had quietly been concerned with obtaining as much information appertaining to the journey as possible, he was a practical man and his approach was to ensure he did all that was necessary to eliminate hardships and shortcomings. He had plied

Dan and his father with questions concerning possible courses of action he might take to ensure this. One recommendation made by Dan would help to ensure the safe keeping of personal property during the voyage. Wooden boxes in which their individual belongings could be stored would be a great asset on board ship and still have a useful life in Australia. Trade in the sawpit was at rather a low ebb, Sam therefore, set his mind and skills to the task of preparing sufficient timber for constructing the required boxes. Also at hand was the necessary hoop iron from which he would fashion the decorative reinforcements for the banding, he intended each recipient should find great satisfaction in his creation. Thus occupied he realised he was now consenting to travelling to the far side of the world and there to establish a new life. He fumbled in his pocket for a piece of chalk with which to snap a line, as he did so his fingers came into contact with the two clover leaves given to him by Ding. He had not forgotten his friend, or the summer palace, but since his marriage and the birth of his son these things had slipped into the back of his mind. Now he was making preparations to travel to the same destination as Ding, who in all probability was already in residence in that far off land, and so too was Richard.

The die had been cast, there had been since Rebecca's expressed desire to accompany the party, a movement towards unanimous agreement, which had culminated in a firm decision with the inclusion of Emma. Sam had been carried along on the tide of approval, gradually he was coming to terms with the situation, his boxes helped him in this respect and once the news travelled around the village, the folk in the chapel gave a solemn promise to uphold the whole party in prayer. Ruth was further strengthened by this assurance from her fellow worshippers and she confidently told Sam all would be well. Mr Manpitt gave support by concerning himself with the details of the voyage and the possibility of paying extra monies to secure reasonable accommodation on board. He also agreed when it was opportune he would obtain passages for all the seven travellers.

Tom inadvertently heard these details but was unable to identify all the adults in the party and shared his thoughts with Dan.

"The answer to your question is standing here beside you, my friend. Do you recall, when I first arrived and we met in Bath, I informed you because I do not now have a family of my own, your family is now my family, and I cannot stand by while they all sail away into the unknown. The composition of the party is such that the responsibility on Sam's shoulders is far too great, so it is my firm intention to travel with them in order to support Sam and to be of service for a while in Australia. I have some knowledge of the conditions they will have to endure and although the ladies share a number of skills, I am confident Sam will welcome a second pair of hands to help with the heavier, manual tasks. We both are aware there will be plenty of these, and should the going get rough the ladies and the boys will have an extra bodyguard. In my heart I know I must take this course of action but as yet I have said nothing to Sam, I am planning to ask him to construct one more box, strong enough to endure a return journey. How long I shall be away is not certain my intention is to make sure your family is safely settled, then return to you and Hannah, as I am desirous of sharing our twilight years together, I am also hoping Cook will be willing to join us. But that is another secret my friend, do not share it with anyone."

The days were disappearing in a rush of enthusiasm when the whole venture was suddenly put in jeopardy. The Squire came to the end of his long life. A respected master, a loving family man and a friend to every villager, he would be sadly missed. His funeral would take place in a neighbouring village where the family grave was situated in a churchyard looking out over the river. Somewhat dejected by the fact the chapel in Annum would not be his final resting place, many of the villagers, in particular those employed at The Hall, paid a final act of respect by making a pilgrimage to the neighbouring village on the day of his interment. Cook accompanied by Dan and Sarah plus all the members of the family, spent the day travelling to and from the service, then on returning discussing the various implications of the Squire's death.

Cook likened her master to an autumn fruit, "He was ripened by age as well as divine grace and, like an autumn fruit, he finally fell," she declared, "but during his ninety five years he helped and supported countless villagers who were going through bad times. There will be many good folk who, God willing, will follow his example but I doubt if there will be any who will reach such a ripe old age."

"What are the future plans for The Hall?" Asked Dan. "I understand from local gossip the place will be put up for sale. The members of the Squire's family are moving away to a smaller property and this presents a problem to people like Cook, who may not only lose their employment but also the roof over their heads. This imposes a huge burden on folk who have served many years of loyal service and it appears to me to be a great injustice, but this is life and you have to cope. It is possible some of the servants may move away with the family to their new abode, but this I think is very doubtful. I am very much aware the village has been robbed of a man who was loved by all, for in the short time we were acquainted; I noticed his compassion was applied to everyone who came into his life there was no selection. The worshippers at the chapel will be deprived of his leadership, although I am given to understand a full time Pastor has now been appointed and this augurs well for the future. The financial burden will be harder to bear, as a stipend of sixty pounds per annum is required to support the Pastor and this has to be accomplished without the aid of the Squire, his family and all the stalwarts who are emigrating."

"I know the Fellowship will survive and prosper," commented Ruth, "if you think back to the years when the chapel was enlarged, the worshippers were greatly concerned with the financial cost of the building work carried out. I am aware that much was accomplished by voluntary labour, but the required funds were raised and the witness in the village has grown. We must have a strong faith like those who have gone before us, we worship the same God and believe in the same Saviour and I know that, whether we are here in the village or in Australia, 'He' will guide and protect us."

Sarah and Cook added their 'Amens' to Ruth's statement, further endorsing their belief in a guiding hand in good times as well as in adversity, then added their own incidents to prove the point. Sam became somewhat embarrassed when his deliverance from the 'summer palace' was cited as a shining example, but he had to admit that his merciful escape from certain death was due to the faith and concern of certain ladies present, to whom he owed a great debt; in fact his very life. He hoped he would live for many years to come as he now shared that life with the very lady who had instigated his timely rescue.

During the next few months Rebecca's health showed good improvement giving the doctors the confidence to grant permission for her homecoming to be arranged. Cook had now left The Hall, she had no desire to work under a new master, so she shared the cottage with Sarah and they were both stalwarts in the life of the chapel. They were also very hospitable and opened their door to Rebecca so she could sojourn with them until her departure with the others. In the adjoining cottage Sam and Ruth cared for the two lads living there as one happy family. The boys were as close as brothers and were delighted to have Cook and Rebecca as neighbours.

In the spa city Hannah and Tom vowed they would never be parted again, it was their full intent to make up for the years lost to them, and as he could now earn a reasonable living working for Mr Manpitt they were seldom separated. The articles in the broadsheet were proving extremely popular, they had contributed to the increase in sales thus giving financial help to both parties and although Dan would be leaving in a few months, Tom knew he would continue to supply articles for some time. Use of the printed material was instrumental in advancing the interest in this far off land, and became a source of knowledge to those in the area who were of a like mind to Sam and Ruth. It thus became apparent there would be a contingent of folk from the West Country included in the number of travellers preparing to sail with the small fleet being equipped for the journey to Australia. Three chartered merchantmen loaded with stores and carrying those who wanted to make a new life on the other side of the world, would be escorted by a supporting naval vessel. This ship would transport the marines and redcoats who were ready to protect everyone during the voyage, and then on arrival, oversee those who were travelling against their will.

As the day for embarkation approached the congregation in the chapel arranged a service of valediction, in this they gave their blessing to all who were travelling on the voyage and a promise of prayer support. Sam had been greatly moved of late, the healing of Rebecca, the secure bonding of the family who were making the journey, the resourcefulness of Ruth, Cook and Emma who together with Sarah prepared for every eventuality Dan could bring to mind, all combined to convince him of the reality of a guiding hand.

Rebecca too was displaying the mother's love, which had lay dormant during the time she and Mark had been separated, and it warmed his heart to see them together. As they left the service he revealed to his wife that he felt obliged to be baptised before they sailed. Ruth was delighted to hear of her husband's desire.

"Sam my love, I have been praying for many months for this to happen, and now my most ardent request has been granted, you have made me extremely happy. I know Cook will be overjoyed."

Together hand in hand they returned to the sanctuary, and confided in the Pastor the fact which Sam had made known. His elated reaction echoed that of Ruth's and he readily agreed to arrange a service of baptism for the final Sunday of their life in Annum.

~*~

Two months later the family were assembled on the quayside awaiting embarkation. The weather was fine, the boxes constructed by Sam had been packed to capacity and the provisions supplied by Cook were secured for use on the voyage. Mr Manpitt had been influential in his dealings, managing to obtain reasonable accommodation for the party to travel with a degree of comfort, an arrangement also promising greater safety. The long, snaking queue of would be travellers was composed of folk of all ages, a number of them ill clad to face the possible ravages of a lengthy voyage. Some guarding their pitiful possessions were very apprehensive of the scene in front of them, as they waited their turn to be ferried out to one of the large craft anchored in the river. Meanwhile the confident, redcoat officers, accompanied by their ladies, strutted along the wharf observing the long-boats being rowed to and fro carrying assorted supplies, to be followed by the travellers themselves. When families and friends were parted there were lengthy, fond embraces, tearful farewells and goodbyes, as folk realised they may never be united again.

The moment those at the front of the queue gained a nervous footing on the deck of the long-boat, the first step on their watery journey; re-assurances were given by those remaining on the quay, and a steadying hand was offered by a crew member, this enabled the great majority to retain a certain amount of dignity. Dan remarked the first time he and Tom had embarked in this way they had been roughly handled with no civility and were completely devoid of personal possessions, in fact Tom was unaware of what was happening to him until he finally regained his full faculties on the deck of the Man-Of-War.

The boys plied Dan with questions seeking information on the ship anchored in the dock area, and sundry items springing up in their imaginations so Dan's store of knowledge was taxed to the full. They required to know more about the sailors pulling on the oars of the boats, the tall ships with a web of rigging and furled canvas, the soldiers waiting on the quay, and the trows helping to load supplies. Sam too was deep in thought, he had not visited the dock area since the time he and his mother were searching for his press-ganged father, and memories came surging back. The butcher, the sparrow, the forest, the summer palace, the Squire, Sarah, the chapel, Emma, Cook and his lovely Ruth. He looked across at her as she was talking to Rebecca, her hair blowing in the breeze from the gorge, and her face alive with life. Ding had called her his angel, but she was now his wife and at this moment he recognised he had a great responsibility towards both her and their son. He suddenly asked himself if they were doing the right thing, were they travelling down the proper path? He felt rather vulnerable, the voyage; no one in their party with the exception of Dan had ever sailed before, a new land, a new life; these would hold challenges of which only Dan had knowledge and experience. Time would tell, he must endeavour to capture some of the confidence and enthusiasm of the others, or the innocence of the boys, whatever they encountered he could have no better companion than Dan. He fingered the two clover leaves in his pocket and wondered if at some time in the future they would be matched up with those belonging to his forest friend. Would they recognise each other if by sheer chance they met again? He would live in hope.

Those Travelling Against Their Will

Chapter Twenty

Five Years Later

During Dan's absence the village and its surrounds had experienced a number of changes. The sawpit, together with the timber yard and wheelwright's facilities no longer existed. In its stead two small cottages nestled behind the Blue Bowl at the bend of the lane, and looked out over farmland with crops, grazing sheep and cattle. A number of gardens producing fruit and vegetables were also established, providing a limited amount of employment, but contributing to the welfare of the villagers by improving the produce available. The coal pits had spread their underground tentacles many miles in all directions whilst the quarry was maintaining a good trade.

The religious revival, inspired by the outdoor meetings conducted by the field Pastors, continued apace and provided the chapel with new converts; it also fostered a calm patience among the folk within the village. The highways and byways in the area were now far less dangerous to the traveller, as the message delivered by these stalwarts of the gospel continued to change many lives. A regular mail coach ran its scheduled way from London to Bath and continued to Bristowe along the once infamous London Waye, demonstrating the decline in lawlessness among certain elements in the Kingswood area of the forest, where the men were now greatly subdued.

A few weeks prior to Dan's return, the unexpected death of Mr Manpitt resulted in Tom and Hannah moving from the spa city to occupy the cottage vacated by Sam and Ruth. Much to Dan's delight he found all his friends gathered together in Annum and was welcomed with great joy and pleasure, without more ado he began to unravel an account of the events since they last met.

"I will recount some details of the voyage, these I hope you will find of interest, even if my dear friend Tom is already aware of such happenings," he said, "he never would have envisaged the response of the ladies in our party to the challenges they faced, several instances occurred where their reactions left me speechless. I am pleased to say all the ships in the small fleet arrived without serious mishap, the immigrants disembarking safely in Sydney Harbour. Many of them took some time to find their 'land legs,' especially the boys who had great fun endeavouring to run along the shore without falling, thankfully the rolling gait gradually left us."

Looking at his old shipmate he continued, "it was known as Port Jackson when we were there Tom, and many changes have already taken place, but I am the bearer of a long letter, written by Ruth with contributions from the others, and I will leave you to glean the family news from that particular source. I can truthfully say the voyage proved to be far less hazardous than most of the party imagined, as a group we understood each other very well and after a week or so all of us had certain responsibilities to carry out. The boxes, made by Sam proved a great boon, not only did they afford a safe haven for our personal belongings, including the monies we had with us, they were also useful as seats and for a variety of other purposes Sam had never dreamed of. During the first part of the journey, the sea was fairly calm and we decided to make good use of Cook's mouth-watering creations, these we set out on the lid of one of the boxes, and pretence was made of having a picnic in the forest. The imagination displayed by Rebecca on these occasions surprised us all and the boys would often scream with delight at some of her comments. Unfortunately, the gifts provided by Cook were soon depleted by voracious appetites sharpened by the sea breeze, and we were soon existing on the weekly rations handed out to all the passengers. It was then that the ladies displayed the skills they had learned from Cook, for together using their initiative and imaginations, they made our little group the envy of many. It was a revelation to see the dried beef or pork, the rice, the flour, the butter, the sugar, the biscuits and on occasions there were pickles to enhance the meal, all undergo an amazing change to something far more palatable. The one item very precious to everyone was fresh water, and we took great pleasure in watching supplies of this life saving commodity being loaded whilst we were anchored off Tenerife. I told the boys if they could fly over the island they would not believe their eyes, for in the clear air and bright sunlight they would look down upon a gleaming snow-cap of a single mountain to the north of the island, unfortunately from our anchorage point we were unaware of its presence. During the daylight hours we watched with great glee the antics of the dolphins and the darting of the flying fish as they appeared to soar from wave to wave, but no-one had any success in catching any sea creature to supplement our diet."

Dan stopped for a few moments and thoughtfully resumed his story, "It would be quite remiss of me to give you the impression that every day was a glorious holiday. Tom knows, as I know, that the moods of the sea can change extremely quickly and several times we huddled together, hanging on for dear life, whilst the wind ripped the top sails to ribbons, whipped the sea into such a frenzy that we feared for our very lives, and a great number of passengers became ill. During these turbulent times the calming influence of Ruth was amazing, she would be found with the boys clasped tightly to her as she offered a prayer for deliverance to her Saviour. As a group we attended service on Sunday mornings, these were well supported, being conducted by a Quaker gentleman who had a passion for the gospel combined with a great love for his fellow man. Following one violent storm, when he had taken note of Ruth's calming presence, he co-opted her aid for the rest of the voyage and she displayed great sincerity in all her undertakings. Her compassion endeared her to many whilst Sam watched with protecting, loving eyes and was always willing to help in any way he could.

It was following one of the sudden storms we encountered that we were all extremely sad to learn of the death of a young lass who had been thrown against one of the hatches on deck with a force strong enough to cause severe injuries, and these led to her demise. I had never experienced the burial of a child at sea before, but this simple service held just after sunrise the following morning proved to be extremely moving. As so often happens, when the storm had blown itself out the new day was bright and the sea calm. I have to admit my tears flowed as the body of the young girl, sewn neatly into a weighted shroud, slipped gently down a plank over the side of the ship and disappeared beneath the waves, several of the seasoned, rough deck hands were moved to tears.

Three times we were becalmed for several days, no wind, not even the slightest breeze, it was then we could look out across a glassy sea and signal to our companions in the accompanying craft, if we were close enough the captains used their loud hailers to share information on the progress of the fleet. On one of these calm days we crossed the equator and as there were three young members of the crew who had never crossed the line, they had to undergo a special baptism in the name of Neptune, it was a kind of initiation ceremony and provided the travellers with almost a day's entertainment.

Some seasoned members of the crew came on to the deck

clothed in fancy dress representing some rather grotesque figures, the main reason for this being the intimidation of those undergoing baptism. There was huge pretence at all sorts of actions, including being tarred and feathered, and having heads shaved with wooden razors before the youngsters were immersed in a large tub of seawater. The youngest of the three was obviously a little scared by the whole proceedings, and I must admit that they were being roughly handled, but he was spared his humiliation by being redeemed. The older members of the crew let it be known that on payment of one shilling to his persecutors, he could be spared the worst aspects of the ceremony. Rebecca readily agreed to pay this ransom and the boy, who appeared to be not much older than her son, was released without hurt. He was so grateful to her for rescuing him from a situation where no real harm was done, but one that had obviously caused him great apprehension, and he admitted he was afraid of letting himself down in front of everyone present. The long and short of it is Rebecca has made a friend for life.

I am rambling on, my final act at this stage is to pass a letter to Sarah, who as an interested but neutral party had been nominated by the boys to read its contents. They also made the comment she is probably the only one who will be able to understand their scribble, although I must add that during the voyage Rebecca, Ruth, Sam and Emma all helped to advance the reading and writing skills of our young gentlemen. They were not the only ones to benefit because other children together with some of their parents joined in, forming a floating school with lessons being held on most days. I too, had my share of instruction."

He suddenly came to an abrupt close, producing from inside his cloak the letter to which he had made previous reference, passing the scroll to Sarah, who carefully opened it up and began to read.

My dear Cook, Hannah, Sarah and Tom,

We are enjoying a wondrous spell of weather and hope that your November days are not as cold and foggy as they can be. When we first arrived we were at out wit's end with regard to the basic demands of living, and came very close to seeking a passage back to England. I can honestly say the presence of Dan was divine providence, not only did he instil confidence in Sam, but he inspired us all to face our difficulties with a smile and to work and plan for a day at a time. Much of the first year was horrendous, we managed to create a shelter from timbers, canvas and sections of bark cut in a special way from a species of gum tree. The shelter was not really large enough to be comfortable for all of us, we therefore spent much of our time in the open air, cooking, fishing and carrying out the menial tasks that are a part of daily life. It gradually became apparent we could not stay in the particular bay in which we had settled so we decided to seek pastures new where we could build a good home. We obtained a piece of land towards the north of the main harbour, the transactions for the deal was a master stroke by Dan, I am sure, had we been on our own, we would have lost the chance, but we finally secured it. Having decided to make the move we required transport to effect it, Dan in his wisdom suggested we endeavour to contact a livery stable where we could hire both horse and wagon. As you can well imagine transport of this kind is in short supply and those who own such concerns are in no mood to place them in a situation where horse or wagon, or both would just disappear. Having found a stable it was then incumbent upon the men to strike the best bargain they could, and the dealing seemed to go on for ages. I do not intend to tell you the rest of this story, as I shall be robbing Sam of news he is longing to impart to you,

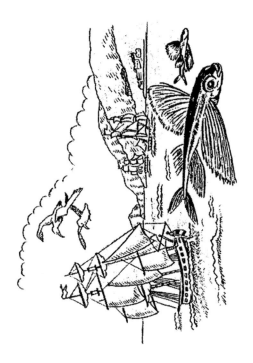

The Darting Of The Flying Fish

I will therefore confine myself to what you may term as 'my news.'

We have Cook to thank for the knowledge and skills she instilled into us when we were at The Hall. So much of it has been of great value and we all seem to remember various aspects, tips, and special dishes to complement each other's knowledge, thus we are now living on a much-improved diet. With the establishment of good trade links there is far more choice offered by local traders and, as you do in Annum, we supplement what we buy with what we grow and rear. As you are fully aware this takes time, but the benefits of our labours and others like us, are now making them manifest. We usually cook, and very often eat, in the open air, there is no shortage of timber for kindling, and bacon, eggs and chicken are available although vegetables are scarce. Sam's skill and knowledge, which he gained at the butchers, has also proved to be of great value, although he remains very reluctant to kill any living creature, which might serve as food for us. Recently a windmill has been put into use to power a mill for grinding grain; we now look forward to such luxuries as our own bread and cookies. I must admit the food we shared when we first arrived was meagre and lacking in variety, I firmly believe Dan could have eaten all our victuals as one sitting.

Dan may have mentioned the Quaker gentleman whom we befriended on board ship, he has founded a mission in one of the bays, and is extending a helping hand to some of the lost souls who have served their time but are now broken men and have nothing. We are unable to spend too much time with him but enjoy supporting him, as we are able, usually on a Sunday when he conducts an open-air service, we help provide succour and companionship. Once or twice a week he invites the local children to his school. They sit on the ground under a huge tree where the overhanging branches offer shade to about a score of eager, ill clad lads and lassies who receive instruction in reading. He tells us his vision is to build a school with his own living accommodation attached, but it may be some years before it is realised.

I have digressed from the news I was imparting before I mentioned the Quaker. Referring to his vision of a school has helped me to regain my train of thought. I told you about the land we obtained but said nothing as to what we did with it. By the time Dan is with you and you are reading this letter we shall be occupying what we all call our 'palace'. Sam, Dan and the boys, who are now old enough to be helpful, together with the help of one other gentleman, have worked very hard to build our home. It reminds me of the cottages in which you are now residing, except that it is a wooden structure and is kept clear of the ground to keep out unwelcome guests, especially snakes, thus it rests on small, stone pillars. When Dan decided he had accomplished his mission and was returning to England, the house, apart from a veranda, was complete, we therefore decided to give him a well-earned rest as a gesture of our grateful thanks for all he has perfected since our arrival. The boys and Sam have now erected this feature and we are able to sit together at the end of the day in the warmth of the evening and talk. Just at this moment we are being interrupted by the amazing noise of a creature akin to a large grasshopper, I expect Tom can tell you more about them because he could not have ignored their activities when he was here, and Dan told us to expect such interruptions. I will leave my news at this point and hand you to Sam who I know is bursting to tell you his incredible story.

Hullo my dear friends,

I must start with the livery stable where we hired the horse and wagon to affect the move to this site. A young man and myself were discussing terms but could not reach agreement, I therefore asked if I might see the owner of the establishment in order to finalise the deal with him. As we were talking my brow began to sweat – it was hot that day – so I felt in my pocket for a kerchief and as I pulled my hand out my two cloverleaves fell to the floor. The young man looked at them, declaring his boss had a similar pair of leaves and he wore them on a wire around his neck. I was awestruck and enquired if the boss was available at the moment. The young man said he was sorry but he was in the large paddock at the rear of the premises trying to break in a rather nervous yearling. He had acquired this particular horse because no one had been able to completely subdue the creature, so his boss had argued, if he could succeed where everyone else had failed, then the horse was his. Much to the disgust and consternation of the young man, I ran through the stable in the direction of noises coming from both man and horse. I suddenly stopped, there was only one person who could handle a situation like the one I saw in front of me and that was Ding. Closing on my quarry, I suddenly had an idea, I had to be certain my intuition was correct so I bent down and plucked a blade of grass, placed it between my thumbs as Ding had done near The Hall, and blew hard to create the piercing whistle given as a signal to the angel. To my surprise the grass seemed tougher than our meadow grass, producing a much lower but audible note. The attention of the rider had been attracted and there was no mistake. It was Ding!

I cannot find words to describe my feelings as we embraced each other, the way we both began asking questions, demanding answers and news of the intervening years since last we met. I informed him of my requirements and since that moment he has accomplished so much on our behalf, his kindness has known no bounds. We were loaned the transport free of charge, furthermore, he accompanied us back to the hut and helped with the removal of our belongings. His delight at seeing Ruth again was only surpassed when he was introduced to Luke and the rest of the family. I felt sure when he met Emma there was a quite a reaction from both of them and I am happy to tell you the friendship is now much stronger. He has helped us in so many ways that I dare not start to describe them to you; I will let Dan share his thoughts on this because it has helped to quicken his return. It seems Ding was fortunate in some respects; he endured a full year of hard labour on road gangs and clearing scrubland, before he came face to face with the trooper who brought him to the Bristowe gaol. The trooper, now risen in rank, recognised Ding and must have had a good deal of admiration for him because he decided his talents were being wasted.

Not many weeks after this encounter Ding was placed in the army stables, and served his time quite happily doing what he loves doing more than anything else, looking after horses. Even when his sentence was completed he remained for another year, and earned himself sufficient cash to make a very small start with a livery stable owned by a fellow Irishman. Since then, he has gone from strength to strength and now has quite a thriving business. The contacts he has made are legion and there appears to be nothing he has not put his hand to, or has knowledge of. However, when Emma asked him if he knew of a haberdashery concern within the area, he firstly had to be told what it meant and then within a month, he had established a place for Emma sharing a small stall run by another trader. She had with her some stock from her shop in Bath and this augmented by further supplies from a Chinese gentleman helped to give her a good start. The business is now growing and her own skill with the needle is adding to the impact her presence has already created.

I shall be eternally grateful for the presence of Dan during the voyage and establishing our home here in Australia. We cannot say all our troubles are over, our life style is now as good as the one we enjoyed in Annum and there are advantages, like the climate, the wonderful sandy beaches, some extraordinary wild life and the fact we are now trying to build a future of our own rather than fit into a society where changes are not easily made. Some of the timbers I have found are exotic and I fully intend to create more furniture of my own, I may even find time to fashion a chess set so Rebecca can teach the boys to play this fascinating game. Time is the one commodity we require more of, it seems to fly and had I been alone with the ladies and boys our situation would not have advanced to its present state. I know Dan is leaving, we wish him God speed, safe travelling and happy days with you all; we shall miss him very much. He will have many more tales to relate to Mr Manpitt and hopefully earn more cash. Emma is ready and waiting to give you her news, no doubt we will all remember things we wanted to say and have not done so, but I feel certain there will be another time.

My dear family and friends,

I think I have almost recovered from the shock of the voyage and the privations we have endured since our arrival. When we were with you, discussing, reading, talking of what we thought would be a great adventure I could not, in my wildest dreams, imagine the happenings since that time. Father and Dan gave us hopes they knew could be realised and they were right to do so, and gradually we are realising some of those hopes but the struggle to obtain them has been beyond belief. We now appreciate each other very much, and we know together we have endured the worst times so that we can look forward with real confidence. Many times during the years since we departed my thoughts wandered back to my haberdashery establishment in Bath, where I could leave my assistant in charge and wander along to the tea shop near the Abbey to purchase a special bun. My imagery was so intense I sometimes smelled and tasted such a treat.

Australian Shelter

During one of these flights of fancy, my mouth watered to such an extent Rebecca asked me why I was dribbling. When I explained the situation to her, she told me as a young girl her father had taken her to the same tearoom on many occasions, and commenced to dribble herself. We are now living in more civilised surroundings than when we first arrived and are exploring the possibilities of opening a small tea room, Rebecca welcomes the idea and I feel certain we could combine it with our other interest and create a more homely place than some of the rough establishments which have sprung up and are now making a reasonable living. I feel Rebecca and I, if we plan carefully, will be able to contribute to the family fortunes in this manner, and we are certain of obtaining help from the others. Ding has offered his support and backing to any ventures we undertake and he seems to have our interests at heart, in fact he and I have become good friends. I can understand how he and Sam became close, as Ding does not share the rather shy approach to life as displayed by Sam, he is far more outgoing, he is prepared to take a risk, but at the same time he is kind, thoughtful and has been very generous. He is not practical in the sense that he possesses the skills to create beautiful and useful things like Sam, but he has a dynamic outlook on life, which carries him along, and at the same time he takes others with him. I am of the opinion they compliment each other perfectly and this is why they are such good mates. He also has a cheeky sense of humour and this endears him to us all. We are really blessed to have these two men to call upon, Sam has slaved without stopping since we arrived, he has toiled and planned and together with Dan they have been instrumental in making our lives so much more comfortable. I must add the work force has now been enlarged by the boys who desire to take part in any way possible and it is already apparent Luke has inherited his father's love of timber, and shows signs of possessing the same skills. Both the boys are growing into helpful members of the family and remain as close as brothers, indeed they are seldom apart.

Although our parents are not here with us and therefore we cannot be a complete family, Sam and I are overjoyed to renew our relationship, and the same family bond exists between us as existed during our early childhood in the city. In fact my own impression is the bond is now much stronger, and we often talk about the days we spent with Joseph and Grandfather, but we always rejoice in the great day when he walked into my shop to shelter from the rain. I often give thanks for that special day, it not only re-united us but it also presented me with the opportunity to share the childhood years of Mark and Luke, an experience I cannot put a price on. We miss you all very much, but we know in our hearts all is well and you will be enjoying life together without all the trials and tribulations of this younger generation. I am now of the opinion we made the right choice, circumstances can only improve and we have already established contact with two other families from the West Country who live fairly close by, so we talk of the forest, the two cities, and the Bath Waye with understanding. I must come to a close, Rebecca and the boys are ready to add their stories, and in fact I understand the boys have gone fishing, as they were tired of waiting. Ding has gone with them and as he gets plenty of luck with his line we are hoping for a good fish supper, we only wish you could share it with us. Cook, the fish we catch from the local beach are marvellous, they are horrible to look at but they have a delicious flavour and the flesh is as white as snow. We are also enjoying crab, caught at the same beach and now looked *upon as a delicacy. My love to you all, you all deserve a very contented and trouble free time. I am sure that better days are ahead and our future here will be secure. Rebecca is ready to proceed.*

My dear, dear friends and relatives.

My first duty is to thank all of you from the bottom of my heart, because you cared for my son and me when we were at our wit's end, and did not know which way to turn. We have endured and come through those dark days and I am indebted to Mr Manpitt for the kindness he showed during my stay in Somerset. His visits, sometimes with Hannah, sustained me through those long months and were doubly enjoyable when he was joined by Dan. All praise too for the love shown by all of you in the early years of Mark's life, he has grown into a young man of whom we can all be proud. I do not know how to tell you the news that is dearest to my heart, but I will try to relate as best I can and you will have to forgive me if I do not make myself clearly understood. I have seen Richard and we are endeavouring to steer a safe passage through some very rough water. It happened this way:

I expect Dan has told you about the little mission run by the Quaker and how he gives help to ex-convicts, well it was from the mission that Mark delivered a message. He came in one day with Luke, they had both been busy using a mould for making candles, this had been given to them by Ding and they could not wait to try it, they were over enthusiastic because they forgot to insert the wick. Having made a couple of candles they wandered down to the mission to get the opinion of the Quaker and hopefully an order for their product. The Quaker was deep in conversation with a gentleman who the boys had not seen before. Mark said he was very thin, quite tall, very poorly dressed and he looked as though he had an illness of some kind. What attracted Mark's attention were his feet, they were bare and he had a toe the same as his, a hammer-toe. The Quaker told him these deformities are quite common but it is the first one he has seen among the men visiting the mission and he suggested he returned home to tell me the story. After he congratulated the boys on their candles, but stated they would be more useful with wicks, he added the man's name is Richard and they will be meeting again in a few days time. He does not know any more about him or where he lives, he suggests that I contact him and he will do his utmost to arrange a chance meeting between us.

Naturally, I embraced the idea with all my being and attended the mission at the appointed time. The gentleman is my husband! He is Mark's father but he is a lost soul, he did not recognise me, although the Quaker holds the opinion this kind of memory loss is quite common and usually disappears when certain facts from earlier experiences are re-established. I do not know, I have found Richard, I came all this way to seek him and now he has to find me and his son! All I can hope for is that you will pray for us, for myself to be given the strength and patience to be guided down the right path, and for Richard to be receptive to anything which might prompt his recall and change all our lives. Ruth has suggested it would be helpful to ask the folk in the chapel for their support and I feel sure Sarah or Cook would seek their petitions on our behalf. I know I do not possess the same faith as Ruth or Sam, but if you do this for Richard and me, I shall be eternally grateful.

There is one other line of approach suggested by the Quaker and already partly implemented by Ding. We are making an attempt to help Richard through the media of printing. Ding has hunted high and low to see if there are any tools of the trade he could purchase, or loan for a while, to see if they stimulate Richard into some form of activity. One of his faults, if we can name them as such, is that he is quite prepared to do nothing and this means he would simply fade away if left to his own devices. The initial effort had some response but obviously the equipment at our disposal leaves much to be desired, therefore Dan is going to ship back to us the things which Mr Manpitt would suggest might be required to set the wheels in motion. Thank you for listening to me, we have a difficult road ahead but it will finally lead to a happy ending, of this I feel sure. The boys are back with Ding, they have been successful in catching our supper, so I am certain their testimony will not be lengthy, God bless.

Hullo Aged Ones,

We did not know what to call you and as the younger members of the family are here it must be true to say all the aged ones are back in Annum. The new country (we can't spell its name) is very different but very nice. Now we have a real house to live in and we are getting real food it is much better. It seems funny to have the sun shining really hot when it is Christmas, but it means we can have our dinner out in the open, which is very nice. There are some lovely birds here, one is like the kingfisher we used to see down by the river, it is called the laughing jackass and if you are not careful it will steal food from your plate then sit up in the tree and laugh at you whilst it eats it. Luke lost a pork chop to one of these birds and we all laughed except Luke There is a lovely little bird we see in the scrubland bushes by the beach, its tail sticks up like our wren's tail does but the little bird is blue in colour. Everything here is blue, the birds, the jellyfish, the water, and the sky, even the mountains. Ding, or should we say Mr Bell, tells us we should call the bird a blue wren, but we think that sometimes he is teasing us. We like Mr Bell, but then everyone likes Mr Bell, even Auntie Emma. We saw them kissing one night down by the beach but we have promised

225

not to tell anyone.

We had a big shock when we were fishing with Ding some weeks ago; a man's body was lying dead in the sand. He had been stung by a jellyfish, they are not very big but their sting is terrible and the poor man had drowned before he could get back to the shore for help. When Ding saw him he said he thought he had seen him before, but he was not sure. There was something about his face, it was the rather big, hooked nose and he could recall a man with features like his being in the gaol the same time as he was. He was of the opinion the man had the nickname Dewdrop. We were sorry he was dead and we shall watch out for the jellyfish, but we could not see why he was called Dewdrop.

We are glad we do not have all the smelly stuff running down the middle of the street, like in the big cities where you are. Sam has a big augur and with this he can drill a large hole deep into the ground, so all the smelly stuff goes into the hole and then after a few weeks we fill the hole in and drill a new one. Luke says we have not mentioned the animals who carry their babies in little pockets on their tummies, some of them are very big, as tall as a man, no, not the babies, I mean the grownups. They can move very fast because they hop on big, strong legs, you will have to ask Dan to show you. We loved being on the boat and watching all the sailors working in the rigging, but it was very scary at times. It is nice to go to the harbour and watch the boats, but we are not allowed to go without one of the grownups. We hope you are all well and enjoying a peaceful time without us. I can smell the fish; supper must be ready. Goodbye for now, we love you all although you are getting old.

Chapter Twenty-one

The Confession

The harbour was now the scene of many comings and goings, during the years since Ding had arrived the number of ships had more than trebled, to the point where most days saw new arrivals and departures. It was therefore common practice for the men to wander down to the jetties simply to observe the goods, as well as the human cargo, being discharged on the dock. There were still many convicts being sent to disembark in Sydney harbour, those serving their time were being exploited, and many ill-treated. The tripod and the lash were ever visible and if you did not observe the public flogging, the scarred backs of many working in the dock area bore witness to a very brutal regime. Richard had no such physical scars, he had escaped the cat, but he had witnessed men being strapped to the triangle, beaten to within an inch of their lives, their backs torn to shreds, then as they passed into unconsciousness being revived with sea water to receive the remaining lashes. Every time he watched this tortuous procedure he felt every stinging blow whilst the cries of the victims remained with him to haunt his restless, sleepless hours. He was a survivor of years of hard labour, making roads, clearing scrub, digging gullies and cutting stone and timber. He, like Ding, had the chance to pursue his trade, but he was betrayed by a jealous rival, it was a very minor affair, but he was returned to the work gangs. Now he too observed the activities in the harbour area and noticed the two men who collected some wooden crates, loaded them on a cart, then made their way towards the Quakers.

At the Quakers they unloaded the crates and then proceeded to a house where two ladies joined them and all four adults returned to the mission. The Quaker was certain he could house the crates for the time being until they could ascertain what space would be required for the printing equipment, should their experiment prove a success. They decided to open up one crate to inspect its contents and, as they made to do so, the door of the mission opened and Richard entered.

Quietly the Quaker told Sam to proceed with the job in hand as he welcomed Richard and introduced him to Ding and Ruth, "and this lady," he stressed, "you have already met, this is Rebecca."

There was no comment from Richard, no flashes of recognition, he was staring at the crate and Sam endeavouring to ease a plank from the top so he could behold the contents. The nails finally gave up their grip with a screeching sound which made the ladies cover their ears and Richard was seen to shudder. Reaching inside the box Sam brought out a neatly tied packet, it appeared to contain papers as well as some small items and he placed it on the top of the crate to inspect it further. The packet contained other small parcels, all of them carefully labelled with the name of the recipient. Sam read the names, passing a parcel to Ruth, then adding one for Luke, he placed one bearing Emma's name on the crate adding one bearing his own name. Mark's name emerged next and this was followed by Rebecca's, who took charge of both parcels. Sam peered inside the packet, it contained one final, small parcel and withdrawing it he read the name Richard.

Richard sat on the edge of the crate and everyone held their breath, he looked at Sam and like a little child he took the parcel and began to open it. His hands trembled, a letter fell to the floor, this he reached down to retrieve and as he did so a paper knife, a special paper knife, a gift from his father, slipped from the packet to the floor, the single diamond in the handle sparkling in the sunlight, its amazing lustre astounding everyone. He did not pick it up, he dropped to his knees beside it, looking around at the faces watching him he suddenly burst into tears, crying, "I did stab him, I did not mean to, I acted in self defence, but they would not believe me. You do believe me Rebecca; you have always trusted me although I was not worthy of your trust. As long as you believe me, I do not worry about anyone else."

Rebecca had joined him on the floor of the mission, her tears were also flowing as she reassured her husband everything would be well, he had recognised her, called her by name, he had broken the spell of whatever it was that bound him. The Quaker looked on, he gave Rebecca an endearing smile and simply said, "His troubles are not over, he has made his first step by confessing his guilt and he will move on from there. I feel it would be wise to leave the crates here with me, and this could be the opportune moment for Richard to accompany you back home, you are a family again."

Rebecca slowly rose to her feet, in her hand the letter Richard had dropped to the floor. She opened up the sheet of paper and read:

My dear Rebecca and Richard,

Thank you for your moving letter, I have passed your prayer request to The Fellowship and they are more than willing to comply. We are very sorry to impart to you the news concerning Richard's father. He passed peacefully away almost a year since and we have been wondering how to inform you, then when Dan came back with the desire to send out goods to you, we thought it an opportune moment to make contact. His death means all his estate now belongs to Richard, thus he is now a very rich man. We do not know your desires, but whether you remain where you are or return here, you will not want for the rest of your days."

We are all well and despite the passing years we still enjoy life. Tell the boys we are not as old as they suggest.

Our united love and affection. God bless. Sarah

Rebecca looked at the startled faces around her.

"Richard," she said, "you must tell me what you wish to do."

Without any hesitation he held her close and whispered, "We are a family again, you, Mark and I, we will remain here, this is now our home, we can fashion a new life together and the Quaker can have the best mission and school in Australia."

Ruth and Sam exclaimed: "Amen to that."

**Extract from the diary of
Charles and Martha Curtis
written on their voyage from
Liverpool to Melbourne in 1862
*(Some forty years after our story)***

Charles and his wife Martha were married at Christchurch, Hanham on 27th July 1862, they were both twenty-one years of age. They sailed on the ship *Champion of the Seas* on an unassisted passage, leaving Liverpool on Friday 9th August 1862 for Melbourne.

Friday August 9th At six o'clock in the morning after having raised the anchor, the *Champion of the Seas* with 332 souls on board were towed out of the River Mersey by one of the Liverpool steam tugs but with a head wind blowing straight against us. After going about fourteen miles and finding we were fast drifting on to the Bar, the ship was put back into Liverpool where it remained until Saturday when it was again towed out into the Mersey but this time by two steam tugs. We went along very well although the wind was against us and on Sunday morning about four o'clock one of the tugs left us. It was a beautiful day and service was held in the saloon, both morning and evening, the Preacher being a Scotch Minister.

Monday August 11th The wind having shifted and being favourable, we sent the other tug away. We were now outside of Cork Harbour. There was plenty of fun every evening on deck when it was fine, as there was plenty of music, fiddles, flutes, concertinas and lots of dancing during the week. There was a little sea sickness, Martha was sick once, but I got off without any. Our provisions were given out once a week, that was Fridays, which consisted of Beef, Pork, Preserved Meat, Preserved Potatoes, Biscuits, Butter, Peasoup, Rice, Flour, Oatmeal, Sugar, Raisins, Tea, Water, Limejuice, Vinegar, Pickles etc. There were four of us in the berth, but six mess together and we must say we agreed capital well.

Monday August 18th And the rest of the week was very fine weather. Lots of flying fish were seen and dolphins, but nothing happened out of the common until Sunday when we passed a French vessel called *The Joseph Brenan* we cheered her as we passed and our captain spoke to her captain through a trumpet. As it was very hot we slept in our beds with only a sheet over us and every Saturday the beds and bedding were taken on deck and aired.

Monday August 25th The weather was very hot and there was scarcely any wind blowing. There was a good deal of lightning which did no harm. On Friday a sudden gale came on about eleven o'clock with awful hard rain, there were eleven sails split to pieces and Martha was very much frightened but she was not herself as there was a great many of the other passengers that shared the same. The ship however nobly bore up against it and it carried us along at eighteen miles an hour a great many porpoises were seen swimming alongside of the ship.

Monday September 1st The weather was beautiful but awfully hot, and Martha and I felt unwell and began to get very thin. On Wednesday we crossed the Line and as it is the customary rule for the sailors to have a spree on that occasion it was postponed until Saturday, lots more flying fish were seen.

Monday September 15th Beautiful weather, the ship going at about nine knots per hour. On Friday a perfect gale was blowing and it rained very hard, the tins and boxes were rolling about the ship in all directions and it was laughable to see the passengers falling about the ship as though they were tipsy, it was fun to see them. I and Martha got on very well. We sailed from the Line to the Cape in fifteen days that is 2,400 miles.

Monday September 22nd Very calm, two young men caught some pigeons that were flying around the ship, they were what is called Cape Pigeons and were very pretty birds. The ship sometimes twelve, sometimes fourteen knots an hour, there was some whales seen in the distance. On Sunday we passed a ship called *The Mauritius* from Greenock, Scotland and bound for Singapore, she had been out to sea sixty four days and during that time she had lost her rudder, we could not render her any assistance.

Monday September 29th Weather cold and wet although we kept going at a rapid rate. The Cape Pigeons were still flying about the ship. Fourth of October being Martha's birthday, we spent a jolly evening in the 3rd Mate's room, drinking our brandy and smoking cigars with all the Mates of the vessel. Chief Mate, 2nd, 3rd & 4th Mates. Likewise the Head Steward and Storekeeper, they all drank our health wishing us health, happiness and prosperity and especially to Martha. We were both first rate in health and very happy together we had a beautiful passage so far.

Monday October 6th Very cold and some snow fell, we saw some snow balling on deck and the ship was going at a frightful rate, fifteen knots an hour, it was truly gratifying to us.

Monday October 13th Thieves now began to plunder, one poor Irishman had his box broken open and some clothes taken from it, worth five pounds, the poor fellow was in a sad way about it. The week rather squally. There was a Scotch Ball held under the saloon where non but Scotch people were invited, they amounted to about 40 altogether and the English being determined not to be outdone by them, got up a Ball the following evening being about 30 in number. I and Martha were invited, we had it very pleasant and we enjoyed it first rate. It began at five o'clock when the Captain and saloon passengers honoured us with their company. Our honourable Captain stood up and delivered a short speech and afterwards drank all our healths, wishing us health, happiness and prosperity in the colony where he expected to be in five days sail. The Captain started the Ball with a set of quadrilles and he chose Martha and led her out for his partner in the first set and chose me to be the musician with the concertina. The Ball broke up at half past twelve o'clock with three cheers for the Captain and his wife and three cheers for the Officers and crew of the old *Champion* and concluded with the National Anthem of *God Save The Queen*. Sunday evening there was one poor Irishman as belong to the ship's crew who was confined to the hospital with consumption, after being three weeks on board, dying in the evening. As the doctor saw him he told him to be prepared for the last home.

Monday October 21st The poor fellow expired at half past five o'clock in the morning in the Catholic faith. His body was sewn in canvas with a lump of lead at his feet, at eight o'clock the body was brought up on deck by six sailors and taken to the saloon. The prayers were read over it by a Roman Catholic then the body was inter'd to the sea. It was a melancholy sight to witness the English colours flying at mast head during the burial, as the last respect shown to him, the sea was very calm. Thursday the wind changed all in our favour and everything was got in order ready for landing. Friday, we only got three days provisions, the ship sailing at fourteen and a half knots an hour. Saturday morning at five o'clock we were in sight of land called Cape Otway which is 150 miles from Melbourne. The sea was very calm and not making any progress towards the Heads. At ten o'clock in the evening the wind was too powerful to take the ship through the Heads which is one and a quarter miles wide and forty miles from Melbourne, and on Sunday morning the ship tack'd round three times before it got in the right course to go through. At eight o'clock the Pilot came on board and took charge of the ship from the Heads and through Hobson's Bay until we came within 500 yards of Sandridge Pier where we cast anchor. The end of the voyage of *The Champion of the Seas*. Here's a health to the Captain, Officers and crew and all that belong to the jovial crew on board. *The Champion of the Seas* arrived at Sandridge, Sunday afternoon, October 26th 1862.

We rose at six o'clock the next morning and got all our things together ready for the tug boat which came alongside. All the luggage was put on the tug boat then all the passengers got on board and away we went leaving the Old *Champion* far behind us. It was a beautiful day and so pleasant to us going down the Yarra Yarra River in the old steam boat. We arrived at the landing stage, put our luggage together and went up to Melbourne and had some dinner, and a good one, which only cost one shilling each, then I left Martha with the luggage.

~*~

Charles continues to describe going to Victoria Railway Station and taking a 45 mile rail trip to Geelong. They still had a further twenty miles to Queenscliff and, as it was dark and raining very hard, they left their luggage in the cloak room and went and slept in the Casher's Hotel. The following day he hired a conveyance to take them and their luggage to Queenscliff, it cost one pound and was called 'the colonial riding through the bush'. They then surprised his uncle and aunt who had left Hanham some ten years before, and were unaware of their coming. However, they were made welcome and treated as their own family. He concludes with much affection for Queenscliff, saying: 'uncle's house is only five minutes walk from the beach and even more affection for their parents and friends and grateful thanks to God for all the mercies they received at his hand in the travelling of sixteen thousand miles.'

Little is known of Charles and Martha after they arrived in Australia and set up home. He became a ticket collector on Victorian Railways at North Melbourne Station but he died in his thirty-seventh year from spinal meningitis. In his will their children are listed as follows: Alice, 13 years; Mary, died; Henry, died: Edward, died; Harold, 4 years; Ellen, 2 years; Arthur, died. His assets amounted to £758, a sizable sum in those days. What became of Martha or her surviving children is not known.

Author's Note: *My grateful thanks are due to Mrs Iris Tucker, nee Curtis, for the copy of the diary of Charles and Martha Curtis. I hope that this information from their travels has been read with the same pleasure as I derived from their real life adventure.*

Epilogue

Connections between the Old Chapel, the folk of Hanham, and various parts of the world are numerous, I would like to acquaint the reader with some of them.

"The song is ended but the melody lingers on." These words epitomise the feelings I have for the building known as Hanham Baptist Old Chapel. It now no longer exists but I treasure memories of the hours we spent within its walls in worship, in business meetings and in the many social events held there.

There are two keepsakes incorporated in the New Hall, a modern building, which will in time have its own history, but at the moment is an inadequate reminder of its predecessor. The first of these is a length of one of the old roof beams set into the brickwork and suitably inscribed to commemorate the date of opening. The second is part of a memorial stone taken from the wall of the old building and mounted in the porch so that as one enters, the name Whittuck is there to remind folk of past glories. The family resided in Hanham Hall and the Squire in my narrative is modelled on Samuel Whittuck, he lived to a great age and was kindly disposed and generous to many of the Hanham poor. The Whittuck's Trust is still in existence, which was established for this purpose, but is now running very low.

Over the years there has been a steady stream of folk who have experienced contact with the Old Chapel and its worshippers and have travelled on to share their faith in pastures new. Australia, Canada, France and many parts of the British Isles have welcomed families as well as individuals in this respect. Australia has received three individuals and two young families. One of the families being my own brother-in-law; Mr Sydney Bryant, who emigrated on an assisted passage with his wife and two young daughters. The elder daughter, Sharon, now Mrs Longman, was baptised in Caringbah Baptist Church in N.S.W. and is now very active in her church in Queensland, together with her husband and three sons.

The son of the Sunday School secretary settled in Canada.

Another young man spent many years of his working life crossing the channel to France on important work on Concorde.

Recent years have shown support for two individuals to become full time ministers, whilst a number of young ladies, seeking Christian mission experience, have spent time in Calcutta and Malawi. Others have worked in children's missions within the confines of this country. Not all of these folk have had personal contact with the Old Chapel, but if they have not, their parents will have had that experience.

Although many of our young men served in the armed forces in the 1939-45 conflict, only one did not return to his loved ones.

In my imaginary story, I mentioned a 'Great Escape'. This is based on a factual tale and during the Festival of Britain, the then secretary of the Sunday School, Mrs A. Carpenter, wrote a short play on this very subject. The minister involved was a field preacher and the first Pastor of the church, the Rev. Andrew Gifford. His part was played by a young lad named Robert Willis. Even at a very tender age his distinctive voice and manner proved him to be an excellent choice. He has gone forward in faith and witness and is now The Very Reverend Robert Willis, Dean of Canterbury. In my heart I know he will have many happy memories of the Old Chapel and these will be entwined with family remembrances of his parents, uncles and grandparents. This combination, perhaps not for three generations, is the delight of many.

Bill Brown